Kenneth Arant

A SNAKE'S LIFE

A Snake's Life – Book 1

PROLOGUE

Hello, everyone. My name is Albert and well... I died. Not in some fantastical way, mind you. I died in my sleep. I lived a good, long life. Far longer than I realistically had a right to. I had children that I loved very much. A wife that passed far too soon. And a home in the southeastern part of the United States of America.

When I finally died, it was an easy death. It was easy to head into the light because I didn't have any true regrets. I was old, tired, and ready to see my wife again.

But fate... it had other plans for me. After I died and went to wherever it is souls go, I met... I hesitate to call it God as it didn't claim to be such. But I cannot for the life of me think of another way to describe it.

It was composed entirely of golden energy and lacking features that would denote a gender. It didn't so much speak, as it projected its thoughts into my head.

"Your wife isn't here," it said, its voice echoing through my mind like a gong.

"Did she... She's not in hell, is she? If so, there must be some kind of mistake. My wife was a kind, gentle woman. Always putting others above herself. If she's in hell, then why—"

"She's not," it interrupted.

Hope flooded through me. "Then where? Where is she? Can I see her?"

"No."

"What? Why not?"

"As I said. She's not here. She's far, far away on another world."

I was rendered silent by that statement. My mind raced as I considered the possibilities. "Is that where heaven is?"

"Heaven?" Its gong-like voice softened to that of a wind chime. *"No, she was chosen for a different path."*

"Chosen for what, exactly?"

"To become a hero. To save the universe from a growing darkness that would otherwise swallow it whole."

"A hero?" It did make sense. Sarah—my wife— spent most of her life saving people. Whether as a field medic with the US Army Rangers, or as surgeon at a hospital in Miami, Florida. She lived to help people. That was also how she died. She'd attempted to save the life of a small boy who had run into traffic. She did manage to get him to safety before the car's bumper snagged her satchel and she was dragged off her feet and into the street. The driver of the UPS truck that hit her swore that he couldn't stop in time.

The doctor that performed her autopsy told me it was a quick death. Painless, even. Which was no consolation for me or the kids. But, after our grief began to subside and we could think clearly, the knowledge that she didn't suffer in her final moments set our hearts at ease.

Whether through chance or providence, the little boy Sarah gave her life to save grew up to marry our youngest daughter and the rest, as they say, is history.

"Can you send me there as well?"

It remained silent.

"Please, I need to see her… I need to know that she's okay."

"I cannot."

"Why?" I asked through gritted teeth.

"Laws far older than your Earth say that it cannot be. Only one hero can be present at any given time."

"I—I can't go? No, wait—the laws said only one 'hero' can be present…"

"Let me guess. I'm supposed to be a hero too?"

"Eventually, yes. Though your time will not arrive for millennia."

"And what am I supposed to do in the meantime while my wife is out there fighting for her life, huh? Am I supposed to just sit back and watch?" I was beginning to yell now. I'd gotten better about controlling my temper in my later years, but this *thing* was trying my patience.

"What if I don't want to be a hero? What if I was something, *anything* else? Could I see her then?"

"Anything?" it asked, its voice resuming its earlier gong-like cadence. ***"Even if you were no longer human?"***

"… Yes," I said after a moment to think it over. "Even then."

"Then I suppose it would be possible. But there would be no going back to the way things were. You'd be giving up your human life, and your chance at an afterlife."

"Afterlife?" I asked. Apprehension settled inside my stomach.

"Yes, the creatures in that place are not allowed to enter the same afterlife as humans. One of the old rules forbids it."

I moved to rub my neck, but my hand passed through it without resistance. I stared at my hand in awe. Wisps of greenish light were seeping through my skin and, if I looked close enough, my hand was entirely translucent. "You swear I'll be able to meet her?"

"On my honor, I guarantee that you'll have a chance."

"A chance, huh?" I weighed my options. On the one hand, I really didn't trust this thing. For all I knew it could be lying to me and I was about to sign my soul away to the devil himself. And on the other, if it was telling the truth, then I could again see the only woman I'd ever loved.

Even if I couldn't have her.

"I'll do it. If you swear on your honor that I can meet her again, then I'll gladly give up my humanity."

"Truly? You'd give up so much for her?"

"And much more."

"...Very well," it muttered after a moment. *"Your request has been granted. It's going to take some work, but I can squeeze you in while there are no living heroes. That should keep the others off my back. Though you'll have to wait a while for her to show up."*

"That's fine. How long are we talking, here? Two—three months?"

"Three hundred years, give or take a decade or two."

"What!?" I protested. "I can't wait three hundred years. I'll be dead and buried long before then!"

"You can, and you will. Provided you can become something capable of living that long. The creatures in this place are not the same as the ones you're used to. They are capable of living for millennia under the right circumstances."

"What's that supposed to mean? Are you going to turn me into one of the creatures?"

"No," it laughed. *"But the world you're going to is… unique. You can grow more powerful there than you've ever thought possible."*

"You're going to need to explain that one in a bit more detail. I'm not stupid or anything, and something tells me it's not going to be as easy as you're making it sound."

"Very astute of you," it admitted. *"Yes, it will not be an easy journey. The path you're about to embark on is similar to one an infinite number of others have walked and will walk on. It is a path fraught with danger. A path that so few beings have completed the percentage cannot even be calculated… the path of evolution."*

I felt my right brow quirk in amusement and had to pull it back down. I knew what the thing was telling me should have freaked me out, but the overly dramatic way it was speaking was almost enough to make me laugh. Or maybe that was just my mind finally fraying? I was handling this entire situation oddly well.

Maybe I had finally lost it.

"And… how am I supposed to evolve, exactly?"

"All will become clear in time. Evolution follows rules so simple even children can comprehend it without instruction. I have faith that you will also be able to figure it out on your own—" It stopped mid-sentence. Its head swiveled to look at my feet before trailing back up to my head. *"It's starting…"*

"Mm? What's started?"

"The translocation process. In a few moments, your body will begin the transformation into your new form,

and you'll be transported to another time and place. If you have any questions, now is the time to ask. I will not be able to contact you for a while after you leave this place."

I racked my brain for any questions and realized I had a few pretty serious ones that I didn't know the answer to. "Will Sarah still look the same as she used to? Where can I find her?" I fired off my questions as fast as I could. A coldness was beginning to seep into my body, as if I was slowly being lowered into ice water.

"In a sense. She is being reborn much in the same way you are, though her body will remain closer to her original form. She likely will not be human once she's been reborn. Possibly an elf of some kind? As for where you can find her, I am not sure. My ability to foresee the future is quite limited at this time. I have a feeling you'll run into her eventually, though I'm not sure when or where that will be."

The cold reached the underside of my eyes and my vision began to blur. "Will she have the same name? Will she remember me!?" I frantically asked.

"Mm... I think her new body will be called Reina. As for whether or not she remembers you, well, we can only hope—"

All sound came to an end as if someone had hit the mute button. Darkness crept into my head as my mind blanked under an onslaught of ice.

I'm unsure of how long I floated in the icy abyss. Time seemed to matter little there, not that I had any way to measure it even if it did. Then something extraordinary happened.

∞∞∞∞∞∞∞∞

Welcome to Planet Rualea

A Snake's Life

∞∞∞∞∞∞∞∞

CHAPTER ONE

I WAS UNSURE OF EXACTLY HOW MUCH TIME HAD passed. Could've been a few days, or a few weeks. During that time, I came up with a plan. That... thing said that I could become more powerful here than I ever thought possible, which also meant that other beings could do the same.

What would happen if Sar—Reina was killed by one of them because I couldn't protect her? What would I do then? I lost her once because some little brat decided to play tag with cars. I… I couldn't afford to lose her again.

So, my plan was twofold and as simple as I could make it: Become something capable of living just long enough to meet her again, and amass as much power as possible, as quickly as possible.

Not long after I'd decided on my future course, I was finally told what race I was to be born as.

∞∞∞∞∞∞

Congratulations on your new life! To accompany your new body, you have been given a new name befitting that of your station/race.

Name: Torga

Race: Non-Venomous Serpent

Classification: Tier 1

Skills: Minor Stealth, Heat Detection, Lesser Gluttony

Traits: Gluttonous

∞∞∞∞∞∞∞∞

Although I didn't care about the new name, since I doubted anyone would use it, the rest of the information displayed did pique my interest.

I would have preferred to be a venomous snake, rather than a non-venomous one. But I'd take what I could get.

The so-called Tier 1 classification also made sense. I wasn't venomous, nor did I feel as if I was all that big, so my choice of prey was limited. That meant my overall power level was, without a doubt, on the lower end of the spectrum.

As for my skills, Minor Stealth and Heat Detection were ideal for an ambush predator, I supposed. I certainly could have gotten worse skills to start out with. Seeing Lesser Gluttony in my list of skills was weird, though. And aside from the Gluttonous trait, which I didn't understand either, I didn't know why I had it.

Focusing on the "skills" in question caused additional windows to appear.

∞∞∞∞∞∞∞∞

Minor Stealth: Your ability to remain undetected is always at its natural peak and will not degrade through aging or lack of practice

Heat Detection: Through the use of the pit organs located above your mouth, you have the ability to sense sources of heat in your general area.

Lesser Gluttony: Your stomach acids are capable of dissolving much denser materials than usual. However, you must also eat more frequently lest you starve to death.

∞∞∞∞∞∞∞∞

And that left me with only one question for the moment. "How do I get rid of this window?" As if it'd heard me, the window vanished just before I felt a pulling sensation near the rear of my body… which, I assumed, would be where my tail was?

A silver portal opened beneath me and I was dropped onto a soft, damp surface. After shaking off my initial surprise of actually being alive again, I took my first cursory look around.

I was in a small clearing surrounded on three sides by trees so tall they blocked out the sky and swallowed the area beneath them in shadows. Luckily the Heat Detection skill activated immediately after I landed and, after a brief feeling of vertigo, I could… er… "taste" the differing heat levels in the area. Currently I was tasting, for lack of a better word, a monotone flavor of nothingness, which led me to believe that I was probably alone.

The sound of flowing water caught my attention. It sounded like it was coming from immediately behind me, but that didn't mean much at the moment since I wasn't sure how much I could trust my ability to detect sound.

It took a surprising amount of effort, and multiple failed attempts, to move my body into a position where I could see behind me. Who knew snake bodies were so awkward to move?

"Maybe there's fish?" I hoped. I could tell my new body was already hungry, which wasn't surprising considering I hadn't eaten in god knows how long. Although, that did lead me to another thought, one I was slightly surprised hadn't occurred to me before now. "What do I have to do to evolve?"

A window appeared before my eyes in response to my question.

∞∞∞∞∞∞∞∞

Consume 50lbs of meat to unlock: Water Boa

Consume 100lbs of vegetation to unlock: Tree Boa

Consume 200lbs of stone/dirt to unlock: Stone Python

∞∞∞∞∞∞∞∞

"That's rather convenient. Can I have a description of each evolution?" Though I waited for a minute or so, no new windows appeared. A disappointed sigh escaped me, and I shook my head from side to side. It was just my luck that it wouldn't be as easy as asking which was the most powerful and going from there.

Reviewing the list again while trying to guess which evolution would be the most powerful from the names alone, I noticed that it didn't say what would happen if I unlocked all three paths. A window appeared in response to my idle thought.

∞∞∞∞∞∞∞∞

Fulfilling the requirements for all three evolution paths will unlock: Titan Boa

∞∞∞∞∞∞∞∞

'Titan Boa, huh?" I did like the sound of that. It sounded strong. Powerful. It would also be more beneficial If I unlocked as many evolutions as possible, even if I didn't see them through to the end.

"I guess that's what I'll aim for. The Titan Boa evolution."

I'd start with fulfilling the requirements for the Stone Python evolution, as It seemed to be the easiest to unlock. Also, it didn't require me to move, which I still hadn't figured out how to do.

Lowering my head to the ground, I opened my mouth and dragged it across the ground as if it were a shovel scooping up dirt. Then I tilted my head back and let the dirt fall down my throat. The loose grass and dirt I was eating tasted like crap, and hurt my throat going down, but I'd tasted worse in the army.

After a few minutes of this, I shifted my head to the side to pick up a stone and felt a tug from inside my stomach. Glancing back, I noticed for the first time that my body had been slowly swelling from the constant influx of "food." However, before my very eyes the mass of "food" began to shrink. "That's convenient." Already, I could feel what I'd eaten being dissolved at a rapid pace. After watching my stomach shrink for several minutes a horrible thought occurred to me: At the rate my meal was being dissolved, I'd be starving again within an hour. So, I began to eat faster.

Every time I filled myself up, I simply waited for the food to be dissolved. During these brief periods of downtime, I gradually got used to my new body. I tried moving around some more, starting with the way I'd seen snakes move in the past. I twisted and swayed my body side to side as I slowly moved around the wide, shallow hole I'd found myself digging.

I also discovered that I could move like a caterpillar… unless I had something in my stomach; then it just made me sick. I continued to test out my new body; twisting, turning, swaying, until I felt my stomach was empty enough, then I resumed eating.

By the time a window appeared to tell me it was okay to stop eating dirt and stones, I was able to decently move around. I was slow as a slug in a puddle of molasses, but I could move.

ꝏꝏꝏꝏꝏꝏ

You have unlocked the following evolution: Gluttonous Stone Python

Would you like to evolve?

ꝏꝏꝏꝏꝏꝏ

"No." The window disappeared. The gluttonous part was new. I wondered if it was because of the Gluttonous trait. That thought led to me wondering if the other paths also gained the trait. A window answered my question.

ꝏꝏꝏꝏꝏꝏ

Consume 50lbs of meat to unlock: Gluttonous Water Boa

Consume 100lbs of vegetation to unlock: Gluttonous Tree Boa

Fulfill the requirements of the other evolutions to unlock: Gluttonous Titan Boa

ꝏꝏꝏꝏꝏꝏ

"So, it appears they did." It also made me wonder what effect this had on the evolutions. Were they stronger or weaker because of it?

They were most likely stronger for it, I decided. The trait made it so I could eat more than a normal snake, which would most likely make it easier to evolve in the future. That thought inevitably led to another. "I wonder how many creatures have this trait?"

Deciding to forget about it for now, I crawled across the ground in search of my next meal.

"Should I go for vegetation or meat?"

CHAPTER TWO

I EXPLORED THE DARK FOREST FOR WHAT FELT LIKE several hours, but not once did I see an animal. It was almost as if they were avoiding this place for some reason. So, lacking any easily accessible sources of meat, I decided to go for the Tree Boa evolution. That should have been the easier task to accomplish, right? I was in a forest after all... But in my time searching, I had yet to find anything on the ground that could be considered a "plant." Trees, grass, and wild weeds aside, the forest seemed to be barren of any plants.

What else could I do at that point? Simple... Climb a tree and eat the leaves and smaller branches.

Now, If I could only figure out how to climb. I could barely move as it was, so climbing was most likely out for the time being... but I'd give it a shot.

My first, second, and third attempts at climbing ended with me crashing to the ground after less than a second. I took a few minutes to try to remember the few times I'd seen a snake at the zoo, and the nature documentaries I'd watched on TV. My fourth attempt went slightly better since I only ended up chasing my tail around the tree for a few seconds instead of falling to the ground... again.

Through the fifth, sixth, and seventh attempts I learned a valuable lesson: Forgetting to keep my stomach muscles contracted when climbing led to sliding... which led to splinters piercing my soft belly.

Ouch.

"This is seriously irritating me," I grumbled as I coiled myself around the base of the tree for the tenth or eleventh time. I'd lost count. Inch by agonizing inch I pushed myself up the tree, only stopping a few times to catch my breath and to get a better grip so I wouldn't slide back down.

"Almost... there," I groaned when I was a few feet from one of the lower branches. I stretched out my body... and immediately knew I'd messed up. My body lost its grip on the rough bark and I started to slide.

"Crap crap crap crap crap." I used what little grip I had left to push myself up and away from the tree. I opened my mouth and sunk my teeth into the bark of what seemed to be a relatively young branch. Its bark was still on the softer side, and it was thin enough for my desperate move to work. But now I had another problem.

"How am I supposed to pull myself up without any arms?"

The answer to that question was "very carefully," by the way. It took a while, but I eventually managed to haul my scaly tail over the branch. I quickly decided that it was better to be cautious than to plummet towards the ground, so I wrapped myself around the branch and settled in for a well-deserved rest.

I stripped a few leaves from the branch and tentatively swallowed them once I'd caught my breath. "Gross," I muttered. The leaves were extremely bitter and filled with some thick, jelly-like substance. I didn't stop eating though. I stripped more leaves from the branch and swallowed them.

It's amazing what flavors you can ignore when it feels like your stomach is trying to dissolve you from the inside out.

Sooner than I'd hoped, I'd cleared the branch of its leaves and had to carefully move to another one for more food. At some point after I'd started eating, I realized that I could feel a warm sensation on my back. I couldn't see anything coming from the ground, but now that I focused on the canopy above me, I could see small specks of light filtering in.

The warmth felt amazing on my scales, and I was beginning to feel sleepy.

"Hmm... Now that I think about it, I have been awake for a while. Maybe I should just find a nice warm spot to take a nap?" I continued stripping another branch of its leaves, even though I almost fell several times during my meal. I eventually cleared the lower part of the tree of its leaves and was in the process of climbing to a higher branch when I happened to glance up at a break in the canopy.

"What the hell is that!?" Towering above everything, and I do mean everything, was an off-white, cylindrical structure so large I couldn't see the top. It seemed to reach into the clouds high above.

"Is... is that a building?" I wondered. No, surely not. No way that thing was man-made. But if it wasn't man-made, then what was it?

"Mm... Suppose I could head in that direction later. Not like I have anywhere else to go." I coiled myself around one of the higher branches and settled in for a nap. I could see the ground after clearing out the tree's leaves, so I had a decent place to watch for any animals that might wander in this direction.

"Maybe I should head back to the river? The water there is most likely fresh, and it could have fish. Of course, it could also be a hotspot for animals. Predators and prey alike need to drink, after all." Then again, there was just as much chance that it wasn't a gathering place, and I'd be wasting my time. I'd been exploring this forest for hours, and I hadn't seen a single animal as of yet. River or not, unless the entire forest was nocturnal, I should have seen or heard something by now. And yet I hadn't. The forest remained as quiet as the grave.

"Oh well. Not like I have anything but time to lose by going back. Maybe I'll clear out the trees surrounding the little clearing I arrived in and make that my temporary base while I get my bearings."

My decision made, I retraced my "steps" back to the river after taking a nap. Kinda. I got lost for a while and wound up wasting a few hours trying to find the clearing again. Only once I did manage to find it, it wasn't quite as empty as I'd left it.

"Damn." I pressed my body into the grass as much as I could, before hiding behind a tree to prevent the animal from seeing me. After listening to it shuffle its feet for a few seconds, I slowly peeked my head around and looked at it. The all-encompassing shadows of the treetops made it difficult to see fine details, but the animal had its head up and was sniffing the air, presumably to detect any nearby predators. I didn't know if it'd noticed me before I had the chance to hide. But what I did know, mostly thanks to my ability to detect heat sources, was that it was large and warm blooded, and its outline against the darkness made me think it was likely to have four legs.

"Can I take it down?" I wasn't sure of this body's capabilities. Hell, I wasn't sure if I could eat it if I did

take it down. It was easily twice my size. *"Not going to stop me from trying, though. I'm starving."* I slowly moved around the tree, while making sure that I was at the creature's back. Then, I crept up on it. With every foot I drew closer, I could make out more details. It was pretty big. Easily over six feet tall and covered in shaggy fur. Two large horns that ended in several points sat on its head.

Its head popped up and I stopped moving. I could swear it looked directly at me, but it didn't react in any way. It returned to drinking after taking another cursory glance around the clearing.

"If I'm going to do this, I need to hit it where it'll do the most damage." After making sure that it still hadn't seen me. I moved to its left side. Then I got even closer, so close I felt like I could touch it if I still had arms.

Just when I felt like I was in position to strike, the damn thing looked down.

It let out a startled scream and rose onto its hind legs.

Using the same muscles I'd used to push myself off the tree earlier, I launched myself at it. I sunk my teeth into its hairy neck and bit down as hard as I could, then held on as it thrashed about. It tried to buck me off for a few seconds, and then one of its legs stomped down on my back, which was the only part of me it could reach. I felt my bones groan in protest, but I held on. It tried to do it again, but I swung my tail up onto its back, causing it to miss.

"How do I get it to stop!?" I panicked as my body was swung around like a rag doll. An image of me climbing up the tree flashed through my mind. *"That's it!"* I started trying to wrap myself around the animal's waist and neck. Though it took several tries, and I now

had a newfound respect for bull riders, I eventually succeeded. Then, I started squeezing, causing it to whimper in pain.

It continued to thrash around, apparently hoping to either throw me off or stomp on me again, but neither happened. In fact, I started squeezing even harder in response. I was probably squeezing harder than necessary, but better safe than sorry.

However, its struggles soon came to an end when it moved to stand on its hind legs… and stepped right into the hole I'd dug earlier. It crashed to the ground; the sickening crunch that preceded its screams told me it'd mostly likely broken something.

I tightened my grip on its neck and body; causing even more of the poor creature's bones to snap under the strain. I planned to continue squeezing until I knew it was dead, and only a few minutes later, I was sure. Its breathing slowly stopped, and it didn't take another. I gave its neck one last squeeze, causing its neck to break and its head to loll to the side.

"Finally," I sighed. "I was beginning to think it would never die. Now I just need to figure out how to eat this thing.

I released my hold on the creature and circled around it. The butt end wasn't the most appetizing option, but its horns were too much of an obstacle for me to swallow it from the front. "I guess I'll just start at the back." Moving to its hind legs, I bit down on its rear. That's when my body's instinct took over, and I began to pull the animal into my mouth.

It took a long time, but through careful tugs, pulls, and twists, I'd finally managed to swallow over half of the creature when I developed a problem. The beast was too large for me to swallow it in one go. However, as I could already feel it dissolving inside me, I decided to just wait for it to dissolve before I swallowed the rest of it.

Which took a while.

I actually fell asleep while I was waiting, and when I woke up, it still wasn't completely dissolved yet.

This became even more problematic when I noticed another heat signature coming towards me. It was similar in size and shape to the first creature.

"Damn... That's not good."

I could only think of one thing to do in this situation. I spit my meal back up and made a break for it. The "leftovers" looked like someone had dipped them in a vat of corrosive acid, but I had no time to marvel at the power of my stomach at the moment.

I quickly made my way over to a tree I believed I could climb, then did just that. By the time I reached what I deemed to be a relatively safe branch, I'd started hearing some odd noises coming from beneath me.

I hesitantly looked down, and immediately regretted my action. *"Oh, God... What is that thing?"* The second animal had found the corpse of the first and, from what I could tell, was tearing into its neck.

A pop-up answered my question.

∞∞∞∞∞∞∞∞

Alpha Deer

The carnivorous cousin of the common white-tailed deer.

Tier 2

∞∞∞∞∞∞∞∞

"Ah... That's probably why I haven't seen any other animals. These things have been eating them." I decided after that to just wait up in the tree for the other deer to leave.

"The most depressing thing about this is that I'm hungry again."

CHAPTER THREE

"*WELL... THIS OFFICIALLY SUCKS.*" I WAS still hiding on the tree branch. The Alpha Deer that decided to steal my food was still hanging around. But my problems soon tripled when two more Alpha Deer showed up to join the feast. One had horns like the first two, while the other did not.

If they followed the same rules as the deer back home, then it appeared I had two males and a female on my hands... and it didn't look like they were going to leave anytime soon.

Now, if it was only one or two of them around, maybe I could do something—whether it be escaping or trying my luck at bringing them down. But with three of them here, no way was I taking that risk.

"Hmm? What are they doing now?" The male deer were staring each other down. One would stomp its hoof, then the other would stomp in response and huff at the other. This repeated a few times, and then they would step towards the other before stepping back again.

"What are you doing?" It almost looked as if they were getting ready to fight, but surely they weren't, right?

They repeated the cycle a few more times before I got my answer. The larger of the two raised its front legs into the air and kicked a few times before ducking its head down and charging. The other followed only a moment later. *Crash!* Their horns clashed together and interlocked. The smaller of the two buckled under the force for a moment, before straightening its legs and standing its ground.

The two's horns would come apart for a moment, only to be slammed back together in a fight for dominance.

While the males were having their little spat, the female began to wander the clearing. And if I wasn't mistaken... It looked as if she would walk directly beneath my branch.

At the moment I was much too far up the tree to take advantage of this… but that could be changed.

"Is it worth the risk, though? If I somehow manage to pull her into the tree with me, I might be able to stay up here until she's dissolved. Of course, I might not be able to pull her up here at all. The branch could break under our weight or she could weigh more than I think..."

Deciding to give it a shot, I slowly moved to a branch only about twelve feet above the ground. Once there, I waited for my chance to strike. Thankfully, I was correct in my assumption. The deer walked directly beneath my branch… and I struck.

My teeth sunk into her neck, and with my lower half still wrapped around the branch, I started to pull her struggling body into the tree. Of course, her cries alerted the two other deer that something was wrong, but instead of trying to help like I thought they would, they bolted in the other direction.

"So much for protecting the women and children." Though the branch creaked a few times, I managed to pull the deer into the tree and wrap my body around both her and the branch. After I secured her in

place, I slowly squeezed the life out of her while being careful not to break the branch in the process.

After two or three minutes of this, the deer lay still and never took another breath.

"This would be so much easier with venom," I sighed. Maneuvering my head into position near hers, I opened my mouth and began my meal. As this deer was approximately half the size of my first deer, I somehow managed to swallow her whole.

Of course, my stomach was now swollen to approximately three times its previous size, and I couldn't have moved to save my own life. But it was nice to have some proper food in me for a change. Eating rocks, dirt, and leaves did not a happy snake make. Venison, on the other hand, was much tastier than I remembered it being.

Now, I could either stay up here and wait for my meal to digest, or I could make my way down and leave. After thinking about it for a while, I decided to wait up here until the food was completely digested before I left the tree. I didn't want a repeat of last time, after all.

With my body still wrapped around the branch, and a digesting deer in my stomach, I thought I would get a bit more sleep while I waited, so I closed my eyes and drifted off to sleep.

I'm unsure of how long I slept, as I couldn't see the sky from here. However, when I did wake up, a pop-up was floating before my eyes.

∞∞∞∞∞∞∞∞∞

You have unlocked the following evolutionary path:
Gluttonous Water Boa

Would you like to evolve?

∞∞∞∞∞∞∞∞

"No." The window disappeared, and another took its place.

∞∞∞∞∞∞∞∞

You have eaten the following species for the first time.

Alpha Deer: Tier 2

∞∞∞∞∞∞∞∞

"I guess now would be a good time to go." A tremble ran through the tree. *"Hmm?"* The surrounding trees all began to shake as if they were afraid of something. *"What's going on?"* I wondered.

I noticed a large heat signature heading in my direction, but before I could make out what it was— *Crack!* The branch snapped under my weight and fell to the ground. After I landed, and after taking a moment to shake away the spots in my vision from where I'd hit my head on the branch, I heard trees being knocked over. Something big was coming my way.

"Ooh, that's not good." Raising my head up as high as I could, I looked into the darkness of the forest for any sign of what was coming. I could see the large heat signature running in my direction. And I was right, it was big… really big.

"I'll—I'll just be going now." The large heat signature entered the clearing at a full sprint, and I got a good look at it before I started to flee. It was an Alpha Deer like the others. Well, it would have been, If the others were the size of an elephant and glowed like they had the fires of hell trapped within their eyes.

Following a safe distance behind the much larger, more pissed off version of an Alpha Deer were two more Alpha Deer, and they looked almost like...

"Went and tattled on me, did you!?" Apparently, the two from before had gone and gotten either the dad or big brother to come and fight their battle for them.

The big one came to a stop a few dozen feet from me and the light burning in its eyes grew in intensity.

"Um... Hello. My name is—" It roared at me, the sound reverberating through my bones like a gunshot. "And you obviously don't care!" It tried to stomp on me, but I managed to dodge around it at the last second.

Weaving through its legs, and doing my best to avoid being stomped on, I got around behind it and bit into its left hind leg. The beast howled in pain and began to kick its legs out in panic.

One of the other deer, while trying to help the large beast, attempted to bite me while I was distracted. It received a kick to the face from the big one for its trouble. The kick snapped the much smaller deer's neck and sent it tumbling into the river over thirty feet away.

The big deer stopped thrashing around and looked between its front legs to see what it had kicked. Judging by the low growl that tore from its mouth, it saw the much smaller deer floating down the river.

"I think that's my cue to leave..." I released the leg while the deer was distracted and attempted my getaway.

I heard another growl from the big deer before I could make it more than five feet.*"...Damn it."* Moving to the side as fast as I could, I barely dodged a massive hoof as it slammed into the ground in the exact spot my head had just occupied.

"Think, think! What can I use to get out of here?" I weaved my way around the beast's legs, occasionally

snapping at an ankle whenever it got too close. I needed to come up with a plan or I was going to die.

The river caught my eye.

"If I'm gonna do this, I only have one chance." I snapped at the big deer's leg one last time before making a break for the river. My plan was to see how well this body could swim, while hopefully not dying from either drowning or the deer.

I was moving my tired body as fast as I could when I noticed the other deer charging at me. I used my tail to propel myself the final few feet, and narrowly dodged the smaller deer's charge. I landed in the water headfirst and immediately started to sink. I tried to swim, but the current was too strong for my tired body to fight against. So, I relaxed as much as possible, and let it carry me downstream.

"Hopefully, I won't run into anymore extra-large deer, for a while..."

I could see the two deer chasing after me in the distance, but the current was too fast for them to keep up with me for long. I had managed to survive my first encounter with the Alpha Deer race.

Chapter Four

I T WASN'T LONG AFTER I ESCAPED THE ALPHA DEER that I figured out how to swim. Except, unlike when I was on land, in the water I had to move my body side to side in order to move around. Doing the "caterpillar crawl" wouldn't get me anywhere except a watery grave.

I also quickly caught up to the deer the big one killed, so at least I had a snack for the road... er, river. However, since I couldn't swallow this one whole, I wrapped my body around it and pulled it along with me.

I swam through the river for a long time before I'd had enough and wanted out. Though I didn't see any fish while I was swimming, I did see several underwater plants, so I could eat as much vegetation as possible. I didn't plan on straying too far from the river for a while.

"Alright, I should be far enough away now. Come on snack, let's get to shore." Tugging my snack along behind me, I swam over to the riverbank.

Once there, I had a little trouble getting the deer out of the water, but I somehow managed it after trying, and failing, several times.

"You're heavier than you look. Did you ever think of going on a diet? Maybe dropping the whole meat-eating thing and eating grass... like a normal deer?" I asked the dead deer. What? I was bored and alone out in the middle of a strange forest. Talking to a dead body wasn't the weirdest thing I'd done today.

Dropping the body at the base of a tree, I climbed up to a branch near the top to get some rest, and I ate some leaves while I was up there. After I cleared out a rather large area, I was able to look up at the night sky. It was... beautiful. I could see the innumerable stars shining brightly in the dark space above. And the two moons were... wait, moons?

"I guess, I really am in another world." The two moons were on different sides of the sky. One was an extremely large bright orange moon, while the other was a much smaller green moon. After watching them for about an hour, I noticed it was the green moon that slowly followed in the wake of the much larger orange moon.

"That's amazing." I watched the moons move across the sky for a few more hours before I called it a night and went to sleep underneath their light.

When I woke up the next morning, my first instinct was to head down and eat, but the deer was gone. "Okay. Either the deer became an undead and left on its own, or there's another scavenger around. Either way, I'm not happy with the current situation," I grumbled.

Moving around the tree, I tried to spot another heat signature, but I didn't see any. I was worried about being ambushed by something I couldn't see, so instead of heading to the ground to look for the scavenger, I moved along the upper tree branches.

When I was confident the coast was clear, I slipped down from the tree. I searched for a while before I smelled the tell-tale scent of old blood. I'd smelled enough of the stuff during the war to recognize it anywhere. I followed the smell until I found the culprits.

A group of rather large bugs was carrying the deer along the forest floor.

"You know what? It isn't worth the trouble it would bring if I attacked them," I thought. Deciding to leave the bugs to their prize, I headed in the opposite direction.

Every now and then, I would see more of the large bugs. Their six legs and dark carapace stood out among the green of the forest.

"I wonder how they taste?" The next time I found a solitary bug, I decided to find out and snuck up on it. It was in a tree about ten feet above the branch I was on. I slowly climbed up until I was behind the bug. It was even bigger up close. It looked to be about a foot high without its antenna, and over two feet long. It had a set of large pincers, which it used to strip the bark from the tree.

"I'd rather not get bitten by those pincers, so I'll have to kill it quickly." Getting even closer to the bug, I waited to strike until it bit into the bark again. I tried to bite down on the back of its carapace, but my teeth couldn't pierce the armor-like shell. After my failed attack, the bug attempted to turn around. I stopped it by switching my target to one of its back legs. I grabbed it as tight as I could with my mouth and lifted it off the tree, then slammed it back down. Since I was unable to bite through its armor, and since I didn't want to take the chance of wrapping myself around it, I planned to slam it into the tree until it could no longer move.

After about ten slams, the bug stopped squirming and was leaking a bright green fluid.

"Is it dead yet?" I wondered. It was still twitching slightly, but that could have been residual energy moving through its body. I held it for another minute or two while being ready to slam it again. When it didn't move, I

wrapped myself around it and rearranged my head in order to swallow it whole.

I was successful in my attempt, though the pincers were annoying to get my mouth around, and it now sat in my stomach like a rock.

"I can already tell this one is going to take a while to digest." I moved on before one of the other bugs could see me and call for reinforcements.

I traveled through the forest for another few hours, until I found one of the most wonderful things I had seen yet. It was a large tree covered in red, star-shaped fruit. It had an overbearingly sweet scent even from my position more than a hundred feet away.

"Jackpot!" Moving to the base of the tree, I found a few fruits that had fallen to the ground and ate them. The taste was extremely bitter despite their sweet scent, but it was still fairly good. It tasted like a strange combination of an apple and a lemon.

"Hmm... Not bad." I ate another, then another. Before long, I had eaten all of the fruit lying on the ground and was climbing up the tree to eat more. Over the course of several hours I ate every fruit on or around the tree. Then, I ate the leaves as well. After I'd eaten the last leaf, I got the pop-up I had been waiting for.

∞∞∞∞∞∞∞∞∞∞

You have unlocked the following evolutionary path:
Gluttonous Tree Boa

Would you like to evolve?

∞∞∞∞∞∞∞∞∞∞

"No." The pop-up vanished and was replaced by another.

∞∞∞∞∞∞∞∞∞∞

You have unlocked the following evolutionary path: Gluttonous Titan Boa

Would you like to evolve?

∞∞∞∞∞∞∞∞

"That's a yes." The pop-up vanished, and yet, nothing happened... at first. Then a severe pain assaulted me. It was so intense I fell out of the tree and landed on my head. I writhed on the ground in agony as a milky white substance covered me, and I was left in the dark again.

∞∞∞∞∞∞∞∞

Your evolution is underway, and a shield has formed around you until it is complete. Time remaining until completion is 23h 59m 47s.

∞∞∞∞∞∞∞∞

"Looks like I'm going to be here for a while. Oh well, at least I'm safe for the time being... Probably."

CHAPTER FIVE

I SLEPT THROUGH MOST OF THE EVOLUTION countdown, and only woke up to read the pop-up on the bug.

∞∞∞∞∞∞∞∞

You have eaten the following race for the first time.

Obsidian Beetle: Tier 1

∞∞∞∞∞∞∞∞

I dismissed the pop-up and went back to sleep. Not being able to see or hear anything for an entire day would have driven me crazy, otherwise. When I awoke for the final time, the pop-up I had been anticipating was waiting for me.

∞∞∞∞∞∞∞∞

Your evolution is complete, and new skills and traits have been added.

∞∞∞∞∞∞∞∞

While that could be a good thing, I had a feeling it would become more annoying than anything else. I don't know why I believed that to be the case, but that's what instinct told me.

I dismissed those pop-ups so the next one would appear.

∞∞∞∞∞∞∞∞

Name: Torga

Race: Titan Boa

Classification: Tier 3

Skills: Minor Stealth, Heat Detection, Gluttony, Minor Durability Up, Major Strength Up, Lesser Growth

Traits: Gluttonous +2, Growth +1

∞∞∞∞∞∞∞∞

I focused on the new skills I'd gained, which prompted more windows to appear.

∞∞∞∞∞∞∞∞

Minor Durability Up: Your ability to resist or completely ignore damage has reached its natural peak and will not decrease through time or age.

Major Strength Up: Your strength has reached the peak for your race and has broken through the natural limit. Your current strength is double that of what could be considered the "peak" for your race.

Lesser Growth: A rare ability only certain races may acquire. Your body grows by one foot every year you live.

*Warning: Due to the Gluttonous trait, you also grow a small amount with every meal

∞∞∞∞∞∞∞∞

As soon as I dismissed that last window, a new pop-up appeared in front of me. This one looked slightly different from the previous ones, however.

∞∞∞∞∞∞∞∞

*Warning: Your Gluttonous trait has gained a level. As a side effect, your stomach acid is now capable of dissolving some metals and you must now eat more often.

∞∞∞∞∞∞∞∞

"Damn," I sighed in annoyance. "I was already perpetually starving, and now you're saying I need to eat even more?" I wanted to seethe at the injustice of it but knew it wouldn't do me any good. My stomach chose that moment to make its displeasure known, as a loud gurgle echoed inside the tight space.

A sudden feeling of claustrophobia hit me. I started thrashing around inside the darkness. My body felt heavy, much heavier than it had ever felt before, and it had grown bigger too. The darkness seemed to press in on me and I knew right then and there that I was ready to get out. No, I *needed* to get out.

My head hit something hard as I swung it to the side and a crack appeared in the darkness.

"Guess that's my way out," I decided. I slammed my head into the hard thing again and again, with each hit making the crack bigger. The darkness finally shattered, and I heard what sounded like a tree falling over.

Lifting my head out of the milky-white shell, I began looking around for whatever had knocked down a tree, but I couldn't see anything nearby. Then I looked back and spotted the fruit tree lying on the ground and saw how close the shell was to the trunk.

"Did… did I do that?" I had hit the shell on something hard in order to get out, but... was I that much stronger? Deciding to try out my new body, I raised myself out of the shell and lifted my head up... and up... and up. "I guess, it wasn't kidding about the size of my new race." By bracing against one of the nearby trees I was able to extend to my maximum height. Fully stretched up, I could almost grab one of the uppermost branches. And my weight was nothing to scoff at either. I tested it by knocking my head against a branch, and the branch easily broke off—a testament to just how heavy I was, as I could climb across those branches before my evolution.

"Maybe I'm the one who should go on a diet." Though there was nothing I could really do about it, I was much more concerned about predators now that I couldn't hide in the trees. "Hmm… I suppose I should also test out how strong I am. I'd hate to end up on the wrong side of an Alpha Deer's stomach because I didn't know my limits." The last time I'd had the misfortune of running into one I barely got away. I might not get so lucky next time.

I wrapped my body around a tree and squeezed as hard as I could. It groaned and protested for a few seconds, then—*Crack!* The tree was crushed beneath my new body and collapsed as soon as I untangled myself from it.

"Well, that's certainly useful." Though I shouldn't need to break down trees often, I was going to assume that most creatures were easier to break than a tree.

"Now, I just need to know what my next evolution choices will be and I can be on my way." A few seconds later, a pop-up gave me the new list.

∞∞∞∞∞∞∞∞∞

Consume 1,000lbs of anything to unlock: Basilisk

Consume 1,000lbs of anything and a creature of Fire to unlock: Flame Basilisk

Consume 1,000lbs of anything and a creature of Wind to unlock: Wind Basilisk

Consume 1,000lbs of anything and a creature of Earth to unlock: Earth Basilisk

Consume 1,000lbs of anything and a creature of Water to unlock: Water Basilisk

Complete the requirements of all other evolutions to unlock: Elemental Basilisk

∞∞∞∞∞∞∞∞∞

"Well, I can easily consume a thousand pounds of food, but what are the creatures it wants me to eat?" I wondered aloud.

∞∞∞∞∞∞∞∞∞

A creature of the Elements is something born into an area saturated with that magical energy.

For example:

A Large Alpha Deer is a creature born of an Earth saturated zone.

A Wyvern is a creature born of a Wind saturated zone.

A Mermaid is a creature born of a Water saturated zone.

A Flame Salamander is a creature born of a Fire saturated zone.

∞∞∞∞∞∞∞∞∞

"Hmm, looks like I'll need to have a round two with that big deer. I'll worry about the other creatures later." My goal was to find that deer to unlock the Earth Basilisk, then find the other listed animals or animals like them in order to unlock the other evolutions. However, I only had one thing on my mind at the moment..."I'm so hungry!" I complained.

Moving to a bit further up the tree I'd broken earlier, I found a section that had been completely broken apart after the fall and started eating the pieces. Then I snapped off the remaining branches and ate them as well. "That took the edge off, but I'm still hungry." I moved out of the clearing. My destination was the river, which I would then follow back the way I'd come.

"I need to grab a few of those Beetles as a snack for the trip." Though hunger was a major part of my decision, I also wanted to be as large as possible when I ran into the Alpha Deer again. "That reminds me—didn't the window mention that eating would cause me to grow with every meal? I wonder by how much?" I had yet to notice a big change, but I didn't want to suddenly grow ten feet because I ate a branch, either. "Eh, I'll figure it out later, I suppose." This stomach of mine was going to be a problem in the future, I just knew it.

Chapter Six

I RETRACED MY STEPS THROUGH THE FOREST AND managed to find my way back to the Obsidian Beetles. With my new size and strength, crushing and eating the beetles was easy, but also left me unsatisfied. Because of my new size the bugs barely filled me up. Even then my stomach acid was dissolving them at a rate that I couldn't hope to keep up with. So, I reintroduced tree branches to my diet in an attempt to slow down the hunger pains. That helped a little, but no matter how much I ate, it was never enough to completely subdue the pain.

I left a path of destruction in my wake as I ate everything in my path. Beetles, tree branches, not even the smaller trees were safe. If I could swallow it, I ate it.

When I finally reached the river again, I chose to move along the riverbank so I could continue to eat anything unfortunate enough to get in my way. Awhile later, I detected a heat signature up ahead. It was small, but I was so hungry I didn't care how big it was. It was food, and that's all that mattered.

I circled around behind it. My heat sense allowed me to find it in the darkness, while it remained oblivious. *"It's a deer... good. Maybe it will take a little longer to digest."* It appeared to be eating something and was sufficiently distracted for me to sneak up on it.

I lifted my head off the ground and raised it until I was looking down on the deer. *"Thanks for the meal."* I struck. My massive size and strength meant I no longer needed to squeeze it to death. Instead, I bit into its back and threw it into a tree. It slammed into the tough bark with a sickening *Crack!* as the bones in its back were reduced to splinters.

It somehow managed to survive the impact and was now whimpering in pain. Its body was wracked with tremors as its eyes stared into mine. "Don't worry, little deer. This won't take long," I assured it. I gently lifted it by the neck… then bit down until I could no longer feel it twitching. I leaned my head back and swallowed it whole.

Once the deer was safely inside my stomach, I moved over to the thing it had been eating and swallowed it as well. It wasn't that big, and since it had apparently been dead for a while before I arrived, it'd lost most of its residual heat.

I didn't know what I had just eaten, but I figured it didn't really matter. With the hunger pains in my stomach pushing me on, meat was meat. And If the deer could eat it, so could I.

I moved on after that and stopped again a few minutes later when I found myself back where I'd started. The hole was exactly where I'd left it, but the traces of my first kill had been cleared away as if they were never there to begin with. Only an old blood stain remained, dyeing the green grass a sickly copper color.

However, that wasn't the deer I was looking for. The big deer and its miniature accomplice were gone… Or was the deer I'd just eaten its accomplice? If so, good.

The little tattletale deserved it. If not, then I still owed a deer a good thrashing.

"I don't think they'd go too far. Vicious they may be, but they haven't given me the impression that they're incredibly intelligent—Hmm?" The smell of meat, bloody meat to be specific, caught my attention. And it was close.

I followed my nose while periodically using my heat sense to search for any signs of living, or recently deceased, creatures. After a few minutes of searching I found the source of the smell. Several deer were surrounding a group of smaller heat signatures... and it looked like a battle was underway.

One of the larger heat signatures yelled in a strange language that sounded... wrong, somehow. The smaller source quickly turned and blasted the deer with a wave of dark blue flames. Another deer charged into the fray and stabbed its horns through one of the larger sources and carried it in my direction.

Another heat source yelled, its voice seeming to carry a sense of... sorrow?

"Oh, free delivery. Normally I'd have to pay extra for that service." I waited until the deer was close before I struck. I attacked its head to prevent it from alerting the others, and quickly crushed it in my jaw. I swallowed both it and the other signature a few seconds later, then went back to watching the battle. Though the other signature had a metallic taste to it, it wasn't bad.

The other large heat source bellowed before charging at a couple of deer. It somehow managed to kill one deer before the other stabbed it in the back. The smaller signatures were quickly overwhelmed by the remaining deer without the two larger signatures to defend their backs.

"Oh well, more food for me." As the deer were feasting on their hard-won meal, I slowly took them out. One. By. One. I would move up to a deer's hind legs and then sneak around and attack its head. After I had it between my teeth, I would quickly jerk my head to the side. *Snap!* and its neck would break. Then I'd gently set it back down and move on to the next deer. I killed three of the five deer before I was discovered and though one of them managed to get away, the other was going into my little stockpile.

"Maybe that's a good thing. Maybe it'll bring the big deer to me like the others did and save me the trouble of hunting it down myself."

I ate every one of the bodies lying on the ground, then settled in to wait. If the escapee didn't bring the big deer to me by the time I was done with my nap, I would continue my search and hunt it down myself. My stomach was pretty full, after all. Aside from the five deer and the four other signatures I had eaten, I also needed to wait for the first deer and its meal to digest.

I went to sleep not long after settling in and only awoke when I heard the sound of a pop-up appearing. I opened my eyes and saw it floating before me.

∞∞∞∞∞∞∞∞

You have eaten the following race for the first time.

Wood Elf: Tier 3

You have eaten the following race for the first time.

Dark Elf: Tier 3

You have eaten the following race for the first time.

Human: Tier 3

∞∞∞∞∞∞

"Hmm... so that's what they were." I strangely didn't feel any guilt about eating them. After all, they weren't my wife. They weren't my friends. For all intents and purposes, they were just... meat. I wasn't sure if I was more disturbed by that thought, or by the fact that I'd managed to think it without feeling any remorse.

"What's happening to me?" I wondered as I dismissed the pop-up and began looking around. I didn't see any sign of the large deer. *"I'll hang out a while longer. Maybe it'll show up eventually."* I lay back down and began to wait.

A long time passed before I noticed two heat sources coming my way. A small heat signature was leading a much larger signature. *"Ah... and that's the dinner I ordered."* I moved out of the way to let them pass and circled to their backs before they could spot me. The big deer stood protectively in front of the small one while it searched the area, presumably for me.

"An appetizer before the main course, eh?" I grabbed the little deer by the head and jerked my head to the side, snapping its neck and throwing it away. The big deer must've heard the impact of the smaller deer hitting the ground because it turned its head in my direction—and I struck as soon as I could. I bit down and coiled my body around its midsection. It tried to thrash back and forth, but I was bigger now, stronger. It wasn't going to throw me around anymore.

After about a minute of its struggling against me, the big deer changed strategies. It stumbled over to a nearby tree and began slamming itself into it.

I groaned under the repeated impacts. I had to release my hold on its neck after the fourth time my head was slammed into the tree, but I quickly sunk my teeth into the side of its head. I jerked it around and smashed it into the tree, breaking off one of its antlers in the process. It recoiled at the pain and let out a reverberating scream that shook my bones.

"Not so fun, is it?" I mentally snarled.

The deer made to slam me into the tree again, but I quickly jerked its head back around and drove it into the tree instead. It desperately tried to make me release its face, but I held on. I switched directions at that point and began pulling its head towards the ground. A few seconds later I had the deer on the ground and pinned beneath my body. It struggled for a few more minutes, whimpering, and moaning all the while… then its struggles ceased, and it lay still.

"Glad that's finally over," I sighed. I uncoiled myself from the deer and repositioned my head at its back legs. *"Time to eat."* I slowly worked my way up its body and swallowed the giant deer whole, though I had to snap off its other antler against a tree so I could close my mouth around its head. Then, I moved over to the little deer and ate it too.

"I should probably get out of here. I don't want anything to interrupt my meal being digested." I slowly moved deeper into the forest in search of a place to rest until I was hungry again. My stomach was weighing me down as several thousand pounds of Alpha venison was dissolving.

CHAPTER SEVEN

I KEPT HEADING DEEPER INTO THE FOREST FOR WHO knows how long before finally growing too tired to move and deciding to sleep wherever I stopped.

After waking the next morning (or was it night? I didn't know or care anymore…), I continued to move through the forest.

"Everything looks the same," I grumbled. "I was hoping to see some form of civilization by now, but all I've seen since coming to this world are these damnable trees."

Of course, the humans and elves that I'd eaten the previous day had to come from somewhere, right? "Speaking of... I have seen one other thing. Maybe it's time I head in that direction?" I was thinking about the giant cylinder I'd seen the other night.

"Now, if I could only remember which way that was…" I decided to do the first thing that came to mind and use my new height to my advantage. I doubted I could see over the trees, though there was no harm in trying. I used a tree as a support while I raised my head up as high as I could.

"Oh, wow. I have gotten bigger—" *Crack!* I accidentally put too much weight on the tree, and it started to break. "Shit... Shit... Shit!" The tree finally snapped, and it collapsed, taking me along for the ride.

"That... hurt," I groaned. Luckily, the tree didn't land on me, but my head did bounce off the trunk a few times.

"Great. I didn't even get the chance to see the giant cylinder." I shook my head to clear it, before moving on. "Alright, new plan. Find something other than a tree to lean against, then try again." Having a tree almost fall on me once was enough, thank you very much.

"At least I'm not hungry anymore, so I have that going for me." I hadn't felt the hunger pains since consuming the large Alpha Deer. That meant I could focus on exploring the forest instead of eating my way through it.

Using my new freedom from hunger, I traveled through the forest for a long time and managed to make some real progress... I hoped. I couldn't be one-hundred percent sure, however. Since I still hadn't found something sturdy enough to lean against, I hadn't managed to get my bearings yet.

"It would be just my luck if I've been heading in the wrong direction this whole time."

"That's not possible," a female voice said from directly behind my head. The words were accompanied by a bell-like laugh.

"Huh?" I spun around trying to locate the source of the voice but didn't see anything.

"Psst. Over here." I heard the voice from my right. I quickly turned in that direction, but again didn't see anything.

"Where are you?" No matter where I looked, I was alone.

"Aww, and I was having fun too," the voice groaned. A source of heat suddenly appeared in front of me as someone climbed onto my head and leaned over to look me in the eyes.

"Hi!" a little girl chirped.

"Hello..." I trailed off. After being unable to understand a word of what the elves and humans were saying during the battle earlier, I had just assumed that no one would be able to understand what I was saying. "How can you understand me?" I asked.

"I wouldn't be much of a druid if I couldn't understand animals. You're a bit weird though," she said, a mischievous grin appearing on her face.

"Am I?"

"Yeah," she giggled. "You don't sound like a serpent. Most serpents tend to roll their S's and R's when they speak, but you don't. Your voice reminds me of an old man I used to know. You're also a lot bigger than most creatures on this planet. What race are you?" she rambled.

"Er… I'm a Titan Boa. And I probably sound like an old man because I am both old and a male," I lazily replied. I continued moving through the forest after deciding that she wasn't a threat. And she was light enough that even though she was riding on my head, she didn't bother me.

"Whoa, you're really a Titan Boa? That's so cool!"

"Yes, I'm really a Titan Boa. Now, if you're quite done asking questions, can I ask a few?

"Sure. I've got nothing else to do today," she admitted. I felt her readjust her legs into a more comfortable position.

"Why aren't you afraid of me?"

"Should I be?"

"Not at the moment. I had a large dinner, so I'm not really in the mood for pipsqueak."

"Then no, I'm not scared," she replied after she stopped laughing. "Besides, I'm a druid. You couldn't hurt me if you tried."

"Why do you say that?"

"Druids are nature mages. One of the perks of being a druid is that non-magical animals can't harm me. Of course, since I can't harm them either it works out for both sides."

"Why can't you harm them?" I asked curiously.

"Granny says that it's a rule of druid magic," she sighed. "Should we break that rule, we lose our magic in return."

"I see..." I nodded my head. I didn't understand a bit of what she'd just said, but it didn't really matter. Wasn't like I could use magic.

"Got anything else you want to know?" she asked after a few minutes of silence. From the way she was tapping on my head with the heel of her foot, I guessed she wasn't comfortable with the silence of the forest... which I thought was odd for a druid. If old books and video games had taught me anything, it was that druids loved nature and a quiet forest was right up their alley.

"How is it impossible to go in the wrong direction?"

"That's easy," she said after a moment. "This planet is so small it's barely larger than some mountains. No matter which direction you go, you'll eventually return to where you started."

"Wow. So, I'll always find my way back to that clearing?"

"Clearing? I mean, I suppose. Though I was referring to the branch."

"What's the branch?"

The girl was silent for a few seconds before she started giggling. "Oh, this is going to be good. I can't wait for you to see it."

"See what?"

"Nuh-uh, I'm not saying," she said coyly.

"Tell me."

"Nope. It's a surprise."

"I hate surprises," I grumbled.

"Don't be that way," she laughed. "I'm sure you'll like this surprise."

"That's not likely to happen. I *really* hate surprises."

I heard, rather than felt, her slap the back of my head. "Don't be an old grouch. Just sit back and enjoy the ride."

"Says the one riding on my head."

"Yeah, yeah. Whatever." She flippantly waved her hand in my face.

"Damn annoying brat."

"So, what's your name?"

"Torga, my name is Torga. What's yours?"

"Pleased ta meet ya, Torga! I'm Ayla Ulafaren."

"Likewise, brat."

"Ya know, we should probably hurry if we're going to make it before nightfall."

That stopped me in my tracks. "What do you mean 'nightfall'? It's always dark, so how can there be a nightfall?"

"We have night and day, silly," she said in the kind of voice you would use for a particularly dim-witted child. "You're just not looking in the right direction."

"Forgive my ignorance. I assumed you had to look up to see the sky," I grumbled.

"Yes, but on this world, you're not looking for the sky. You're looking for those." She pointed towards a tree that had a large Obsidian Beetle eating through it.

"The... Beetle?"

"Yep. The Obsidian Beetle is only active during daylight hours and they sleep at night. While a race known as the Alpha Deer are the opposite. They only come out at night... unless they're hunting something."

"Oh? What happens then?"

"Well, the deer are a vindictive bunch. They'll hunt down anything that smells of their kind's blood."

"Is that so?"

"Yep," she immediately agreed.

"Mm."

We traveled in silence for a little while before she started asking questions again.

"Say, you wouldn't happened to have killed any of the deer, would you?"

"Why?"

"Oh, no reason. I was just wondering why we were being followed by deer for the past twenty minutes."

"*What*?" I snapped my head around and saw well over ten deer following behind us in a half-circle formation.

"What're they doing?" I asked as I slowly rotated my body around to face them. I didn't want to provoke them into attacking before I was ready.

"I'm not sure. I think they're waiting on something," she replied quietly. I felt her hunker down and a pair of slender arms fastened themselves to my neck.

"Damnit!" I felt the trembling ground long before I saw what was causing it. I quickly raised my head into the trees and threw Ayla off onto a branch. "Stay there," I ordered.

"What's happening?" She leaned off the branch to get my attention.

I glanced at her before focusing on the large deer that was charging at me. "I think this one might know my last meal."

"You ate an Alpha Deer!?"

"I've eaten several of them," I replied with a snort of amusement. "I was referring to the big Alpha Deer I had for dinner last night."

"Oh... that'll do it. Alpha Deer mate for life, so you probably ate its partner."

The deer was only a few tens of feet away when I heard what she said. "Well then, I'll just have to reunite them." Right before the deer reached me it ducked its head, showing me its two small, needle-like horns. Unlike its mate's giant, dull horns, these appeared to be quite sharp. I moved my head out of the way as it charged by. I bit into its leg and yanked it backward, causing the charging deer to lose its balance and slide to a stop. I wrapped my tail around the base of a tree, bit into the deer's spine, and quickly jerked my head to the side. The large deer was lifted off the ground and I used the tree to get enough momentum to sling it away from me.

"Whoa! You're strong," I heard Ayla cheer. I chose to ignore her in favor of focusing on the deer that was climbing to its feet.

"Wait—hey, there's a small one behind you!"

I looked back in time to see a deer with thin horns ram into my side. The sharp horns pierced through my scales without effort. "Ow! You annoying little shit." I closed my jaws around its neck and yanked it away from my body. I slammed it into the tree I'd wrapped my tail around and grunted in satisfaction as its body crumpled like a Styrofoam cup against the hard bark of the tree.

The remaining smaller deer chose that moment to split their attention; half of them charging at me, while the rest started to devouring their fallen comrade.

The large deer made another pass at me, one of its horns tearing a line across the underside of my mouth as it passed. I ignored the sting of pain that followed and attacked its neck before it could get out of range. I flipped the deer sideways, before quickly coiling part of my body around it. The deer managed to continue its charge for another few seconds before I slammed my full body weight into it and threw it to the ground. I twisted my body around and lifted the deer a few feet off the ground, then drove it headfirst into a tree trunk. Its horns pierced completely through the hard tree bark as if it were made of paper. The deer screamed in pain and reflexively attempted to free its head. But because of the angle I'd left it in, it couldn't get enough traction against the ground to free its horn.

The deer was well and truly stuck.

I bit into its neck and was about to deal the killing bite when I heard Ayla scream. "Torga, help!" her little voice pleaded.

I looked in her direction and immediately noticed the problem. A group of male Alpha Deer were rhythmically slamming their antlers into the trunk of the tree she was standing in. Each hit shook the branch she was perched on and it was beginning to bend into a bad angle.

"Use your magic!" I snarled before I bit into the large deer's neck again.

"I can't!" she hollered. "I'm just a trainee. I don't know any spells yet!"

"What?" I couldn't afford to just let this thing go. If I did, who knows what I could miss out on by not eating it.

"Help me, Torga!" she cried.

I could just leave her. Let them eat her while I escaped...

"Albert," a familiar voice said. "Save her, Albert," it continued.

"Sa... Sarah?" I asked, surprised. I hadn't heard that voice in years—

"Save her, or I'll never forgive you!" The sound of my wife's pissed off voice never failed to clear things up for me.

"Yes, ma'am!" I immediately replied. I latched onto the large deer's neck and pulled until I heard the bones snap, though its horns were still buried inside the tree. The move fulfilled its purpose. Every small alpha deer surrounding us had frozen up as soon as the large deer stopped moving. As one, their eyes tracked over to me and the large deer.

They began to advance on the large deer, and I took that as my cue to leave. While they were distracted I moved over to Ayla and picked her up by her shirt. We made our escape while the small deer consumed the barely breathing large deer. Alive.

INTERLUDE: A GODLY CONVERSATION

ON THE HIGHEST PEAK OF MOUNT VYENS STOOD A small bronze temple. And inside this temple, two beings made of pure energy were sitting at a table. On one side sat the owner of the temple, a being composed of golden energy. On the other side sat a smaller figure made of bright silver energy.

"Niabus, you cannot continue to interfere in the affairs of mortals. You know this," the silver being said.

"Spare me your lies, Forna," the golden being scoffed. **"You and your 'siblings' have all been interfering in mortal affairs. Or was it not you who caused that woman's premature death, so you could have your 'perfect' hero?"**

Forna tapped her fingers on the table and stared at Niabus, who was returning her look with an intense glare.

"That was... different. I saved a pure soul from a life of misery, while you brought her tormentor here to interfere."

"That's my sister, always so 'justified' in everything that you do." Niabus leaned over the table and stared into Forna's eyes. **"Admit it, sister. Your hatred of men is what drove your actions. Not this**

drivel about 'saving' a pure soul. You ripped her away from a family that loved her and forced her to reincarnate into an incredibly dangerous world, all so you could appear to be her benevolent 'savior.' Tis only natural I do something to protect her from your schemes."

"Since when did you become the type of person to care about mortals?" Forna scoffed. **"Your very existence is their natural end. Isn't that right... God of Destruction?"** The golden energy dissipated and revealed a tall, overly thin man with burning red eyes and two curved black horns protruding from his brow.

"Of course, sister. But I've never claimed to be the 'good guy.' Unlike you and the rest of my 'esteemed' siblings, I'm only honest in what I want." The silver light faded away and revealed a small woman with long white hair and eyes as dark as the abyss.

"Are you saying I'm not honest, dearest brother?" she asked, as the pressure in the room began to increase and cracks formed along the walls and ceiling.

"Of course." Niabus offered a half-hearted shrug. **"After all, you wouldn't be much of a life goddess if everyone knew the kind of person you really were, now would you?"**

"You always were my favorite sibling, Niabus." She laughed. It was a musical sound that had driven many a man to his knees... and a fair few women. **"But do not interfere with my business again or there will be consequences."** Her black eyes began to release an oppressive mist that slowly filled the room.

"I'm looking forward to it, sister." Niabus' eyes ignited in a pure red blaze and a crown made of blue flames appeared above his head.

"Hmph!" She vanished in a silver whirlwind and left Niabus alone.

"You always were too easy to rile up, Forna," Niabus laughed, after he was sure she'd gone. **"Now, what're you planning for my new 'friend'?"** Niabus waved his hand, and a ring of fire appeared before him. The ring shimmered for a moment, before a crystal-clear image of Torga and Ayla appeared inside it.

"Sorry Albert, I can't allow that girl to die just yet. She's my wild card in this game." Niabus cleared his throat and began speaking.

"Albert..."

"Save her, Albert." Niabus could see Torga begin to look around.

"Sa... Sarah?"

"Save her, or I'll never forgive you!"

"Yes, ma'am!" Niabus watched as Torga snapped the Alpha Deer's neck and then proceeded to make his escape with the girl.

"Sorry for deceiving you like that, my friend. But I'm sure you'll thank me for it... one day." He swiped his hand through the flames, dissipating them before he leaned back in his chair. **"Of course, you're probably going to hate me for it first."**

Chapter Eight

YLA AND I HAD LONG SINCE ESCAPED THE ALPHA Deer, but I refused to stop until I was sure we were safe. I moved for over an hour before I slowed enough to check on Ayla. "Are you okay, brat?" I slid her off of my head and watched her for a few moments as she lay on the ground.

"Yeah, I'm fine... it's just," she said through gasping breaths.

"It's just what?"

"That was..."

"Scary?"

"That was awesome!" She jumped up and began running circles around me.

"You're so strong! The way you just lifted that deer and hurled it through the air was amazing!" she squealed. I watched her run around for a while before I said anything.

"You do realize that you almost died, right?"

"Oh, sure I do. But out here in the wildlands, that's a common occurrence."

"The wildlands?"

"Oh! That's what we call the areas populated by magical creatures. Since we don't really know the names of these areas, we just call them the 'wildlands.'"

"Is that so?"

"Yep!" she chirped, but then she got really quiet.

"Brat?"

"Granny's gonna kill me," she mumbled.

"Why would your granny kill you?" She looked up at me with her bottom lip quivering.

"I snuck out to play in the forest, but I was supposed to be back before nightfall."

"Okay... and?"

"The Beetles are gone. That means Granny has probably already discovered that I left." She began to run around for a different reason.

"What am I going to do? If I don't make it back soon, Granny might send out a search party to look for me. I'll be in big trouble then!" I silently watched her panic for a few more minutes. Then, I decided to leave before she attempted to drag me into her problem. Unfortunately, I wasn't as stealthy as I'd hoped, and she noticed me.

"Where are you going?" she asked. Though I still couldn't make out her facial features. The way she tilted her head and began tapping her foot reminded me of Sarah when she was mad... or at least growing impatient with me.

"Um... away from here?" I replied. She tilted her head to the other side and her foot sped up.

"Why?"

"Because I wanted to." Her foot sped up even more.

"So, you were just going to leave me here. In the middle of the wildlands. Alone. Were you?"

"Okay. That's just creepy." She was acting like Sarah used to after I'd said or done something she viewed as "wrong."

"What's creepy?" She tilted her head again.

"Never mind, it's just old memories," I assured her. "I take it you expect me to escort you back to your granny?" The foot stopped tapping then.

"I mean, I wouldn't want to impose or anything..." She looked at the ground.

"Oh, alright then. Bye." I turned to leave again.

"Hey, wait!"

"Yes?" I turned my head to look at her.

"I thought you were going to take me back?"

"No, I asked if you would like me to take you back, and your response was to try manipulating me into feeling guilty. If you want something, speak clearly or not at all."

Her foot started tapping again and I could swear she clicked her tongue at me.

"Did you just *Tsk* me?"

"What, are you, my dad now?" she asked, her voice dripping with sarcasm.

I froze at her words and stared at her. Something akin to déjà vu struck me. I knew I'd heard those exact same words, in that exact same tone before... but where?

"Um... Are you okay, old man?"

"I'm fine. So, do you have anything to ask me?"

She folded her arms and looked at the ground in response. "Will you take me to my granny?"

I stared at her. When she looked up and saw me, she seemed to realize what I wanted because her face grew pink.

"Please."

"Eh, why not. I don't have anything else to do until my meal digests."

"Why only then?" she asked as she clambered onto my head again.

"Because, brat. Then I get to eat again."

"Is your next meal all you think about?" she snickered.

"Of course not. I also think about snacks in between meals," I replied in a serious tone.

She almost fell off my head because she was laughing so hard.

While moving through the forest and listening to Ayla ramble on about her granny, I began to think about the voice I'd heard. *"Was that actually Sarah?"* I wondered. For the entirety of my time here, Sarah had never said a word. So, what could have caused me to suddenly hear her voice?

Was it my conscience feeling guilty about leaving a little girl to die? But then, why didn't I feel anything when I ate those bodies? It could have been because I knew saving Ayla was what Sarah would have wanted me to do. After all, she died to save a child. And regardless of the pain it brought me, I knew it was just who she was.

"Or maybe there's more at work here than I currently know." I wanted to throw a suspicious glance at the little chatterbox riding on my head, but didn't. I seriously doubted Ayla was involved, but another druid, perhaps? I was unfamiliar with their capabilities, so I couldn't rule out some rudimentary form of mind control.

"Hey, Ayla?" She stopped rambling long enough to look at me.

"Yeah?"

"How does your magic work, exactly?"

"What do you mean?"

"How does it affect the world? I've never encountered a druid before, so I'm curious."

"Oh!" She brightened considerably, which was quite a feat considering she was already a squirming mass of positivity. "Well, according to Granny, our magic connects our minds to the plants and animals around us, to allow us to communicate with them and ask them for assistance."

"If they refuse, could you force their compliance?"

She was quiet for a few seconds, then she asked, "Are you worried I'll force you to do something?" She leaned over to look me in the eye.

"You?" I laughed and shook my head. "No, It's not you I'm worried about. It's others like you that concern me."

"You don't have to worry about Granny either. She's the nicest woman I know," she assured me. It didn't do any good, but it was the thought that counted.

"Is it just the two of you?"

"Well... no, there's a camp of us," she admitted.

"Should I worry about any of them?"

"Hmm. There are a few that may try to suppress you."

"Oh, and why's that?"

"A druid is only considered an adult when they have successfully bonded with an animal. While most of us believe this is a sacred bond that should be voluntary on both sides, some of us believe it to be a show of strength, so they force the animal into submission."

"Would I be an animal they would try to 'force'?"

"Probably. I mean, since you're so strong, and your race so rare. A lot of people will want to bond with you."

"Wait... my race? Are Titan Boas that scarce?"

"Yeah... I mean, I think so. Granny's mentioned before that most large Serpents are hunted for their meat and skin, Titan Boas even more so. You'd be a rare thing among my people."

"Hmm, Is that so..."

She must have mistaken my words for fear because she spent the next twenty minutes assuring me that I would be fine. What she didn't seem to realize was, I wasn't speaking from fear.

"It sounds like I'll have all the food I could ever want if I'm so 'rare' that people will actively try and hunt me down."

"What was that?"

"Nothing, nothing. So, tell me about the other druids at camp."

She began listing names and a description of each person. She also told me which ones she liked, and those she didn't.

"Especially Aurae. Don't trust her. Ever."

"Rivalry on the playground, I take it?"

"What? No!" she vehemently denied. "Aurae is my granny's age. She's also the leader of the camp's warriors. She's one of the people that likes to force animals into serving her, and my granny has never gotten along with her.

"Hmm, I suppose I should probably avoid her then?"

"Yes! You definitely should!" Then she went back to rambling off names as we ventured through the forest with her leading me to the druid camp. Then something appeared in front of me.

∞∞∞∞∞∞∞∞

You have unlocked the following evolutionary path:
Gluttonous Basilisk

Would you like to evolve?

You have unlocked the following evolutionary path:
Gluttonous Earth Basilisk

Would you like to evolve?

∞∞∞∞∞∞∞∞

"No." A phantom smile spread across my face. *"If any of them tries to "force" me to do anything... well, I could always use a snack on my way to the next animal."*

"Huh? Did you say something, old man?"

She's annoyingly perceptive sometimes. "Nothing at all," I lied. I was almost eager for one of them to try, now.

CHAPTER NINE

I FOLLOWED AYLA'S DIRECTIONS AND ONLY THREE hours later I could smell smoke in the air. My first thought was that the forest was on fire, but I quickly calmed down when I remembered that we were heading towards a camp, and a camp meant cooking fires. We must be getting close.

"Okay, how did you manage to get us here so fast?"

"Hmm?"

"I smell smoke in the air, so I'm assuming we're close to this camp of yours. Now, are you going to tell me how you managed to get us here so quickly when everything looks the same?"

"I'm just that awesome, old man!" I didn't need to see her face to know she was smirking at me.

"Alright, brat, you've earned a little praise."

She jumped off my head and ran a bit ahead of me. "Hurry up, old man!" She took off running towards camp.

"This damn brat. Does she ever get tired?" I followed after, and before long I saw a large break in the trees. After passing through the tree line, I found myself in a large clearing full of leather tents and campfires, and standing directly in the center of the clearing was a large group of people. I could hear them yelling about something, but I was too far away to make out the words.

Ayla, however, apparently could hear them fine because she started sprinting for the group.

While she was running, I got my first good look at her. She had long blonde hair and was wearing some sort of gray cotton dress. She was also barefoot, though I had suspected that for a while as I didn't feel anything rough on my scales.

I followed her, hanging back from the light of the fires in case the people carrying bows got jumpy or the few carrying spears suddenly decided to get all stabby on me.

"Granny! It's okay, I'm here!" Ayla ran and jumped on the back of a young woman.

"That's her 'granny'?" The woman Ayla jumped on looked to be in her late twenties with short silver hair. When the woman turned her head to the side, I saw the ears. *"So... they're elves."* In the light of the fire I could see their tanned skin and golden eyes.

"Ayla, where have you been!? You've had me worried sick about you!" Ayla's granny yelled.

"Sorry Granny, but I was just so bored waiting around the camp all day." Her granny pulled her off her back and placed her on the ground, presumably so she could inspect her.

"So, you thought running into the Myrkr Forest alone was a good idea, did you?" Granny bopped her on the head. "You idiot! What would you have done if you ran into an Alpha Deer, huh!? You knew we already lost one group to this damnable forest!"

"I know Granny, but it's okay, I made a friend!" Ayla said, while trying to dodge her granny's arms.

"Oh? And just what good would this 'friend' have been if you ran into a group of deer? You both would have been killed!"

"No, it's okay. We did run into a group of deer, but he protected me!"

"What!?" She seemed utterly surprised at Ayla's confession.

"Are the Alpha Deer truly so dangerous?" I wondered to myself. Sure, they seemed like it at first. But they proved themselves to be fairly dim-witted. Surely the elves could outsmart them?

"Where is this man, then?" Granny asked. "I'll have to reward him for saving your life."

"Yay!" Ayla ran to the edge of the firelight and began looking for me.

"Old man! Where are you!?" she hollered into the darkness.

"Oh well, might as well get this over with."

"Old man?" Ayla called again. Though this time her voice sounded nervous.

"Yeah, yeah. I'm coming, ya damn brat." I watched the gathered elves' faces as I entered the light. At first, they didn't seem to react… though that could have been because they were frozen in surprise.

The ensuing volley of screams told me they weren't frozen any longer.

One of the men wearing leather armor with a bow strapped to his back yelled something in that odd language. The other armed men and women quickly surrounded me, while the unarmed people fled. Those with bows notched their arrows and prepared to fire.

"Is this how you repay someone for helping you?" I raised myself up and glared down at them.

"Wait, no! He's my friend!" Ayla yelled.

"Hold your fire, hold your fire!" Granny yelled.

"You should listen to them; I'm beginning to get hungry."

The leather-clad elf said something to Granny and Ayla without taking either his eyes or his bow off of me.

"There are children inside the camp, Elder!" a female elf yelled. I was surprised that I understood that one.

"You think I don't know that!?" Granny yelled back before she cautiously looked up at me.

"If this... serpent, actually protected Ayla, then I owe him."

"Well, aren't you the honorable one?"

She looked up at me. "Some think me 'foolish,' not honorable."

"Sometimes," I laughed, "those aren't mutually exclusive."

"Agreed," she said through a tight smile.

"Smart lady."

The other elves were watching us talk, though they appeared confused. "What's it saying, Elder?" a woman asked.

"It?" I asked curiously.

"Don't get upset, Titan. They don't understand you, the way we druids do."

"My name is Torga, and yes, I figured that out when they started speaking gibberish. Though I was led to believe this a druid camp?"

"Well, Torga, this is a druid camp. However, as we cannot defend ourselves in these lands, for fear of losing our magic, we hired guards to protect us. They cannot speak to the animals as we do."

"From... the deer?" I guessed.

"Yes," she nodded.

"I see. Well then, I'll be going now." I turned and began to head back the way I'd come.

"Wait, old man, where are you going?" Ayla ran ahead of me and stomped her little feet.

"I'm going to hunt, brat. Unless you want me to eat some of your camp to satisfy my hunger?" I asked, knowing full well the answer I'd get in return.

"No, definitely don't do that!" She rapidly waved her hands in front of her.

"That's what I thought. I'm going hunting now, and I'll return tomorrow to receive whatever reward your granny decides to give me," I assured her.

"Promise?" She looked at the ground.

"Yes, Ayla. I'll be back tomorrow." Her face began to heat up as I moved around her on my way to the forest. Once inside, I began hunting for as much food as I could find. A portion of the surrounding forest didn't survive the night, and I fell asleep only moderately satisfied.

The next morning, I reentered the druid camp and was quickly surrounded by the guards, which I expected. What I didn't expect was the dark-skinned elf with silver hair and red eyes standing at the forefront of the group. "Hello," she purred, walking up to me. "My aren't you a beautiful creature." She reached out to run her hand along my scales.

"If you desire to keep that arm, then keep it to yourself," I said in a neutral tone. I wasn't in the mood to deal with this right now.

She quickly withdrew her hand and glared up at me. "Well, aren't you a feisty one?" She waved her hand in an intricate pattern, and I felt a force enter my mind. *"Now, you're going to let me touch you, aren't you?"* Her voice reverberated throughout my mind, and my body attempted to obey. My head was lowering to her eye level when I stopped.

"Get. Out. Of. My. Head," I hissed.

"My, you are a strong willed one. I'll have to break you of that. Now, Bow!" she commanded.

Her order caused an instant and severe migraine. Even so, I refused. "You. Pretentious. Elven. Bitch. Get out of my head!" I struggled against my body as it tried to obey her. The pain was getting worse for every second I disobeyed.

"You'll comply eventually. They always do." She smirked up at me. I was about to respond again when I got a pop-up.

ᘯᘯᘯᘯᘯᘯ

Because of your repeated resistance to druidic mind control, you have gained the following trait.

Strong Willed: Increases resistance to mind altering effects.

ᘯᘯᘯᘯᘯᘯ

Almost instantly, the pain began to lessen, and my body stopped fighting against me. The elf seemed to notice that I wasn't struggling as much and appeared to believe she had won.

"There, you see. I knew you would comply eventually." I lowered my head to her level.

She grew excited and quickly raised her hand to touch my scales, but the instant she did, I whispered, "I warned you."

"Huh?" she asked an instant before I bit her arm and quickly spun my body away. She was pulled off her feet and slung into the air. She screamed as she traveled through the air until, at the peak of her motion, I quickly pulled in the opposite direction. Her arm couldn't take the strain and was torn off, while she fell out of the sky and onto the hard ground. I quickly swallowed her arm before anyone could stop me and began glaring at the surrounding elves.

The previously confident elves were now nervous, and terribly angry.

One of them screamed, which alerted the rest of the camp. They drew their weapons and tried to corral me. However, a voice froze them in their tracks. "Stop this at once!" Granny and Ayla ran inside the circle of guards and stood in front of me. "What the hell do you think you're doing?" Granny demanded.

One of the guards yelled something, and Granny took a step towards the guard in response.

"She's not dead, you incompetent oaf!" She pointed over their heads at a group of druids surrounding the downed form of Aurae.

The guard seemed much less confident now. His words came out staggered, almost as if he were stuttering.

"Shut your damn mouth! I told Aurae last night to leave Torga alone, and what does she do? She tries to force him to bond with her." She took two more steps forward. "She's lucky we need her, or else I'd let nature take its course!"

"So... I can't eat her?" I quietly asked.

Granny glared at me over her shoulder. "If that is what you desire as payment for saving Ayla, be my guest."

"No, I'd rather receive information as payment," I immediately replied.

Granny's body seemed to sag for a moment before her back straightened. "If it is information you desire, then follow me and I will answer any question you have.

However, I would ask that you leave after that to prevent further incident."

"Very well." I nodded my head.

"Come along, then. We'll talk over at my campfire." She turned and walked off.

I glanced down and saw Ayla fidgeting in place. "Relax, brat. I suspected that would happen before we arrived."

She peeked up at me. "You're not mad?" she asked. The nervous tension in her voice was as clear as day.

"Not at you. Though if that woman comes near me again, I'm going to eat her."

"I think Granny was hoping you would pick that as your reward." She leaned up to whisper near my head. "She's been trying to get rid of her for years now. But Aurae was given her position by the previous Elder, so Granny can't do anything directly."

"I think your Granny and I could really get along," I admitted after a moment.

Ayla perked up at my words. "So... you'll stay?"

I shook my head. "I can't stay. I have something I need to do, and I can't do that with people around."

"Oh. Will you come visit?"

"Yes, brat, I'll come visit you and Granny."

She glared up at me. "Promise?"

"Yes, I promise I'll come to visit."

Her glare vanished and she smiled up at me. "Good!" She took a few steps back. "You better keep your promise, or when I'm bigger I'm going to come looking for you!"

"Understood, brat."

Her smile grew wider. "Okay! Bye, old man!" She turned and walked deeper into the camp.

"Bye, brat." I moved to follow Granny and headed up to her campfire for our talk and hopefully, some information on my next target.

CHAPTER TEN

I FOLLOWED GRANNY TO A TENT ON THE OUTSKIRTS of the camp. I noticed that it was one of the simplest among the several tens of tents scattered around the area.

"I'll be honest. I expected something a bit more..."

"Lavish?" she asked, glancing up at me.

I nodded.

"What can I say. I prefer simple." She shrugged. She sat down on an old tree stump near the campfire and motioned for me to move closer. I did, and after fiddling with something in her bag, she looked up at me. "Bantil?" She held out an off-green stick for me to inspect. It smelled like peppermint.

"Sure." She tossed it and I snatched it out of the air before it could travel more than a couple of feet. And I was right, the damn thing tasted like a less sweet version of a piece of peppermint candy. "Say, aren't you supposed to be the leader?" I asked after taking a moment to glance around the area. "Why're you over here by yourself?"

"I am. Though you'd never know it by asking most of the people here. And I prefer to be by myself. Easier that way," she admitted offhandedly.

I tilted my head in confusion. "Why?" I asked. I decided to ignore the various stares pointed in my direction and refocused my attention on Granny.

"Too many people with differing opinions have caused a divide. On one side, you have my family and a few of the older druids. And on the other…" she scoffed. "Aurae and her lot. She's been luring the younger generation over to her way of thinking for several years now. Most of them have already turned against the old teachings."

"And your attempts to stop her have failed because… she's more powerful than you? Better connected politically, perhaps?"

"Something like that," she agreed. She stood up and began pacing back and forth in front of her tent while a bantil stick hung loosely from her mouth. "My grandfather, the last Elder of the clan, gave her that position. Whether I like it or not, that's given her a... a modicum of leeway in what she can and cannot do. And I can't interfere as long as she claims her actions are for the camp's 'protection.'" She bit off the end of the bantil and let out a frustrated sigh. "Credit where it's due. She's quite good at manipulating the truth to fit her needs. The bitch is as slippery as a snake—er… sorry, no offense meant."

I wanted to laugh at how red her face turned, but I did a mental shrug instead and chose to ignore it. "None taken," I assured her. "I still don't understand why you haven't put a stop to it, though."

"I told you why. If I can't prove she's done something wrong, then I can't punish her for it. Without proof, the people would believe I was just pushing her around because I didn't like her."

"So? Who cares what they think as long as they're safe? Say, can I have another one of those stick things?"

"What?" She stopped pacing and was now staring at me.

"Can I have another one of those stick things?"

"No, I mean, yes, but before that. What did you say?"

"Would you mind?" I asked while motioning to the bag with my head.

She pulled a handful of bantil out of her bag and tossed them to me one at a time. Once I'd eaten all of them, she stared expectantly at me as she waited for me to explain myself. After a few seconds of my not saying anything, she started tapping her foot impatiently.

"Okay, maybe things are different here. And I'm certainly no leader, so take what I'm about to say with a grain of salt. But, if it protects your people, who cares if they think you're being mean? Her path could, and probably will, lead to a lot of deaths. So, which is more important: the lives of your people or whether they remember you as a nice person?"

Her foot picked up speed as I spoke until it settled into a rhythmic beat that I could imagine accompanying a rock song of some kind. She seemed to be doing it without conscious thought since she appeared to have zoned out after I was finished talking.

"Guess she got that from you, huh?" I wondered out loud.

My offhanded remark must have caught her off guard because her foot stopped tapping. "Huh?" she asked a few seconds later, which confirmed it.

"Ayla does that too." I motioned to her foot.

She looked down and quietly laughed. "Oh, yes. Ayla's picked up a few of my habits. And I suppose you're right. I've been too soft on them. Treated them like they were my misguided children instead of the adults they actually are. Perhaps, I really am as foolish as they say."

I immediately disagreed. "No, I don't think you're foolish. Perhaps a bit too kind for your own good, but that's not necessarily a bad thing."

"Fair enough." She sighed. She returned to her spot on the tree stump and, after a few moments of staring at the ground, she looked at me with a refreshing smile on her face. "Alright, tell me what it is you want to know, and I'll do my best to answer."

"She's made a decision, then..." I collected my thoughts for a few moments before asking my first question. "How big is this planet?"

She waved her hands in a series of circle and line patterns and a dirt ball floated into the air. Then, she waved her fingers and a line carved its way around the planet. "This is a representation of the planet we are currently standing on. That line in the center is the only source of water on this rock."

"The river?"

She smiled a little brighter. "Exactly."

"But, what about civilization? I mean, surely this camp can't be all that exists."

She shook her head. "Of course not." She waved her hand and a small tree grew underneath the ball of dirt. The tree suddenly sprouted innumerable branches, before it finally stopped growing. "This," she motioned to the tree, "is Yggdrasil."

"What's that?" I asked as I stared in awe at the miniature model.

She closed her eyes, for a moment to think. "Maybe it's better if I called it the 'World Tree.'"

"Oh... *that* Yggdrasil."

"So, you have heard of it? Good, I was hoping I wouldn't have to explain everything. No offense, but sometimes animals, even intelligent animals like yourself, aren't the most self-aware creatures." She coughed into her hand and quickly looked away. "That saves us a *lot* of time and a general overview should be enough for you to get by. The rest you can figure out on your own." With a few more waves of her fingers, the model began to gain detail.

"Okay, first things first. We're currently here." A tiny orb attached to one of the highest of Yggdrasil's innumerable branches turned a pale green color. "We're on a dwarf-planet called Rualea. Rualea is little more than a wildlife preserve in terms of usefulness to the outside world, but it does have its purpose. Certain plants and animals are unique to this planet due to the extreme levels of earth mana found here." Another finger wave caused an orb slightly further down the tree to glow pink. "In the outside world, and away from the relative safety of the upper branches, it can be *very* dangerous for the unprepared."

"I see." I nodded along with her words.

"For instance," she pointed to the newly glowing orb, "This is Rhan, and it's currently the farthest down the tree anyone has managed to get."

"What's there?" I asked curiously.

"Not much at the moment. It's a planet on the edge of the 'civilized' world, so I'm not sure if they've even managed to build their first gateway yet. A few towns and villages maybe, but nothing really worth talking about."

"Where's the current seat of power?"

"Depends on who you ask," she muttered while fiddling with her model.

"Multiple kingdoms?"

"Yep. Thousands of them, possibly hundreds of thousands. The exact number is impossible to guess due to the sheer size of Yggdrasil. Honestly, no one is even sure if Rhan is the farthest down we've gone. It's just the best guess of the Lusan Kingdom, which I happen to be a citizen of." She pointed to an orb that glowed faintly yellow a few branches down and to the left of Rualea. "Aside from us, the other two that I'm familiar with are Dadora, the beast-man kingdom." An orb that glowed blue appeared a few branches to the right of Rualea. "And the Shazar Empire." An orb lit up with an eerie black light a few branches over from Rhan.

"What's with the creepy color?"

She shrugged. "Considering the Shazar Empire is ruled by and named after an Elder lich, it fits."

"One creature has its own empire?" I accidentally hissed my response. Luckily, she didn't seem to mind my outburst. Or if she did, she didn't react to it. Instead, she stuck another bantil in her mouth and bit down.

"No, the reason it's called an empire is because of the massive undead horde under the lich's control."

"And, this lich... it just stays there?"

She nodded. "Most of the time. Although, it has been known to travel to a new planet every... hundred years or so."

"Oh." I suddenly had the feeling that I'd run into that lich eventually. "Very well." I let my annoyance at the thought go. "I only have one more question."

"Alright," she nodded. She bit off another piece of bantil and waited.

"Can you explain the tier system to me?"

"Sure." She took a moment to collect her thoughts then began speaking. "I'm assuming you know your own tier?"

"Titan Boa, Tier 3."

She seemed to hesitate for a moment. "While that is certainly true, I doubt that's all of it. There are certain variables that affect the actual 'tier' of a creature, even if the system that governs such things disagrees with us. You're most likely closer to a Tier 4 beast than you are a Tier 3."

"I'd like to circle back around to that 'system' you mentioned, if that's okay?" At her nod, I continued. "But why do you think I'm closer to a 4 than a 3?"

"I saw the way you ignored Aurae's commands. That, coupled with your massive size and intelligence… well, you'd have to be close to, if not already, a Tier 4 creature."

"I see. And, what about this 'system' you mentioned. What is it?"

"No idea," she admitted, her shoulders shrugging upwards. "It's just what we call the little boxes that pop up to inform you of a change. As far as I'm aware, no one knows how or why it works. Only that it does."

Out of the corner of my eye I saw a heat signature trying to hide behind Granny's tent. It was too large to be Ayla, so I assumed it was one of Aurae's "followers." "I see. Well, thank you for your help. I should get going before I cause any more problems for you and Ayla."

"Where are you headed?" she asked after a moment of silence.

"Hopefully, to find a way off this rock."

"Mm…" She stood and walked to the side of her tent, then pointed at the cylinder. "That's one of Yggdrasil's branches, and your way off this rock. When you get there, merely touch it and you'll find a portal that'll lead you to your next destination. I'm sure you can figure out the rest."

"Thanks again, Granny." I slightly bowed my head and moved past her.

"Oh, and Torga?" She called after me.

"Yeah?"

"Two things. One, my name is Freja. Call me Granny again and I'll smack you. And two, mind the guards at the base of the branch. They're not as… accommodating as I am. Their job is to keep creatures like you from traveling to other planets. So be careful, okay?" I noticed the heat signature leave. It probably heard what it needed to and was going to get help. *"Oh ho... Looks like I get to have that meal, after all."* A phantom smile spread across my face. "I understand, Freja. I'll be careful." With that, I left the camp and started making my way towards the branch.

I soon spotted the multiple heat signatures following me, and one of them happened to be missing an arm. *"Well, well. Look who's here."* I saw them congregate ahead of me, so I ducked down and circled around them. Once I was close enough, I glimpsed them hiding in the trees. *"Trying to ambush me, eh?"* I looked for the signature that was missing an arm and snuck up behind it. Then, I rose to my full height. "Boo," I hissed into her ear.

Aurae jumped at the sound of my voice and quickly spun to look at me. Well, she saw the inside of my mouth. I bit down on her head and neck before she could scream, tilted my head back and swallowed her whole. Then, I left the young elves waiting in the trees. "Consider this a favor to you, Freja," I muttered as I went on my way, while the young elves continued to wait in the trees. How long it would take them to realize their leader was gone, I didn't know, nor did I care.

CHAPTER ELEVEN

I TRAVELED FOR WHAT FELT LIKE DAYS AND ONLY stopped when I was ready to sleep. Otherwise, I kept moving.

I ate almost everything to cross my path, whether it was an Obsidian Beetle or the few large Alpha Deer I came across. None were spared from my stomach. Though I did make sure to avoid most of the humanoids I saw along the way. The few that did stumble upon me, as long as they didn't attack, I left alone. However, the four humans being dissolved in my stomach meant that wasn't always what happened. They chose to attack me, so I ate them.

I arrived at Yggdrasil's Branch on the eve of the fourth or fifth day since I'd left the camp. I immediately spotted the heavily armed guards Freja mentioned and, thanks to my ability to detect sources of heat, I noticed multiple sentries patrolling the forest around the branch.

I rose up to get a good look at the branch and saw what I'd been looking for. *"So... that's the portal* Freja *was talking about?"* A large clear ring was floating just before the branch and had approximately ten guards stationed in front of it.

"Freja was right. They're not playing around." Instead of allowing myself to be seen in the sunlight, I moved deeper into the forest to watch the guards for a while. The clear sky around the branch

would make sneaking through the portal almost impossible, which meant I needed to come up with another way to get past them.

The snapping of a twig drew my attention away from the branch and into the forest to my right. I turned my head and saw a patrol heading in my direction. I slowly moved out of their way and resettled into a comfortable position to continue watching their movements.

I watched them circle once, then I started counting how long it took them to make a rotation around the branch. I watched them head farther into the forest several times, but they always came out after a few minutes.

"If I try to take out the stationary group while the other is out of sight, then I'll only have a few minutes to kill them and get through the portal." As I was watching them, however, I noticed something standing in the forest to my left. *"Or, I could always go with plan B."* It was a stray Alpha Deer that had either gotten separated from its group or was a scout looking for food. Either way, it reminded me of what Ayla said about the deer being vindictive.

With that thought came a plan... Why do this myself when I could sit back and let something do it for me?

I smiled as I moved towards the lone Alpha Deer. *"Time to see if the brat was right, and you really are a vindictive lot."*

~ ~ ~

EREN LEOTRIS

Eren Leotris had been assigned to this post along with the seventeenth regiment of the Lusan Kingdom to prevent any of the native animals from making it through the portal. He was walking next to his longtime friend

Shaun Baldove. The two of them were part of the unit patrolling the forest and were currently walking along the southernmost side of the branch.

"Hey, Eren?"

"Yeah?"

"Why are we doing this again?"

Eren rolled his eyes at him. "You know why, Shaun. We were drafted, so we're stuck here for another three months."

"Do we really have that much time left on our draft orders!? I thought we were down to a few weeks, at most?"

"Yes. Now, be quiet before something notices we're here," he whispered.

"Nothing is going to happen, Eren," he scoffed. "We've been here for six months and haven't seen a damn thing apart from those elves that came through a few weeks ago." This earned him a glare from Eren.

"You don't know that. What if your blabbering alerts a group of Alpha Deer, or silver city forbid, a large one?"

He rolled his eyes at him. "Oh, no—not the dreaded Alpha Deer. Whatever shall I do?"

Their commander turned up just then. "You'll die if you keep up that attitude, boy!" Now, most people would heed the commander's warning. The man had been stationed here for years and obviously knew what he was talking about. But Shaun didn't see it that way.

"Is the great Commander Evart scared of a few deer?" Shaun mocked.

The commander stepped up to Shaun, and though he was a few inches shorter, he was much more intimidating than Shaun could ever be. "Aye, I am scared of the demonic beasts," he said harshly, before continuing in a much quieter voice. "And if you ever encounter them yourself, I guarantee that you'll fear them as well." He turned away and moved to the front of the group.

"Enough lazing around!" Evart shouted. The men jumped to attention and saluted.

"Aye, Sir!" they shouted and continued their patrol. They made it halfway around the branch before they started hearing the screams.

"Double time, men!" the commander yelled.

They hoisted their shields and sprinted the rest of the way around the branch. What they saw there could only be considered a war zone. Bodies lay everywhere as a group of Alpha Deer feasted on them. The few guards that remained alive were desperately trying to protect the bodies closest to them from the Alpha Deer's hunger.

The commander drew his sword and charged, which prompted the guards to shake themselves out of their stupor and copy his actions. They followed their commander into battle as a group of greenhorns who'd never seen combat, but they—or at least Eren—was determined to see it through and come out the other side a veteran.

Commander Evart became a whirlwind of death as soon as he pulled his sword from its scabbard. He hacked and slashed his way through the feasting Alpha Deer. Each slash cleaved heads from their bodies, each stab pierced a vital organ. And only after they reached the surviving members of the seventeenth regiment did he slow down enough to start barking out orders. He told them to pair off and take on the straggling deer, while he directed the remaining portal guards to tell him what happened.

"I don't know, Sir!" one of the men managed to gasp out.

"What do you mean, 'you don't know'!?"

"It's the truth, Sir." The lieutenant, and the man in charge of this group of soldiers, spoke in between heavy breaths. "One moment we were all standing guard, as usual. And the next thing we knew a headless deer body came flying at us. Luckily, we managed to raise our shields in time, but the blow knocked most of us off our feet."

"Hit us like it'd been fired from a damn cannon," a third man groaned. His arm was clearly broken beneath his leather arm guards.

"Right," the lieutenant agreed. "And before we could stand back up, we were already under attack by these beasts."

"A headless deer?" Commander Evart asked. A sense of horror was dawning on him. A few seconds later, his worst fear was realized when he spotted the headless deer lying on top of a dead soldier. "This was a planned attack. Everyone, stop killing the deer and get through the portal. Right now—" The last deer fell to the ground before he could finish his order. And that's when the ground began shaking.

"Oh... Fuck no!" the commander yelled. "Get through the portal, double time!!"

~ ~ ~

TORGA

"Oh, fuck yes." I'd seen the large Alpha Deer walking through the forest since before the battle began but didn't actually expect it to join the fray. Until I bit the head off the lone deer and threw it into the mix.

The large deer crashed into the soldier with the fanciest armor first and speared him through the chest while the soldier was trying to defend a taller man. It was soon joined by numerous Alpha Deer reinforcements, and they made quick work of the surrounding soldiers with their hooves and horns. Only a couple of the guardsmen managed to escape through the portal before the deer could get to them. By the end of the battle, the big deer's legs were covered in blood and bodies adorned its horns like some kind of sick decoration. And it was continuing to take out its anger at losing the lone Alpha Deer on the fallen human corpses.

"Don't worry... You'll be joining them soon." I launched myself out of the tree line and slammed into the deer's side. I bit into its neck, wrapped my body around it, and almost instantly began to crush the air from its lungs. Though it tried to throw me off, I was easily able to hold on until I could get a good grip on its throat with my teeth. I twisted my head and ripped a large chunk of its flesh off; blood sprayed onto my face for a few seconds before I felt the deer's body trembling. A few seconds after the blood shower began, it fell over and remained motionless.

"That... that was too easy." I stared at the corpse beneath me. I wasn't sure what I felt—horror, excitement? My stomach twisted in pain. Hunger, I felt hunger.

"What do I eat first?" Deciding that it didn't really matter since I was going to eat everything anyway. I started with the human bodies as an appetizer, then the large deer and its accessories as the main course. And I ate the little deer for dessert.

I decided to only enter the portal after my meal had digested, because even after eating such a large meal, if I could feel it digesting at a frightening pace, I was ready to sleep. So, I circled my body around the branch and went to sleep. *"I hope the next world has one of the creatures I need to evolve... and that it's delicious."* I drifted off with that pleasant thought in mind.

CHAPTER TWELVE

I WOKE UP SOMETIME THE NEXT DAY AND BEGAN TO observe the portal. As far as I could tell, it was just a clear ring floating in front of the branch. It lacked any identification markings that would give me some clue as to where it led, so I was going to need to be extremely cautious moving forward, lest I get ambushed on the other side… or die because it dropped me into a hazard zone.

"Where will you take me?" I wondered. I moved up to the portal and realized it made a slight humming noise, though it was so faint I could only hear it once I'd gotten close to it. I leaned my head closer until my nose was brushing against it. And that was my mistake.

A strong pull instantly began to affect my body, almost as if the portal had its own gravity field. First, my nose was stretched until it was pulled inside, then my head followed, and my body was pulled through. None of this hurt, though it was incredibly disorienting.

Once I was inside the portal all I could see was a kaleidoscope of colors, and no sound seemed to exist in this place.

"Where... am I?" A pop-up answered my question.

ꝏꝏꝏꝏꝏꝏꝏ

Welcome to the Bifrost

Please select your next destination from the available branches.

∞∞∞∞∞∞∞

"Hmm... Alright, let me see the choices."

∞∞∞∞∞∞∞

Iorus: A majority of this planet is covered by water, and only three islands exist.

∞∞∞∞∞∞∞

"Wait, is that it?" Although I was slightly happy that I had a higher chance of finding a magical water creature in a world that was mostly water, I would have preferred a non-water world first. Swimming in a river was awkward enough as it was, never mind trying to swim in an ocean.

"Oh well, Planet Iorus it is." The force returned and started pulling me along.

I'm not sure how long I was inside the Bifrost, though it probably wasn't a small amount of time. Eventually, a clear ring formed in front of me and my body was pushed through.

After reforming on the other side and clearing my head of the disorientation, I looked around and saw buildings that had been built around the branch in a circular pattern and expanded out into a sprawling city. It would have been an amazing sight... had it not been in ruins. The buildings were made with white stones, which had been overrun by moss and other vegetation. Most of them were still standing high, with the tips appearing to brush the clouds that passed overhead.

"What is this place?" A pop-up appeared.

Kenneth Arant

∞∞∞∞∞∞∞∞

Welcome to Planet Iorus

∞∞∞∞∞∞∞∞

"Well, I suppose that tells me where I am, but not what this place is." I moved around the branch to get a look in every direction. After a few rotations, I believed I had at least some idea of which way I should go. On the portal side of the branch was the ruined city; on the other side was a sheer cliff that led to the ocean. "That's... a long way down," I muttered as I pulled my head back from the edge. I'd been looking over it for a safe way down, so I could try my luck at finding the water creature I needed. But after a few minutes I decided to circle back and head deeper into the city. "There's got to be a way down, somewhere..." I resolved myself to search the city until I found one.

I explored the city for days, sleeping when I felt like it and just enjoying the fact that for some reason, I wasn't constantly craving food. The city was an amazing sight; skyscrapers dotted the cityscape, and it seemed as if a beautiful vista could be found around every corner.

"One day, if it's still here, I'm going to bring Sarah here to see it. She would love it here." I distantly wondered why this place, this beautiful paradise, was left to ruin. Where did the inhabitants go? But I decided it probably didn't matter. Besides, all this thinking was giving me a damn headache. From what I'd seen since arriving, this island had everything. The ocean was an endless supply of food, and I could see fish constantly jumping out of the water below. Massive gardens filled with food were scattered around the island, and yet... no matter where I looked, I hadn't found a way down, or clues to where the previous inhabitants went.

It was like they just up and disappeared one day.

"Come to think of it, this place could have been a prison for all I know." If you replaced the iron bars with all the food you could eat, perfect weather, and scenery a painter from back home would kill to see… though that did bring up the question of *why* anyone would turn this place into a prison... or why I even brought up the prison idea to begin with. My vision began to grow blurry. "Fucking headache," I sighed. "I'm not sure I actually want to know. But, I need to find a water creature. So, I guess I'll find out eventually if I want to or not. If I was going to search the ocean for that creature, then I had to leave this place. Even though I didn't want to. Wait... don't I want to leave?" The thought hit me like a ton of bricks and my headache intensified sevenfold. "Maybe I should go lie down for a while. Actually, yeah, that sounds like a great idea." I slowly nodded my head to avoid making it hurt any more than it already did. "That's what I'll do."

I moved through the city until I arrived at my favorite sleeping spot—a grassy hill behind the branch that had a truly breathtaking view of the ocean. Once I was there, I laid down and allowed my head to dangle over the edge of the cliff. I don't know why, but for some reason, I really enjoyed looking at the water below.

"Maybe I should just jump?" I wondered aloud, already semi-delirious from pain. Instantly, my headache worsened, and I grew dizzy. "Alright, alright. Jumping is a bad idea. Got it." I tilted my head away from the cliff. The farther back I leaned, the less my head seemed to hurt. However, something in me screamed that I needed to do something, anything. A feeling of panic settled in that was so intense it made my body shake. Instantly, everything became clear and I knew what I needed to do.

I threw myself over the edge.

It was slow at first, but as I fell, my mind began to clear. That was also when I saw IT—a colossal creature, or the remains of one, that was holding the city on its shoulders as it stood in the ocean. The water only came up to its calves, which emphasized just how massive the creature was.

The only things I could clearly see were its dark blue skin, which was covered in tribal tattoos, long black hair that almost reached the water below, the two curved horns on either side of its head, and the thick chains wrapped around its huge chest that served to hold the island in place on the creature's shoulders.

I hit the water with the force of a cannonball and was lucky the impact didn't kill me. It might have been due to the lower gravity of the planet or the increase in durability my skill granted me. But slamming into the water at terminal velocity only managed to knock me unconscious and left me at the mercy of the waves. When I came to, I discovered that the waves had carried me far away from the creature and the paradise— or rather, the hell—it carried on its shoulders.

Chapter Thirteen

I WOKE UP SOMETIME AFTER DARK AND FOUND myself floating on top of the ocean. The waves were slowly pushing me up and down, and side to side... Honestly, it was the most relaxing thing to happen since I'd come to this planet.

I don't know what that island was, but it was terrifying. I think I'd only been semi-conscious since the day after I arrived. I was aware of what I was doing, but there didn't seem to be any purpose to it. I knew I was *supposed* to be looking for a way down. My heart was never really in it though. Maybe I was right about it being a prison, after all?

However, that left me with a few questions: What was that place? Why was my mind so cloudy? And what was that creature carrying the island?

"If... Or rather when I see it again, I'll have to be much more careful about keeping track of the amount of time I spend there. I have zero interest in being trapped in a mental stupor until I die." Deciding to push all thoughts of the island to the back of my mind, I ducked my head under the water. The water was crystal clear, but it was currently too dark to see more than a couple dozen feet in any direction. And with the thick rain clouds in the sky above, I wasn't likely to get any assistance from whatever moon was in the sky above.

I completely submerged myself after relaxing for a few more minutes and began exploring.

After swimming straight down for a few minutes. I found an expansive coral reef and bevy of ocean life. Fish of all sizes, colors, and breeds seemed to call the reef home. I could see a few decently large sharks swimming in the distance. *"Guess I won't be lacking in food anytime soon."* I swam closer to an expansive piece of orange coral and found a hole large enough for me to squeeze through.

"Hmm... not bad." I swam inside and "introduced" myself to the occupants, a family of bright orange-and-black fish that were about the size of a house cat. They numbered in the dozens, so it took me a little while to catch them. But since my coiled tail performed its job as a cork admirably, they were easy, and more importantly, tasty prey.

After properly introducing myself to the fish, and throwing my compliments to the chef, I returned to the surface to breathe for a few minutes before heading back down. This was a long and tedious process that consisted of me searching the reef for as long as I could hold my breath, returning to the surface to breathe, then diving back down again.

As I currently lacked any sleeping quarters of my own, I'd catch a few winks during the many times I came up for air, then continue exploring. Luckily—or unluckily for me, I suppose—I accidentally intruded on a long lost cousin.

I'd been searching a massive piece of red coral that could have housed a small building, when I found the entrance to a rather large chamber. I poked my head in to look around, but I didn't see any creatures swimming in there, and my heat sense wasn't detecting anything either.

Naturally, I assumed it was either empty or the owner was out. I was wrong.

Only once I'd swam inside the chamber and something moved to cover the entrance did I suspect that I may have been in trouble.

At first, I thought it was one of the many sharks I'd seen during my time exploring the reef, coming to suggest a particular recipe for shark fin soup for me to try. Or perhaps it was a school of fish swimming past the entrance. The absolute last thing I expected to find was an enormous white serpent with beady black eyes staring at me from the entrance to the chamber. Its head was large enough to completely fill the hole I'd come through, and I briefly saw a pair of gills on each side of its neck before my attention was pulled back to the matter at hand… which were teeth so bright I'd swear I could see my reflection in them.

"… Hello?" I offered my greetings with a slight bowing of my head.

"Greetings, little one," it replied, its fish-like eyes never leaving mine.

"Oh, you're friendly?" A loud rumble followed my words and I winced.

"So long as you provide me with a reason to be," it returned, a gleam appearing in its expressionless eyes.

"Well, uh… I mean you no harm?" I tried.

It shook its massive head. "Try again."

"I can help you?"

It shook its head again. "Still no. Last chance to convince me or you're going to be a late-night snack."

"I taste awful?" I sighed. This wasn't going to end well for me.

It shook its giant head once more. The water inside the chamber rolled from side to side with such force that I was almost slammed into one of the walls. "I'll be the judge of that," it finished, its mouth growing even wider as more teeth appeared.

I quickly turned and swam deeper into the chamber.

"Oh, goodie. I love fast food!" I could hear it crash into the walls in its haste to follow me. But with my smaller size, I had a much easier time getting through the narrow passages of the coral than it did.

Eventually, though, I found an exit and re-entered open water, where I quickly lost any advantage I had inside the reef. The four large fins I caught glimpses of during the few moments I was brave enough to look back and its massive size helped it cut through the water at a much faster pace than I could ever hope to achieve.

I feigned going left, before swimming down and to the right. Then I used my smaller size to dodge around the serpent's gaping mouth and back towards the coral reef.

"Where are you going, little one?"

I glanced over and saw the serpent casually swimming next to me with its teeth glowing in the darkness.

"Nowhere important!" I ducked beneath a large piece of coral and hugged as close to the ocean floor as possible, while still maintaining my speed.

I caught glimpses of the Serpent through cracks and holes in the coral above me. But it was its voice that would've raised the hairs on the back of my neck, if I still had any hair to raise. "Is that so?" it asked in a voice reminiscent of a small child. "Then how about joining me for dinner, my treat?"

"I'll pass, thanks." My mind latched onto the way the Serpent had said, "my treat," and the chills returned to racing down my spine.

"That's not nice. And here I was hoping to have you for dinner." Its voice brought to mind the image of a child pouting.

"I'm sure a nice guy like you can find a dinner date. No need to drag me into it—" A loud *Bang!* startled me so much I almost ran into the cause of the cave-in. The white serpent's head had crashed *through* the reef and was now mere inches away from me.

"I'm a woman!" it hissed. It opened its mouth and sprang at me faster than I thought possible for a creature its size.

I turned tail to run, but it was much too fast for that trick to work a second time. Its mouth closed around me. *"Fuck!"* I was lucky enough to turn my head in time to avoid the teeth now occupying a space a hair's width from my face. But this time I was inside the creature's mouth and a low rumbling sound, followed by a powerful sucking force, told me how screwed I really was.

I was pulled deeper into its body, thrashing against, and biting into, whatever I could to keep myself from being completely swallowed.

"What do you think you're doing!" the creature yelled.

Though I couldn't answer it out loud, *"Something incredibly stupid,"* was my response.

I tore off a chunk of the uvula and was pulled deeper down the throat, then into the esophagus. I swallowed the piece of uvula and bit into the esophagus wall. I heard the creature yell again, but I was too focused to understand what it was saying. I held on until the suction stopped and then I began eating my way through the esophagus wall. The serpent began swallowing other creatures in an attempt to stop me, but I sunk my teeth deeper and held on.

Even when creatures slammed into me and knocked me loose, I quickly reattached myself and continued holding on. I was *not* dying here, in the belly of some overgrown sea worm.

I eventually made it through the esophagus wall, and into the muscle tissue beyond it, where I continued to eat my way out. I did run into a problem at this layer, however. More and more blood began to fill up the esophagus and splash on me. Normally, this wouldn't be much of a problem. Except the serpent's blood felt like acid on my scales—acid that was slowly eating its way through them and into my own muscle tissue.

I started eating even faster than before, only stopping for a few seconds at a time to spit out what I'd ripped off once my stomach was filled to the point of bursting and I could no longer just swallow it.

Finally, after about twenty minutes of eating, I bit through the final layer and was just inside the serpent's scales. It took me another few minutes to dig through them because they were so thick, but at least the acid blood had stopped spraying on me, so I had that going for me, at least.

Once I'd eaten my way through the final barrier keeping me from the outside world, I blindly swam as far away from the now *royally* pissed off serpent as I could. The creature was thrashing around on the ocean floor in severe pain, so I could have taken this opportunity to try killing it, but I was too tired. My body ached too much for me to care at this point.

I managed to stumble into the walls of the reef after swimming for who knows how long. I dragged myself into a little hole near the top of a piece of coral poking out of the water. I could finally rest in relative safety and breathe a sigh of… and that's when I noticed what kind of shape I was in. Large swaths of scales had been either completely dissolved or severely damaged and the muscles beneath were open sores that burned fiercely beneath the onslaught of saltwater. The severity of the pain I'd managed to ignore through a mix of adrenaline and shock hit me like a ton of bricks and I passed out.

I woke up sometime later to a pop-up floating in front of me.

∞∞∞∞∞∞∞∞

You have eaten the following race for the first time.

Leviathan: Tier 7

You have unlocked the following evolutionary path: Gluttonous Water Basilisk

Would you like to evolve?

∞∞∞∞∞∞∞∞

"No..." I groaned before trying to go back to sleep. But then another pop-up appeared, surprising me.

∞∞∞∞∞∞∞∞

You have unlocked the following evolutionary path: Gluttonous Dual Element Basilisk

Would you like to evolve?

∞∞∞∞∞∞∞∞

"That's... new?" I thought for a few seconds before asking, "Can I add the other elements later?" A secondary pop-up answered me.

∞∞∞∞∞∞∞∞

Provided you do not evolve to a new race, you can add the missing elements later.

∞∞∞∞∞∞∞∞

Well, that makes this an easy choice then. "Yes, I'm ready to evolve." Just like the first time I evolved, a white shield formed around me and I sunk to the ocean floor.

∞∞∞∞∞∞∞∞

Your evolution is underway, and a shield has formed around you until it is complete. Time remaining until completion is 6d 23h 59m 42s.

∞∞∞∞∞∞∞∞

"Hopefully, I'll heal during my time in here... because saltwater stings like a bitc—" was the last thing I could think before blissful unconsciousness took me.

Chapter Fourteen

I HEARD A DING THROUGH THE DARKNESS, WHICH caused it to recede, and I was allowed to wake up. Upon opening my eyes, I was greeted with a pop-up.

∞∞∞∞∞∞∞∞

Your evolution is complete. You have gained two new traits and a new skill.

Name: Torga

Race: Gluttonous Dual Element Basilisk

Classification: Tier 5

Skills: Minor Stealth, Heat Detection, Gluttony, Major Durability Up, Major Strength Up, Growth, Minor Mental Resistance Up, Petrifying Gaze, Greater Acid Venom

Traits: Gluttonous +2, Growth +2, Strong Willed, Venomous, Aquatic

∞∞∞∞∞∞∞∞

I went over my new information and was honestly surprised I'd gotten to the fifth tier so quickly. Focusing on my newly acquired skills and traits brought up the expected pop-up.

∞∞∞∞∞∞∞∞

Venomous: As a basilisk, you have very potent venom.

*Note: Due to the Gluttonous trait. your venom also possesses acidic properties.

Aquatic: Due to the water element, you now possess the ability to breathe underwater as well as outside of it.

Petrifying Gaze: Due to the earth element, you have gained a second set of brille. This set is capable of being opened or closed like an eyelid. Should it be opened, anything of your tier or lower that meets your gaze will be turned to stone.

∞∞∞∞∞∞∞

"Finally, I'm venomous. Thank God for that." I internally sighed.

∞∞∞∞∞∞∞

Congratulations on making it this far!

After the fifth tier, your deeds become more important than what you eat. Also, you can no longer combine races should you complete their requirements. Instead, by completing the race requirement you will gain a random trait or skill of that race.

Consume a creature of Fire to unlock: Flame Basilisk

Consume a creature of Wind to unlock: Wind Basilisk

Complete the requirements of all other Basilisk evolutions to unlock: Elemental Basilisk

Survive 100 years to unlock this path: Dual Element Hydra

Consume a Ruby, a Sapphire, a Tiger's eye, a Diamond, an Emerald, an Amethyst, and a piece of ebony ore to unlock: Dual Element Naga

Crush five ships to unlock: Dual Element Leviathan

∞∞∞∞∞∞∞∞

"So, I can become the same as that monstrous serpent, I can also become a Naga or a Hydra... Can I get a description of each?" Like before, it either ignored me or couldn't accept my request for further information. "I thought not," I sighed. "Well, it's not like I have to decide now. I can't get access to the Hydra path for a hundred years, and I still need to unlock the remaining elements for the basilisk path. Rushing myself now won't do me any good in the long run, so I might as well take it slow and do things the right way." I broke out of my shield a few minutes later and immediately swam to the surface to expose my newly healed scales to the warm air.

I also took the opportunity to check myself out for the first time since I became a snake; I had dark green, dinner plate sized scales that covered my sides and back. These scales were much thicker than the thinner gray scales that covered the underside of my body. The places where I remembered having exposed muscle and damaged scales were now merely white patches that gave my body an odd coloring.

"At least I'm alive," I muttered, while staring at a particularly large white spot on my chest. The scars would be a constant reminder for me to always remain cautious. I'd let my guard down upon coming to this new world, because of how well things went for me on the last one. "I won't be making that mistake, again."

I continued inspecting my new body by focusing on my eyes. They were deep maroon with vertically elongated pupils that perfectly separated each eye into two halves.

I ran my tongue along the inside of my mouth and what I felt surprised me. I had fangs… huge fangs! I probably shouldn't have been so surprised. After all, venomous snakes had fangs, didn't they? But my fangs were exceptionally large. And when I opened my mouth, the newly created venom would drop off them and splash into the water. Fangs aside, I also saw rows of razor-sharp teeth lining the inside of my mouth. They reminded me of shark's teeth, only thinner and curved like hooks.

I wasn't sure how much I'd grown since I began evolving. But I could definitely spot a difference in length and overall size, so it was more than likely a decent increase.

My gills were on prominent display on either side of my neck, much in the same way the Leviathan's had been. I also played around with my new "eyelids." Opening and closing them repeatedly became something of a game for a few minutes. When I was done playing with them, I ducked my head under the waves and swam back to the bottom. Once there, I began looking for something to test my new abilities on.

"Hmm... That should work." Three sharks were swimming just outside of my temporary home in the coral reef, so I put them to good use. Waiting until one of them drew close enough, I shot my head out and sunk my teeth into the back and belly of the shark. Unfortunately, I had forgotten about my new teeth as well as the fangs, so I accidentally bit the shark in half.

"Whoops." My mistake alerted the other two sharks. I opened my "eyes" and watched in horrid fascination as the two turned the color of sand, then sunk to the ocean floor like a pile of rocks. I closed my "eyes" after seeing

the two sharks' demise and vowed then and there to be *very* careful with that particular ability.

I consumed the two petrified sharks and what remained of the first one before I started looking for something to test my venom on. A few minutes later I found a large shark with three eyes on each side of its head swimming around near my temporary home inside the reef. I swam up to it and quickly coiled around it while it was facing away from me.

Surprisingly, it started yelling at me.

"Unhand me, foul serpent!" It struggled against my hold. I started in surprise at the thing's accent. It sounded cockney.

"You can speak?" I asked curiously.

Its struggling increased. "Of course I can speak! What, did you think I was some mindless fish!?"

"Honestly... yeah, that's pretty much exactly what I thought."

It stopped struggling momentarily, before fiercely attacking the water in front of it. "Well, I never! How could you, a mere serpent, ever believe that I, the great and *magnificent* Jagno, was but a simple fish! The nerve of you, sir! The nerve!"

I didn't hear what else it had to say because I started tuning it out after it called me a "mere serpent." I bit into its back and injected what I believed to be a small amount of venom.

"Ouch! What are you doing!? I say, unhand me foul beast! The nerve of you serpents these days. Why, I remember a time when sharks ruled the seas, and you serpents were but an inch long—" It continued to ramble on, and on, and on.

"Do you ever shut up?" I asked. The damn thing's incessant blather was giving me a headache.

"Oh, so you think to intimidate me, do you? Well, it won't happen today. Nay, it shall never happen! I am Jagno, a shark king, and I refused to be bullied by a neanderthalic snake with an Oedipus complex!"

"Neanderthalic? Is that even a word? And Oedipus complex? Great, out of every shark in the ocean. I grabbed the one that likes to memorize a thesaurus in his downtime." I bit the shark again. This time I injected a lot more venom into it.

"Oh sure, trying to silence me for speaking out, are you? Well, it... won't... work... I shall... never... surrender... " The shark finally stopped talking after I'd pumped what I believed to be about thirty percent of my venom into it.

"I'd like to thank the god that brought me here for allowing me to rid the ocean of this annoying creature. And to the being that made it: Fuck you." I swallowed the shark and made my way back to the reef, praying that I could sleep off the headache Jagno had given me.

I woke up the next day, and I was headache free, though I had a few pop-ups to go through. Most of them were normal animals. It was the last one that had me curious.

∞∞∞∞∞∞∞∞∞∞

You have eaten the following race for the first time.

Charming Shark: Tier 4

∞∞∞∞∞∞∞∞∞∞

"Someone, somewhere, has a truly sick sense of humor."

Chapter Fifteen

I SPENT THE REMAINDER OF MY DAY SEARCHING THE coral reef for anything that could be useful. Sadly, I didn't find anything besides food. Wait, why am I complaining about finding food?

I decided to leave the reef in search of civilization while I still had my sanity. I spent the night planning my trip and watching the stars. Unlike Rualea, this planet wasn't always shrouded in darkness, so I could enjoy the sights as often as I wanted.

And Iorus was a gorgeous planet indeed. Despite my feelings on the island, and the encounter with my "cousin," I was thoroughly enjoying myself here. The ocean was crystal clear without a sign of pollution, and the silver moonlight bouncing off the waves was incredibly beautiful.

That was another difference between Rualea and Iorus—the nighttime sky was completely different. Iorus, having only one moon, was a stark contrast to Rualea's dual moons.

The moon was gigantic, and easily occupied most of the night sky. And its light, while not being as bright as the sun, still enabled me to see for miles in every direction.

"I should get some sleep before sunrise. I have a feeling tomorrow is going to be a long day."

Early the next morning, I set out on my journey, after stopping for a quick bite to eat, of course. A shark was only too happy to provide me with a decent meal, though I'm sure they would have been adamant that they tasted better than "decent." But I don't like talking with my mouth full, so it was difficult to ask them without coming off as rude.

I traveled from sunrise to sunset. After the long, long day of swimming, I sank to the bottom and buried myself in the sand to better hide from anything that might like a midnight snack.

I'd set out again tomorrow.

I had discovered something on this trip. Namely, that I don't get hungry nearly as often if I eat a lot of meat. Random things like sand, coral, or stone don't have much in the way of nutritional value, so eating them doesn't do much for me. However, there also seemed to be a correlation between the tier of the creature and how long they satisfied my hunger. Tier 1 creatures were little more than tic tacs at this point, whereas a Tier 3 creature of the same size lasted several times longer.

I'd need to experiment more to be certain, but that experiment would have to wait.

I journeyed this way for several weeks without seeing any sign of civilization. The only thing I did find, or rather, that found me, was my "cousin," and she wasn't happy to see me.

"Get back here you worm!" she yelled upon seeing me quickly swimming away.

"No thanks! You seem to be in a bad mood, so I'll just go!" I swam into a cave that she was too large to fit inside and ate my way out of the back while she continued to scream at me.

"I swear it. One day, I'll have you inside me again!"

Yeah, not something most people would want to hear their "cousin" screaming. "Can you please not phrase it that way!"

She didn't seem to get it because her response was to loudly yell out, "Why!? Does it make you uncomfortable that I want you inside me!?"

"Incredibly so!" I returned.

Of course, then she decided to be very vocal about her desires. It even included a song about wanting me in her mouth. Luckily, I had long ago mastered the "ignore everything" skill. So, I focused on eating my way through the stone wall and escaped as soon as I was able.

After making my escape, I didn't stop swimming for several days, as I was desperately trying to put as much distance between us as possible.

Another week passed by without much excitement until I eventually came across something interesting. While chasing down a fleeing shark, I discovered the remains of a sunken city. What this city was before its fall, or how long it'd been down here, I had no idea. But it was a medium sized city with stone walls and gardens scattered throughout.

"Actually, this looks a lot like the city on the island. Are the two related?" I wondered. I guessed they probably were related somehow, but I had no idea what the connection was aside from the way the buildings were built and the stone carvings that littered the area. However, I'd learned my lesson on the island and didn't stick around to investigate. I swam around the sunken city and continued on my way.

After god only knows how long I'd been swimming without seeing any sign of sentient life, I'd almost given up hope. I did end up changing my goal from "finding civilization" to "finding the island-carrying giant," as I was ready to leave this place and continue on my journey. This planet was beautiful, but even paradise got boring after a while.

Just when I'd given up all hope of finding other people, I actually found someone... Well, they found me.

I was sleeping on the ocean floor when I felt something poke me. Thinking it an attack, my eyes snapped open and I prepared to fight back. Then I realized what it was: a child. Or, more specifically, it was a pair of children. A boy and a girl. Both appeared to be between the ages of ten and thirteen. The boy had been the one to poke me.

"What?" I hissed with more force than I meant.

They seemed surprised that I could talk, but the girl resolutely pointed to the surface and motioned for me to follow her.

Deciding to humor the child, I lifted off the ocean floor and followed them up. Upon breaking the surface of the water, the two climbed aboard a ship that was about half my length and twice as wide.

I poked my head out of the water and observed the ship for a few seconds before raising myself onto it. After I'd cleared the side and coiled into a more manageable ball, a woman walked up to greet me. "Greetings, great serpent. My name is Lena, and I request your aid." She bowed her head. The two children quickly copied her, though the boy seemed reluctant to do so.

I watched them for a minute while glancing around the ship. But, aside from a large black object at the back of the ship, it was completely bare. I returned my attention to the three of them, and though the two females were still bowed, the boy was staring at me.

Looking at the top of his head, I noticed a small pair of dog ears poking out of his wild dark hair.

"Dog ears?" I wondered aloud.

It was the woman who responded. "My son, Solon. He and his father are of the Warg race."

I glanced to the daughter, then returned my gaze to the mom. "And yet, neither of you are the same?" I was honestly confused. The two of them appeared to be elves of some kind.

"No, we are of the High Elf race."

"I see. You can stop bowing, by the way." I muttered the last bit. The bowing was making me uncomfortable.

The two raised their heads at my words and smiled at me. "Thank you, great serpent." Lena replied. An open, friendly smile was on her beautiful face.

"Torga."

"Pardon?" She tilted her head in confusion.

"My name, it's Torga. If you want to talk with me, at least use my name. Not this 'great serpent' bull you keep mentioning."

"Understood." She nodded.

"So, I take it the two of you are druids?" I asked, though I already knew the answer.

She nodded again. "Yes. My daughter and I are druids."

I glanced back to the boy. I'd been watching him out of the corner of my eye since the conversation began, but he didn't appear to be following along.

"But, not the boy?"

"No, Solon is following in his father's footsteps and becoming a warrior," the little girl answered. "He can understand a little bit of what you're saying, but he cannot speak the language himself." She finished by patting him on the shoulder and giving him a smile.

Which I noticed he didn't return.

"I see. So, what's your name?"

The little girl pointed to herself and tilted her head in confusion.

"Yes girl, you. I know your mother's and brother's names, but not yours." I sighed.

She blushed in embarrassment and the mother stared at me. The boy, Solon, switched his gaze from me to the girl several times before taking a step forward and putting half his body between me and her.

I rolled my eyes at him.

"I'm Hali," she finally said a few seconds later.

I nodded and was returning my attention to the mother when a large shadow passed over me. I looked up and saw a giant wolf-like creature standing just behind Lena. The beast was easily twenty feet tall and probably thirty feet long. It had bright yellow eyes and pitch-black fur that seemed to absorb the light. And if that wasn't surprising enough, it could talk.

"I'm Fenris, and I'm the one in need of help." It sat down on its haunches and stared at me.

Shaking off my surprise, I responded. "Not sure how I can help you, but alright. I'll listen to your request. What's in it for me?"

The beast seemed to consider the question for a minute. "I'll help you evolve one time, and in exchange, you'll help us get to the portal, so we can go home."

I tilted my head to one side and thought over the offer. Then a question struck me. "Wait... don't you live here?"

It quickly shook its shaggy head. "Do I look like a fish to you, snake? We were betrayed and ended up stuck here as a result."

"Of course, you were," I sighed.

"Alright, I'll help you." I didn't tell them I was heading there anyway because I didn't want Fenris to retract his offer to help me evolve.

I climbed off of the ship after talking with the family for a few minutes more, then swam alongside it as we headed for our destination.

CHAPTER SIXTEEN

I'D BEEN TRAVELING WITH FENRIS, LENA, AND HER children for about a week when I could no longer contain my curiosity. But I didn't want to ask in front of the children, that would be impolite. So, I waited until nightfall, after they had fallen asleep.

"Hey, Lena?" I quietly called out to her.

She looked over the edge of the ship. "Hmm?" She tilted her head in confusion. I noticed the bags under her eyes and assumed I'd woken her up.

"Mind if I ask you a personal question?"

"Uh... Sure?" She covered a yawn with her hand. "I guess that would be fine." She shrugged and motioned for me to come aboard.

I rose my head out of the water and sat it on the edge of the ship. My weight caused it to temporarily tilt onto its side, but it stabilized shortly after. Lena made her way over to Fenris and sat down beside him. She leaned against him, pulled a blanket over her legs, and started watching me with an expectant look on her face. Fenris also opened one eye to watch me, as he'd done anytime I was around Lena or the kids.

"Ask your question, snake." Fenris said after a few seconds. I nodded my head and began speaking.

"I was curious—"

Fenris interrupted me. "Get on with it."

I glared at the beast. "Well, if you'd give me a moment to speak, I would, you sorry sack of fleas," I hissed in return.

Lena smacked Fenris on the leg. He shot her a hurt look, which she ignored. "Don't mind him. He gets like that when he hasn't gotten enough sleep," she explained. "What is your question?"

"Where is your husband?" I asked after a moment.

"I'm sorry?" Lena asked with a tilt of her head.

"What're you asking, snake!" Fenris growled.

I looked between them for a few seconds, noting the anger on the wolfish face of Fenris and the confusion on Lena's beautiful face. I repeated my question. "You mentioned a husband before... Where is he?"

Fenris pushed Lena off his side and stood up. He advanced on me, a snarl twisting his face into an ugly facsimile of the wolf I'd come to know. "I'm right here, you ignorant worm!" His voice sounded gravelly, as if someone had torn his throat open with sandpaper. He advanced until he was nose to nose with me, but I didn't pay him any mind and chose to focus on what he'd said, instead.

"Wait... you're the husband?" I looked around Fenris to Lena for confirmation.

She shyly nodded her head in return.

"Of course, I am! Who else would be the father of a half-Warg, but a Warg?" he snarled.

"Well, for starters, someone... I don't know... humanoid?" I gave Fenris a once over. "No offense meant for Miss Lena, but how did that even work?" I asked.

Fenris gave me a wolfish grin. "Well, when a mommy Warg and a daddy Warg love each other very much…"

"I'm aware of how children are made, thanks. My question was how a creature *your* size, produced said children with a creature Lena's size. Unless you hit the crap jackpot in dick sizes, the body size difference doesn't make much sense. You would have killed her," I explained slowly, as if speaking to a child. I never took my eyes off the hot-blooded mutt. I didn't put it past him to smack me while I wasn't paying attention.

"As a druid, I am... unique," Lena began. She stepped between the two of us, as if her tiny body could hope to stop either of us. At this distance, if we actually wanted to fight, she'd be little more than a stain on the deck before she could cast a single spell and she knew it. Her putting herself between us was meant to convey her trust in us, but the angry snarl on Fenris' face told me he saw it slightly differently than I did.

"How so?" I asked. My eyes still hadn't left Fenris' face.

"What do you know of druid bonds?" she asked.

"Not much," I admitted. "I know, or rather, I've been told, it's the way druids bond with their animal companion—the specifics of which were slightly vague."

She nodded. "When a druid forms a bond with an animal, they take on some of the animal's traits, and the animal gains some of theirs in return."

"Like a form of symbiosis?" I guessed aloud, to which Lena nodded and Fenris' eyes widened.

"That's surprising," he muttered, which earned him a smack on the side from Lena.

"Anyway, the longer a bond lasts, the stronger it becomes. Eventually no separation exists-by which I mean they can share the other's form... for a brief period, anyway."

I slowly nodded to show my understanding. "So, you can turn into a Warg and he turns into an elf?"

She gave me a half shrug. "Yes. Though a difference does remain."

"What kind of difference?"

"I can't get rid of my ears and tail, and she can't get any larger than a Warg pup," Fenris said.

Lena covered her face for a few seconds. I noticed her ears turning a bright pink, and through my heat sense I could tell that her face had grown noticeably warmer. "Yes, that," she admitted.

"I... see," I nodded. "I'll just let you get some sleep now. Thanks for answering my questions." I slightly bowed my head and retreated from the ship.

"Annoying worm," I heard Fenris mutter.

I felt my temper flare at the casual insult, and came up with a fun idea. I moved to the other edge of the ship and slowly climbed back on. I waited until Lena was clear of Fenris, then I shot forward and slammed my head into his side. The impact sent him flying through the air and into the water.

The loud yelp and splashing sounds of Fenris floundering in the water woke the kids up, which earned me a glare from Lena.

"Hey, he deserved that one," I protested.

She shook her head and slightly smiled at me.

"Yes, I suppose he did. Though I'd appreciate it if you didn't do it again. It's cold and he's no good to me wet."

"I don't think he would share that sentiment if your roles were reversed," I muttered before I could stop myself. I heard the wood of the ship creaking, and glanced down at Lena. She was glaring at me.

"Perverted snake!" she yelled. A plank of wood shot up and hit me on the nose. It didn't do much, but it was the sentiment that counted. I retreated off the ship, swam to the other side, and threw Fenris back onto the ship, laughing all the while.

"Damn snake!"

I didn't look, but I did get to hear Lena's next words before I submerged myself.

"Don't come over here until you dry off... you smell like wet dog."

"But Lena, I'm cold!" I heard Fenris whine. And I honestly couldn't stop the smile that spread across my face.

The next morning we continued on our journey through the crystal-clear waters of the Iorus ocean. I had gorged myself while they slept and was good on food for a little while. So, after waking and eating breakfast, the family unfurled the sails and we began moving again.

And everything was going fine... until I heard, "Where are you, worm!?" I balanced the ship precariously on my back and quickly swam in the opposite direction of the sound. I ignored the screams and protests of the family in my desperation to get as far away from my "cousin" as possible.

"What the hell are you doing, snake!?" I heard Fenris snarl.

I ensured the ship wouldn't fall off before I took a quick peek behind me. When I didn't see anything, I slowed down and allowed the ship to sink into the water. I looked up and saw Fenris, Lena, and the children staring at me. "I heard the Leviathan coming," I explained.

Fenris' and Lena's eyes widened, but the children just seemed confused. "Did... did we get away?" Lena whispered.

Fenris began prowling the ship while staring in the direction we came from.

"I believe so," I nodded.

Lena still looked incredibly troubled, and Fenris was still prowling the ship. But the two of them seemed to relax a little. "That... that's good." Lena dropped to her knees and pulled the children into her arms.

"Mom?" Hali asked. Solon yelled something in return and was pantomiming an object being picked up.

Lena smiled at the two of them. "Nothing, nothing at all." She squeezed them tighter.

The sight of her with them caused a severe pain to stab into my chest and Sarah was superimposed over Lena's body in my mind. *"Sarah..."* The thought of her worrying over our children's safety the way Lena was caused something in my mind to snap. *"It wants to harm... Sarah."* Though I logically knew that Lena wasn't Sarah, I couldn't stop the fire that began to rage inside me. *"It wants to take her away from them."* By this point, Lena no longer existed in my mind, as her image had been replaced with Sarah's and the sound of screeching tires rang in my ears.

"Kill it!" Sarah's voice echoed in my mind.

"Hey... Fenris?" I called.

He padded over to the edge of the ship a few moments later. "What is it, snake? I'm trying to spend time with my family here," he grumbled.

"If the Leviathan comes near us again, will you help me kill it?"

He smirked at me. "Of course. Do you even need to ask?"

We didn't see the Leviathan again that day, several weeks passed by in a flash. The five of us traveled across the ocean in search of the island-carrying giant. In spite of our best efforts we hadn't found it.

During that time, the rage inside me continued to build. No matter how often I convinced myself that she wasn't here... that it wasn't her, the anger returned time after time. Lena and Hali sensed that something was going on with me. But every time they asked, I brushed them off.

What was I going to say? What *could* I say? *"I keep replaying my wife's death in my mind and your image keeps being replaced with hers. Isn't that weird?"* They'd think I was crazy. Though at this point, I wasn't entirely sure I wasn't.

I began to eat more often to help me work off my anger. I believe the sight of blood was doing more to calm me than eating was, however.

"Kill it!" Sarah screamed. Yeah, that also wasn't helping. Sarah's voice continued to echo in my mind, and her death was on a loop inside my dreams. And even though there were some variations, it always ended the same. My old human body was always covered in shadows, and Sarah would be standing in the middle of a busy highway, screaming for me to help her. But I would always fail. No matter how hard I tried, or how fast I ran, I was always too late to save her. And, it was driving me crazy!

"I only hope this ends soon."

CHAPTER SEVENTEEN

"**W**AKE UP, MORTAL."

My eyes snapped open and a blank white space greeted me. I quickly discovered that I was on my back. I tried to roll over, but something stopped me. "Huh?" I looked to my side and saw what was stopping me... I had arms. Well, not really "arms," as they were made of a misty shadow, but they felt real. And when I looked down at myself, I realized that I was in a human body. "What's going on?" I tried a few more times to roll over and finally succeeded on my third try. I attempted to push myself up onto my knees, but I fell down repeatedly instead.

"What's wrong, mortal? Having trouble?"

From my place on the floor, I looked up and saw the golden being standing in front of me. "What's wrong with me?" I tried again to push myself up but failed and ended up falling on my face.

"That should be obvious. You've spent so much time as a snake your "other" body has faded."

"What do you mean?"

"Never mind, that isn't important at the moment."

I finally got to my knees after struggling for another minute or so, but any further attempts to stand caused me to fall onto my stomach or back, so I ended up just sitting there.

"Why... why am I here? Did I die?"

"No, you're not dead. Though if I hadn't stepped in, you would most likely have died soon."

"What do you mean? What's gonna kill me?" The being snapped its fingers, and we were suddenly floating over the ship. My body couldn't be seen, as I was submerged, but I could see Lena, the mutt, and the kids sleeping on the deck. Fenris was stretched across the width of the ship, and both his head and tail were hanging off the sides. Lena and the kids were sleeping against him.

"Do you see that?" The being was pointing at the mast of the ship. I followed its finger but didn't see anything.

"I don't see anything." I shook my head for emphasis.

"Of course not," it sighed. It floated over to me and grabbed the top of my head. "You may feel a slight pinch. But bear with me."

"What are you... GAH!!" An intense pain, like fifty thousand volts of electricity, coursed through my mind and a screen appeared in front of me after a second or two.

∞∞∞∞∞∞∞∞

You have been granted a new skill: Detect Concealment

Due to receiving a blessing from Niabus: God of #%@?@# and #%@?@#, You can now see through concealment techniques of magical natures.

∞∞∞∞∞∞∞∞

The being turned my head back to the mast. **"Do you see it now?"** it asked impatiently.

I waited until the pain subsided to crack open my eyes, but once I did... I saw it. A gray squid-like creature was floating above the mast. Its tentacles were wrapped around the top and its single yellow eye was staring into the water.

"What is that?" I groaned.

"A nightmare. A creature that feeds on the anger and resentment buried deep within," the being explained.

"What's it doing up there?"

"Do you really not know?"

I thought back over the past week and the answer was obvious. "It's the cause of my anger."

The being shook its head. **"No, it doesn't cause anger. It only feeds upon anger that already exists."**

"I see. But, why is it only targeting me? If it was truly feeding off of anger and resentment, shouldn't it also target the others, or at the very least Fenris? I know the mutt is harboring resentment too."

"Normally," the being nodded.

"Then, why?"

"It was ordered to."

I fell back over in surprise. "What!? Who would order such a thing!?" I shouted as I fought my way back onto my knees.

"My sister... most likely."

I stared at it in confusion. *"What?"*

It turned to face me. **"My sister."**

I shook my head and regained focus. *"Why would your sister send that thing after me?"*

"I'm sure she has plenty of reasons." It snorted with laughter. **"Though, none of them are entirely correct."**

"What do you mean?" I asked. My confusion would be clear on my face, if I had a face at the moment. As it was, I think my entire body was composed of the shadow stuff.

The golden being held up one finger. **"If you were to ask her, she would tell you she did it to give you courage."** It raised another finger. **"If one of her 'allies' were to ask, she would tell them you were an abomination that needed to be eliminated."** A third finger was raised. **"If I asked her, she would deny everything and blame it on someone else."** And a fourth finger was raised. **"When she asks herself why she did it, she will justify it by saying it was for the greater good. And that you should be killed before you can corrupt anyone."** It lowered its hand.

"What's the truth?"

"The truth is never so easy to explain, mortal."

I tilted my head to one side. "Why not? Isn't the truth just that, the truth?"

"How do you define what the 'truth' is when everyone has their own version of it? Your 'truth' could be entirely different than someone else's based on your perception of an event."

I thought for a few moments, then nodded. It made sense, in a twisted kind of way. "Alright, then what's the most likely reason?"

"That's much easier to explain. She's doing it because you're a threat to her... or her image, at least."

"I don't understand. I've never met this woman before, so how am I a threat to her?"

"Simple," it laughed. **"She's afraid of you 'corrupting' her new protege."**

I looked at it in confusion. *"Who?"*

"Sarah," it explained.

A few seconds later, everything clicked. "Your sister is the one who brought Sarah here. The one responsible for her reincarnating."

The being nodded.

"I don't understand. Wouldn't a god who summoned someone meant to be a hero be happy that said hero had a guardian?"

"If that was indeed why she was brought here, then yes."

I was silent for a few seconds. "Why was Sarah brought here? What is she meant to protect?"

"Again, probably for a multitude of reasons. And I don't know. My sister's thought process is... strange. It's difficult to predict what her intentions are in my current state. But that's not important right now. What is important is I cannot guarantee that what I tell you is correct."

"Okay... Then what's the most likely reason?"

"Power."

I was confused again, and the being could tell. It began to explain further. **"Yes, she's a god, but it isn't personal power she craves. It's power over the mortals. We gods absorb a portion of our power from our worshipers. The more mortals who worship us, the more power and influence we possess."** It seemed to hesitate for a second, then continued speaking. **"We gods police ourselves, much like you mortals do. We also have laws we must abide by, and directly interfering with mortal affairs is a crime. As with every law, there are cases where exceptions are made. But gods are usually forbidden from changing someone's destiny. You mortals are supposed to succeed, or fail, all on your own."**

"I… see."

"People look up to heroes," it explained. **"A genuinely loved hero can topple worlds without lifting a finger. Their words can move the hearts of billions and destroy them just as easily. So, if you're the one responsible for such a hero…"**

"Your power and influence over mortals will increase with their love for the hero?" I guessed.

"Exactly," the being agreed.

The two of us were quiet as I digested that information. Then I asked, "Why'd you bring me here?"

It shrugged. **"I brought you here to interfere with my sister's plan."**

"How?" I was preparing for it to say something like 'Kill her,' but that's not what happened. The golden being let out a sigh and shook its head. **"I don't know. I haven't been able to figure out what her plan is, so I can't decide how to mess it up."**

"What do you want me to do?"

"Well, my sister obviously doesn't want you to reunite with Sarah, so… that's a good place to start."

I nodded. "I was going to do that anyway."

"Good. There is something else I need to mention."

"What is it?"

"My sister has labeled you a 'tormentor' of Sarah, and as such, her followers will try to prevent you from finding her."

"What?" I snarled. "I never harmed my wife, let alone tormented her. I loved her more than anything else in the world." I felt my heart pounding in my chest.

"Calm down. I'm aware that you never hurt her; my sister is also aware of that. However, labeling you

as such will allow her followers to justify themselves while they try to prevent your reunion. "

I growled low in my chest and folded my "arms" across it. "Lying bitch," I hissed.

"Indeed. That's part of why I brought you here when I did. If I'd waited any longer, her lies would have spread much farther than they already have. She's currently bound by the same limitations I am, but that may change by the time Sarah is ready to be reborn. Your path will not be easy, Torga. You need to be aware that you're headed for hardship and possibly death if you continue down this path."

I rolled my eyes at the being and let out a sigh of annoyance. "I was drafted into the marines during the fourth world war and served my country loyally for twenty-five years. I left an arm in a bunker in Russia, and two brothers were lost to the Gobi. 'Hardship' is in my blood… And I've been prepared for death since before I landed on Rualea. I'm living on borrowed time, I know that. But if your sister wants to take it back, she's gonna have to come down here and do it herself. Because I will fight, and I will kill to keep hold of it."

The being stared at me for a long time without saying anything. The golden light its body was emitting seem to dim considerably for a few seconds before it returned to normal and the being shook its head.

"Yes, I believe you will. We're done here," it suddenly announced.

"Wait, really? But I still have some questions," I protested, but the being shook its head in response.

"I've wasted too much time here already. I need to go."

"Will I see you again?"

It shrugged. **"Probably. Oh, before I forget."** It reached out and grabbed my head. The electricity coursed through my mind again, but this time it was even more painful.

∞∞∞∞∞∞∞∞

You have been granted a new skill: Glutti-lingual

Due to receiving a blessing from Niabus: God of #%@?@# and #%@?@#, you can now process, understand, and speak the most common language of any race you have previously eaten.

∞∞∞∞∞∞∞∞

"There. Consider that one a 'good luck' gift." The being snapped its fingers and I woke up back in my snake body. The first thing I did was swim up to the surface and climb onto the ship. Then, I slowly opened my "eyes" and looked into the nightmare's eye. It must have realized that I had discovered it, because it tried to shut its eye. But my power took hold before it could, and quickly turned the creature to stone. I raised my head until I was level with it, then I broke its hold on the mast and carried it down into the water. "I want to do so much more than just eat you, but I can't risk you tampering with my mind anymore." I swallowed it, then curled up and went back to sleep.

CHAPTER EIGHTEEN

ANOTHER WEEK PASSED BY, AND WITH THAT creature no longer influencing my mind, I was finally able to calm down and think again. I also decided to avoid the Leviathan instead of actively trying to kill it. After all, If I didn't need to risk my life, why should I?

Speaking of the creature, I woke up to another pop-up the following day.

∞∞∞∞∞∞∞∞∞

You have eaten the following race for the first time

Nightmare Demon: Tier 4

∞∞∞∞∞∞∞∞∞

While the creature's name didn't surprise me so much, the tier did. Because I expected a demon to be a terrifying creature, and while the squid's appearance was certainly monstrous enough, it was weak. Although maybe this particular demon race was naturally weak, hence the concealment.

"Oh well, at least I got something useful out of this." I was, of course, referring to the Detect Concealment skill granted to me by Niabus. After receiving this skill and waking up the next morning, the first thing I did was to check the kids. Then I checked Lena and Fenris for any other concealed creatures. I didn't find any, but I did spot something on Fenris' forehead. A small blue jewel, about the size of a thumbnail, was sitting directly between his eyes. I decided to wait a few days before asking about it since I didn't want it to seem too coincidental that the day after I stopped having nightmares, I was suddenly able to see it.

"Hey, Fenris," I called out. If I had to guess, it was slightly past noon and the family had just finished their lunch. That meant Fenris would be taking a nap near the stern while the rest of the family operated the ship.

He looked over the edge. "What is it? I'm busy."

I rolled my eyes at him. "Just because you were licking your balls, does not mean you were busy."

"I was not!" he protested. Before he could continue his tirade, I heard Lena pipe up with, "Yes, you were."

"Hey, you're supposed to be on my side!" Fenris barked.

I raised my head up to the railing, so I could see what was going on. I saw Lena walk over to Fenris and kiss him on the ear. "Aww, I am on your side, sweetheart. But there's no point in lying about it."

"Yeah, well ever since the twins were born, it's not like I've been able to get you to do it," Fenris grumbled. A plank came loose and smacked Fenris on the nose, causing him to yelp in surprise. He quickly covered his nose with his two front paws and whined like a little puppy.

"Not in front of the children!" Lena hissed at him.

"Hey, Mom?" Hali tugged on Lena's sleeve to get her attention.

"Yes, sweetie?" She looked down at her daughter with a warm smile.

I suddenly felt bad for Fenris. That mood swing happened *way* too quickly for my liking and I began to wonder how often I'd seen such drastic shifts in her personality. *"To hell with it. It's none of my business, anyway,"* I decided, after thinking about it for a moment.

"What did Dad mean when he said he couldn't get you to do it?" Hali asked with a naïve look of concern on her face.

The veins appeared on Lena's forehead and Fenris jumped overboard, almost landing on my back in the process.

"Don't worry, sweetie. I'll be having a talk with your father later tonight, about that very thing." She told her daughter with a saccharine smile on her face.

I glanced down at Fenris and saw him doggy paddling beside the lower half of my body. "I guess you're in the doghouse now, eh, mutt?"

He glared at me and showed off his teeth. "Watch it, snake. It's your fault I'm in this mess."

I grinned at him. "So, are you still busy?"

"What. Is. It?" he growled.

Lena came over to the edge of the boat and looked down at me. "Torga, would you please bring my husband back on board? I need to have a 'chat' with him."

"Gladly," I cheerfully replied. Fenris tried to swim away before I could grab him. However, my tail quickly caught and wrapped around him, then tossed him back onto the ship.

He landed with a heavy *thud* and I could hear the anger in his voice when he growled my name. Luckily, for him at least, Lena was blocking his path to me. Between a giant, magically enhanced wolf that could probably sheer metal with his claws and tear apart airplanes with nothing but his teeth, and his five-foot-nothing, one-hundred-twenty-pound pissed off wife… it was no contest. I could only hope to get out of there before she shaved the poor bastard's fur off and made him run around naked for a while.

My internal amusement at that image aside, I really did want to talk with him. I interrupted her before she could start her rant and received a grateful look from Fenris in return.

"Mind answering my question, now?" I asked after she'd strolled off with an obvious sway to her hips.

Fenris whined as he watched her walk away, and he had to lie down on his stomach to hide "something."

"What are you, a horny teenager?" I mumbled.

He glared at me. "Don't think I've forgotten that it's your fault I'm in this mess!"

I tilted my head in confusion. "How is it my fault? I'm not the one that made you say something stupid. You did that all by yourself."

He stared at me for a few seconds, then rolled his eyes. "Whatever, just ask your question."

I nodded. "Alright. What's that on your forehead?"

His eyes opened wide. "What are you talking about?"

"The small jewel between your eyes. What is it for?"

"Lena, could you come over here, please!?" he called out in a panic-stricken voice.

She'd been over on the other side of the ship talking with Hali and Solon when she heard Fenris' call. But she came walking over a few seconds later. "What is it?" .

Fenris motioned to me with his head. "Ask her, it's her area of expertise." After pawning me off on Lena, he walked over to the kids and fell down beside them, causing the ship to rock and them to start climbing on him.

"You had a question for me?" she asked, and I nodded in return.

"I did. What's that jewel on Fenris' forehead?"

She tilted her head. "Pardon?"

"The small jewel between his eyes. What's it for?"

She seemed to realize what I meant after taking a moment to think about it, because she took a step back. "You... you can see it?"

I nodded.

She began chewing on her nails... After a minute or two of staring at me, she sighed. "Alright, the jewel is a druid artifact."

"And?" I asked impatiently.

"It's a semi-rare stone that has been enchanted to, well, make things more convenient for us druids."

"How so?"

"Well, since we can't fight against animals to defend ourselves and it would be very inconvenient if we were forced to leave our partners behind when entering a city, the jewel was enchanted to shrink them to a normal size, so they could always be with us."

Her explanation confused me. "Where does it go?" I asked.

"Huh?"

"The excess size and weight. Where does it all go? I'm assuming it doesn't just vanish into thin air."

She shook her head. "No, it doesn't. It's all converted into energy and stored within the jewel. Don't ask me how it does this because I don't know. Enchanting was never my forte, despite what my husband would have you believe. However, if you're that interested, then once we make it out of here you can come with us to the druid home world and meet with Master Uriel. I'm sure he could explain it to you."

"Hmm… okay," I agreed. "Um... You wouldn't happen to have a spare jewel, would you?"

She shook her head. "No, sorry. The jewels are embedded within our partners by Master Uriel personally, and no one is allowed to have more than one. Not even to carry around."

"I see," I sighed. "Thanks for answering my question."

She gave me a quick nod and walked away. I stared after her for a few moments before I slipped into the water and silently continued to swim alongside the ship.

After that rather disappointing conversation, I followed the ship for another three days, and my patience was finally rewarded.

Solon yelled something from the top of the mast, which Lena translated for me as "Land ahead." All of us gathered at the front of the ship and saw what Solon was referring to. An island. Not the island we were looking for, but an island all the same. It was fairly small, with the majority of it seemingly being taken up by a single city. Said city appeared to be densely populated, as groups of skyscrapers covered the center of the island and smaller buildings were built on the outskirts.

Solon yelled again. The boy was looking through a small telescope at the island.

"Hmm, they must live in the towers at the center for protection."

I raised my head up to look at them. "Have you never been here before?"

Lena and Fenris shook their heads in unison. "No, this is the first city we've found in this world." Lena replied.

"The first 'populated' city, you mean. We've found abandoned cities before. Even found this ship in the city we arrived in," Fenris corrected. After a few seconds Lena nodded in affirmation.

"Right." I watched them for a moment, then looked back to the city.

"Well, shouldn't we get ready?" I asked.

"For what?"

"Docking, of course. Unless you plan to pass up the chance to stretch those legs of yours?" My words seemed to strike home as only a few seconds later, they were all in motion.

"Solon, help me lower the sails!" Solon jumped to attention and quickly moved to obey his father's command.

The family got the ship up to full speed faster than I'd ever seen them, and I followed along at a safe distance. I made sure to stay submerged, so I wouldn't panic the locals, though I did manage to see Lena activate the jewel on Fenris' head. After she activated it, Fenris seemed to have the air sucked out of him, quickly shrinking down to the size of a normal wolf.

"Wow..."

"Finish that thought, and I'll bite you."

"Whatever you say, mutt," I laughed.

Only a few hours later, the family ship pulled into port and was greeted by a dark-skinned human and a group of what looked to be soldiers in leather armor. Though I didn't get a good look at him as I was trying to keep myself hidden.

"Ahoy there!" the human yelled in a semi-deep voice.

"Greetings, my name is Lena." I could hear her step up to greet him.

"Hello, ma'am. My name is Jordan Yesyra. I own and operate this here harbor."

"Nice to meet you, sir." I didn't need to see her to know she was bowing to him.

"None of that, now. Though I do need to ask you a few questions."

"Ask away."

"How many people are on your boat, besides you three?"

"It's just us, and Fenris over there."

"Mind if we check?" he asked before continuing. "I apologize for the inconvenience, but we have to make sure nothing is being smuggled in."

"Oh, of course," Lena agreed.

I heard multiple people step onto the ship and spend about fifteen minutes looking around.

"Thank you for waiting, ma'am."

"Oh, no problem."

"That appears to be everything. However, I must warn you to avoid the back alleys and the lower bazaar after dark. Bandits and thieves have been known to target women and children."

"Oh... thank you for the information."

"Anytime, ma'am. And please, enjoy your stay in Edge Haven."

"Guard the ship, snake. It's your scales if I come back and there's a single scratch on her." Fenris called out to me after Jordan and his guards had left.

"Sure," I laughed. "And I'll be sure to start believing that around the same time I start believing in Santa, the Tooth Fairy, and the words of politicians."

"Yes, well," Lena interrupted before Fenris could say anything. "We have a lot to do, and little time to do it. Come along, dear." She yanked on Fenris' tail and dragged the poor mutt off the ship, followed by a stoic Solon and Hali, who'd taken the opportunity to wave at me while they departed.

I coiled around the ship (a recent influx of higher quality food had ensured that I was now long enough to do so), and I went to sleep.

Interlude:
A Godly Confrontation, the Serpentine Security System, and Fenris Fights for His Life

NIABUS WAS SITTING AT HIS TABLE AWAITING THE inevitable "visit" from his siblings. They always paid him a "visit" after he'd gone against Forna's wishes, and now he'd not only helped the mortal but was also the direct cause of his killing one of Oyja's "beloved" minions.

"As if the bitch actually knew what 'love' was," He said to himself. The door behind him opened, and he could hear multiple people enter.

"Who's this bitch you're talking about, Niabus?" Niabus glanced behind him and saw three people coming into the room.

The first was Ewdea, Goddess of Honesty. She was a tiny woman with shoulder-length brown hair. She was so small, she could barely see over Niabus' table and was often mistaken for a child, but she had the power to read and influence the mind to an unimaginable degree.

She called herself the Goddess of Honesty but was really the goddess of manipulating the truth. And she held the "important" position of being his sister's right hand.

The second person to enter was Kalos, God of Justice and Penance, a giant of a man, so large he could barely fit inside the temple even though it had forty-foot ceilings. He had a shaved head and beady black eyes, and though you wouldn't think so because of his size, Kalos was a pacifist. By that, I mean, he hated getting his hands dirty and would prefer it if you committed suicide so he wouldn't have to kill you himself. His powers allowed him to control someone as if they were a puppet, a slave in their own body.

He especially enjoyed making young gods and goddesses into his "playthings," and he'd driven more than a few into insanity.

With these two by your side, no one was safe from manipulative bitches. Speaking of which...

"Forna, so nice of you to drop by. Is it that time already?" Niabus was referring to his yearly "punishment." Forna and her two lackeys would come by every year, and forcefully absorb his power into themselves. It's how they stayed the ruling faction among the gods.

Forna shook her head, and goons one and two smirked at Niabus.

"No, this is a special occasion."

Niabus quirked one eyebrow at her.

"Really? Then don't keep me waiting, sis. What's the occasion?"

"We have reason to believe that you interfered with mortal affairs."

He raised the other brow.

"Oh? That's a serious accusation. Where's your proof?"

Forna smirked. **"Oyja has named you as her accomplice in interfering with a mortal's life."**

Niabus blinked at her.

This was more serious than he'd originally believed. Oyja was one of Forna's closest allies, and if Forna dragging her name through the mud...

"I guess Oyja's punishment has already been delivered?"

"Yes," She agreed. **"As per usual, interfering with mortal affairs without probable cause results in the offender fading. Oyja's sentence was carried out by Kalos earlier today."**

Niabus glanced at the man and saw specks of blood on his face and on the front of his white pants.

"The poor girl was probably raped before he killed her...." Niabus maintained his neutral expression. **"Really? That must have been hard for you. She was one of your closest allies, after all."**

Forna let out an overly dramatic sigh. **"It truly was. But a criminal must be punished for their crimes. I just wish I knew why she agreed to help you."**

"You lying bitch. You gave her the order to drive Albert insane. And you punished her with this farce because she failed to do so before I caught on." Niabus raged in his mind but otherwise didn't make a move.

"How sure are you that she didn't act alone?" Niabus asked.

"I confirmed it myself. Admit it, Niabus. You're still up to your old ways." Ewdea smugly replied.

Niabus glared at her, as memories of times long past raced through his mind. After a few seconds he glanced at Forna and asked..."**What do you think, Forna? Is history repeating itself?**"

She seemed to space out for a few seconds, then glared at him. **"Enough talking, brother. It's time for your punishment."** Goon one and two went to either side of Niabus, while Forna stepped up and grabbed the front of his robes. She leaned her head down and whispered in his ear. **"Your punishment is giving us all of your remaining power and fading. Like you should have millennia ago."** Niabus was pulled to his feet. Ewdea grabbed his left arm, Kalos grabbed his right arm, and Forna reached up and grabbed his face.

Ewdea and Kalos began to manipulate Niabus' body, while Forna drew out his life force... as was her domain. Forna was originally a creature of the purest essence that gave life... not snatched it away. She used to be the very incarnation of the cycle. Life...Death...and Rebirth, they were all under her control.

Niabus felt his life leaving him, and with the temple suppressing his power, Niabus was powerless to resist. An unspeakable pain assaulted his senses as Ewdea and Kalos attempted to keep him in a paralyzed state while Forna drew out his life force.

"Forna... I wish the you of the past could see you now." The draining sped up.

"Shut up, Niabus. What I'm doing is right, and you're in the wrong here, not me."

He gritted his slowly sharpening teeth at her. **"Are you truly so blind, that you believe this is okay!?"**

"What? Punishing a criminal?" She looked honestly confused.

"No. I agree that I broke the law. But only because you. did. it. first."

She rolled her eyes at him. **"Oh, please. I've done no such thing."**

"Look at yourself!" Niabus roared, and his features changed even further. His skin became rough and scaly, his eyes turned to slits, and his horns grew larger.

"You have deluded yourself for so long that you let this monster kill an ally... and that wasn't all he did, was it!?"

She dug her nails into his flesh. **"She deserved what happened to her!"** Forna spat in Niabus' face, as his features continued to change. Niabus' robes were torn asunder as wings grew from his back, scales turned black as ebony, his eyes blazed with the fires of hell.

"No one deserves to die that way!" Niabus roared as his size increased a hundredfold. The growth enchantment on the temple was just barely able to contain his new size. A long serpent-like tail grew from Niabus' backside, and a crown of flames appeared over his head.

Niabus casually threw off Kalos and Ewdea, then continued to stare into Forna's eyes.

"I didn't bring you back so you could turn out this way, Forna." Niabus bowed to her.

She placed her forehead against his and whispered. **"You should have let me die."** The drain increased in speed again.

The memories of their past lives played through his mind, as the woman he used to love like a sister slowly caused him to fade.

"Maybe I should have. But I never would have imagined that you would become like him."

"Take that back!" she roared.

Niabus' snout grew longer and his control over his power began to slip. **"No. I won't."**

She dug her nails deep into his scales and screamed. **"You will!"**

He shook his head. **"No... and I won't let you have my power either. If I'm to die today, it's on my own terms. Not yours."** The crown began to spin faster and faster, as the fires of hell slowly consumed Niabus' body.

Forna continued to hysterically scream at him, and her two goons tried to make a break for it as they knew what he planned to do.

"This probably won't kill you, but I doubt your two lackeys will survive." The flames consumed Niabus' flesh and revealed his true form... A massive black dragon with obvious blue veins filled with the fires of hell that covered his body like a spider's web.

"I, Niabus, God of Fire and Destruction, do hereby relinquish my power, and pass it on to the next Dragon King..." Niabus' power stopped being drained from him, and the veins that covered his body began to glow.

"No! Ewdea, Kalos, stop him!" Forna let go of Niabus' head and stumbled backward. An explosion of power lit up the temple and destroyed it. The mountains were turned to ash, the waters boiled away, the sky was vaporized, and the branch of Yggdrasil connected to the planet was incinerated. Niabus' power spread outside of the planet and deep into space, where it vaporized every planet and star within five light years of him. It continued to spread until nothing remained, and Niabus vanished along with it.

Forna and her two lackeys were vaporized as well, but Niabus knew Forna would live. She was a survivor, if nothing else. And being reborn was her race's specialty, after all.

~ ~ ~

JOHN THE THIEF

John and his gang of five other men were making their way to the docks to set up a trap for some new arrivals, a beautiful elf woman and two children. One child was another elf, the other was a beastman. As it was currently nighttime, they were able to move around mostly undiscovered. And the only people to see them were members of the city guard. But they knew to keep their mouths shut, lest their bribe money be cut out.

"Alright men!" John hissed as they reached the docks.

"We'll set up an ambush for them on the ship. If we're lucky, Mr. Bones will buy them for a grand sum."

One of the younger men spoke up. "Uh, sir... what about the dog?"

John rolled his eyes at him. "We kill it, of course!"

The men nodded at John's order and the gang boarded the ship.

John took a quick look around before turning back to the men, but someone was missing.

"Where's Ri'shaan?" John quietly asked.

The men looked at each other. "I don't know, sir. Maybe he chickened out?" One of them shrugged.

John noticed something move out of the corner of his eye, but when he looked, it was gone. "Did anyone else see that?" He asked, panic beginning to seep into his voice. He looked at the men and noticed another one was gone. Another vanished a few seconds later.

"Form up, we have an attacker!" John ordered the two remaining men. They stood back to back with John so they could watch every direction. John turned around in time to see one of remaining men get yanked overboard by... something.

"What the fuck, was that!?" John yelled, just as the ship was knocked to the side, causing the last of his men to stumble over to the edge of the ship. There, he too was pulled overboard.

John pulled out his sword and picked up another that had been dropped by one of his gang members, Chritar, he thought. John ran over to the mast and pressed his back against it. "Okay... It can't sneak up on me now." A hissing sound coming from above John drew his attention upwards. So, he very slowly looked up and saw the largest serpent he'd ever seen. And it was staring back at him.

"Oh... Fuck me..."John muttered. He couldn't dodge its mouth in time and was quickly swallowed whole.

~ ∴ ~

FENRIS

Fenris woke up the next morning after hearing someone knocking on the door. Lena had rented a double room at an inn near the harbor, as they wanted to set out early. Also, Fenris didn't want to give the snake a reason to come looking for them since there was no way that would turn out well. After all, the only reason Fenris trusted the snake was that Lena assured him that Torga meant his family no harm. Though now that he'd thought about it, that protection probably only extended to herself and the kids. Fenris had seen Torga look at him like he was a tasty snack, but he only looked at Lena and the kids with a fondness that Fenris honestly hadn't seen since they left his home world of Urilia.

And that's not even counting his reaction to the Leviathan. The snake lifted up the ship and carried them away so quickly that Fenris didn't even detect the damn thing until they were out of danger. In fact, for a while, Fenris had assumed Torga was only saying it to mess with him. But Lena told him later on that night that the fear and anger Torga had towards the creature definitely weren't fake. He was serious about trying to kill the Leviathan should it pose a threat to them. Fenris believed that was the moment he'd decided to place his trust in the snake. Not to protect them in the face of danger, no. He still wasn't going to trust their lives to someone he'd only known for a couple of months. But he would trust Torga to not abandon them at the first sign of trouble. If he cares enough to willingly attack the Leviathan, the least Fenris could do is trust him a little bit.

Fenris snapped back to reality as he heard the knock again. He crawled over to Lena and nudged her awake. When she opened her eyes, the first thing she did was try to talk but Fenris covered her mouth with his paw and motioned to the door.

"We have a visitor," He whispered. Fenris nodded when the fog left her eyes. She glanced over to the door and threw off the blanket on their tiny double bed. She climbed to her feet and pulled on her tight green pants and white shirt.

Though Fenris tried to keep it in, he honestly couldn't help himself and whined in appreciation of the sight before him. And she obviously heard it, as she glanced in Fenris' direction with a smile on her face.

"I'm still mad at you," she whispered.

Fenris covered his eyes with his paws. He heard her chuckle as she walked over to the door. After looking through the metal peephole, she slowly opened the door.

She made sure to keep the chain lock on the door, and only pulled the door open enough for her to peek through.

"Hello?" She asked in a friendly tone.

Fenris walked over and stood beside her in case whoever this was wasn't friendly.

"Hello, ma'am. You asked for a six a.m. wake-up call?" The man on the other side of the door replied.

Lena sighed and pulled the door open a little further. "I did. Thank you, we'll be down in a few minutes."

The man must have nodded because Fenris didn't hear anything other than his breathing for a few seconds, then his footsteps walking away from the room.

"You asked for a wake-up call?" Fenris asked, tilting his head to one side.

She nodded and began to explain. "Yes, I didn't want to leave Torga alone at the ship any longer than necessary."

Fenris rolled his eyes, then padded back over to the bed and jumped on to it. "You act like he's a child that needs to be protected."

She shot Fenris a glare as she finished getting dressed, slipping on her boots, then her robe. "Don't act like you aren't thinking the same thing, Fenris. You've been glancing back towards the ship since we entered this city." She walked over to the children and began shaking them awake. Hali, as per usual, woke up almost immediately. But Solon needed several shakes before he woke up. Then she set about getting them ready for the day. She brushed through Hali's hair while Solon pulled on his gray shirt and stuffed his feet into his boots. Hali did the same with her dark red blouse and boots.

The family left the room after gathering their discarded stuff and headed to the checkout desk. There was nobody there. They looked for the young woman that checked them in the previous night, but she was nowhere to be found.

"I don't like this..." Fenris muttered. he stood at Lena's back to ensure no one got the drop on them, and Lena twisted her fingers in an intricate pattern. A burst of energy immediately followed, and she went glassy eyed.

That was something Fenris had never understood about druidic magic. Druids didn't need spells like other magic classes, but their magic required complete focus. Unlike other spellcasters, who could simply say the spell and forget about it, if a druid tried that, the magic would either fizzle out and become inert or would backfire. However, a backfired spell rarely, if ever, happened. Most druids wouldn't use attack spells because they saw everything as a part of nature and refused to harm any of it. Lena wasn't one of those druids, though she did refuse to attack animals. She was quite happy to put another elf, human, or other humanoid creature on their ass if they threatened her.

This was about to come in handy because as soon as she regained focus, the door was kicked open and a group of ten well-armed, masked men stormed in. Though most of them were brandishing swords, a few were carrying auto-casters—small devices with a barrel and a rotating cylinder that, when loaded with an enchanted stone, were capable of firing out whatever spell the stone was enchanted with. However, these devices were exceedingly rare outside of the dark elf kingdoms. Those elves are the only ones who know how to make them, and they don't like sharing their technology with anyone. Either these men stole those auto-casters—which was unlikely, as they're usually enchanted to prevent theft—or there was a dark elf supplying them.

The man at the front of the group took a step forward and raised his auto-caster, then pointed it at Lena.

"What did you do with my men!?" he yelled. His race became apparent, as his voice had an undertone of hissing. And only one known race had that feature.

A Snake demi-human.

The man asked his question again, and this time, Lena answered.

"I don't know what you're talking about!"

The man pulled the caster's trigger, which caused a blue light to shoot into the floor between Lena's legs. "You lying bitch! A group of my men went to your ship last night and haven't been seen since. Now, tell me where they are!" He pointed the gun at Solon. "Tell me!"

Fenris could tell the moment Lena decided to drop her "innocent" druid act... and it was the moment he dared to threaten one of her "babies."

"I. Said. I don't know!" Lena hissed between clenched teeth. The wooden floor glowed green and a spike of wood shot into the hand holding the auto-caster. Then another stabbed into his face, piercing his eye, and puncturing his brain. The other men stood in silence as the snake-man fell onto his back.

"Kids, get behind the desk." Lena commanded in a tone that brokered no argument.

They nodded and jumped over the top, then huddled together.

"Fenris... if you wouldn't mind?" Lena asked.

Fenris nodded. His body glowed a bright green as he revealed his demi-elvan form. Though He'd prefer turning back to normal, inside this cramped space, this form would have to do. When the glowing died down. The men could see a half-Warg demi-elf standing in front of them... naked.

"Please, do make this interesting. I haven't had a good brawl in a while as I've been cramped up on that ship." Two more wooden spikes shot out of the floor and pierced through the casters before they could even be raised. Then, a large wooden spike pierced through a man's gut... and the fight began.

A man to Fenris' left charged at him and swung a broadsword in a horizontal arc at his neck. Fenris ducked under it and punched him in the groin, then grabbed his sword arm and flipped him onto the desk with his head hanging off the edge. Fenris slammed his elbow into the man's forehead hard enough to snap his neck and leave it dangling uselessly.

Fenris picked up the man's broadsword and charged into the other swordsmen, while Lena handled the casters. He blocked one sword slash, then kicked the offender in the knee, causing the bone to snap in the other direction and pierce through his flesh. A wooden spike finished him off. Fenris punched another man in the face, then ran yet another through with the "borrowed" blade.

Fenris had to quickly let go of said blade, as another blade almost cleaved through his hand. Fenris jumped over a second blade, wrapped his arm around the attacker's head, then kicked off a third attacker. The sudden movement allowed him to snap the man's neck, as he simultaneously threw him into a fourth man, which sent the two of them falling back. A wooden spike grew from the ground and impaled both the falling man and the thrown man.

Fenris had to roll out of the way as one of the remaining men bull-rushed him. A wooden spike was awaiting him as he passed. It pierced through his stomach, as another was shoved directly into his eye, courtesy of a pissed off Lena. The last man attempted to run away, but Fenris quickly caught up to him and swept him off his feet, then pinned him to the ground. A spike grew out of the ground next to Fenris, which was quickly snapped off and pressed it against his throat.

"Now... are you going to be a good boy and answer my questions? Blink once for no, twice for yes."

The man blinked twice very quickly.

"Good boy," Fenris answered with a smile on his face. Fenris lifted him off the ground and threw him into the wall, then pressed the spike against his throat again. "First question. Who sent you and why?" The man glanced down at the spike, then back into Fenris' eyes. Fenris pulled it away slightly and the man breathed a sigh of relief.

"Mr. Bones sent us to kidnap the two elves. That's what the men at your boat were for as well."

Fenris nodded. "Who's Mr. Bones?" He asked.

The man glanced around before he answered. "I don't know who he actually is. I've never met him personally. But he's a slave trader who specializes in... uh…"

Lena spoke up. "Sex slaves?"

The man slightly nodded.

"You're doing great. Only one question to go... How many more men are waiting for us outside, and what are their locations?" Fenris asked.

The man's eyes widened. "Tw... twelve," He stammered. "And they're stationed around the front and back entrances."

"Thank you, for being so cooperative." Fenris smiled at him... before slamming the spike into his forehead, pinning him to the wall. As he stepped away from the body, Fenris shifted back into his miniature Warg form. "We need another way out of here."

Lena nodded and went to retrieve the kids, while Fenris searched the ground floor for another way out. And, though he did manage to find one, it wasn't a particularly nice one.

"Is... is it really necessary for us to go into the sewer?" Hali asked, her voice trembling.

Fenris nodded and Lena patted her on the head.

"Sorry, sweetie. It's the only way out that doesn't involve a big fight." The children sighed but complied anyway. Fenris led them into the sewer by jumping down the twenty-foot-deep circular hole and awaited his family. Solon, following his father's example, quickly jumped down as well, with Hali and Lena following shortly after. Once they were all inside, Lena waved her fingers and the hole was closed.

"Alright, that should buy us some time." Lena sighed.

Fenris nodded before allowing his family to climb onto his back and sprinting away.

CHAPTER NINETEEN

WHEN I OPENED MY EYES THE NEXT MORNING, the first thing I saw was a pop-up floating before me.

∞∞∞∞∞∞∞∞

You have eaten the following race for the first time.

Cobra beastman: Tier 3

You have eaten the following race for the first time.

Wolf beastman: Tier 3

You have eaten the following race for the first time.

Dwarf: Tier 3

∞∞∞∞∞∞∞∞

"Hmm... so that's why they tasted slightly different." It wasn't a bad taste, by any means. But, I could definitely tell the difference between them and the humans. They were also slightly harder to sneak up on, and I assumed it was the wolf beastman that managed to spot me, then alerted the others by screaming as I dragged him off the ship. Admittedly, I should have just bitten his head off. But I was trying to prevent the ship

from being covered in blood. I didn't want to scare the children, after all.

"Hmm?" An extremely loud siren was echoing across the city and was causing the populace near the harbor to panic.

"What's happening!?" One man yelled as he tried to keep his wife and children behind him. Several other people began to scream and yell following the firsts outburst. Captains of the surrounding ships started their departure preparations early. And, the only person to stay calm, was the owner of the harbor.

"Please, please, everyone, calm down!" Some of the people calmed enough to listen to him, but most just ignored him.

"I'm sure the guards have everything under control, and the alarm will stop shortly!" Shortly after, Jordan was proven correct. The alarm ceased and the city returned to a state of normalcy.

Deciding that it probably had nothing to do with me, I submerged myself and waited beneath the ship for the family's return. But hours later, I was still waiting. The sun had already passed its apex and was beginning to decline and yet, I'd not seen the family. So, I continued to wait until after the sun had set...

The sound of water being disturbed cause me to looked to my left, where I saw a dirty and bloody Solon rinsing his hands in the water while hanging his upper body off the dock. Raising my head out of the water to meet him, I saw the extent of his injuries. His left arm was missing a bit of flesh and blood was sliding off and into the water. I gave him a once over as he stared at me.

"What happened?" I quietly asked.

"… Ambush." He muttered. He went on to explain that they had been running through the sewer and were closing in on the exit when they were ambushed. Fenris and Lena managed to force their way past the first group, but then Lena fell and the second group took her.. Fenris fought until he was able to get Solon and Hali through, then he was captured as well.

Solon and Hali were separated from each other when a group of guards saw them. Hali tried to ask them for help, but one of them knocked her out and tried to do the same to Solon. In order to defend his sister, Solon pulled out his dagger and attempted to stab the man. He got backhanded for his efforts, then had to dodge a sword swing that took a chunk out of his arm before he could escape and make his way here... to ask for my help.

"Please, Torga. Help me get my family back!" Solon bowed his head to me and begged.

I stared down at him, then looked towards the city. "Stand up, boy."

He raised his head to look at me. "Sir?"

"I said, Stand. Up."

He quickly obeyed. "So... You'll help me?"

I licked my lips as I stared at the towers that made up the city's center, then I nodded my head. "You kept me waiting for so long... I'm starving. And, all those people look... delicious."

He seemed confused for a moment, then the realization hit him. "Dad always said I should embrace the Warg part of me." A grin formed on his face.

"If you come... don't touch my food." I ordered.

He nodded, then scrambled onto my back.

I climbed out of the water and a patrol of guards quickly spotted me.

"M... Monster! Sound the alarm!" One of the guards gasped.

I opened my "eyes" and glared at them. The three guards looking at me were almost instantly turned to stone. The other two had been looking at each other, so they weren't affected. I quickly bit down on one of them, my long fangs and sharp teeth puncturing the leather armor and into the flesh beneath. I could actually see my acidic venom as it flowed into his veins, taking on a bright green glow and dissolving the surrounding flesh. The man died a few seconds later.

Meanwhile, Solon had leapt off my head, landed on the other guard's shoulders and held his dagger to the man's throat.

"Where's my family!?" he yelled, temporarily confusing the man.

"What?" The blade pressed into his neck until it drew blood.

"Where. Is. My. Family!?" The guard snapped out of his confusion and told Solon that those captured were taken to the prison on the other side of the island... the building with the large tower that was used to hang criminals.

"Thank you." Solon hopped off the man's shoulders and seemed content with letting him go. But I wasn't. I snapped my teeth together and bit the man completely in half, then I ate both sides while glaring at Solon.

"Never. Leave. Witnesses." I hissed. "During a rescue mission, two things are the most important. Remaining unnoticed, and failing the first, eliminating the reason you failed the first."

Solon's face went white, then he quickly nodded his head.

"Get on." He complied and I set out for the other side of the island.

CHAPTER TWENTY

WITH SOLON RIDING ON MY BACK, I MOVED over to a tall building and used it to raise my head above the rooftops, then I looked around for the tower the guard had mentioned. Since it was nighttime, I didn't have to worry too much about being seen, so I could focus on the task at hand: reaching the tower, freeing Lena, Hali, and Fenris... and eating a nice meal on the way. However, I was currently having a slight problem. A group of guards was circling overhead on giant half-bird, half-cat things. Each of these things was only a third the size of Fenris in his normal state. So, I was forced to hide between the buildings as they flew overhead, lest I be spotted, and put the family in danger. Solon, after following my eyes and noticing what I was seeing, slid off my back and filled me in.

"Those are Griffins. They're often used by the beast kingdom as mounts and war-beasts." He pointed at them to make sure I understood what he was referring to. I nodded instead of answering him as I didn't want to lose focus on the Griffin that was about to pass overhead. I retracted my body until it was coiled like a giant spring and waited... as the bird flew directly over us. I shot my head out as fast as I could and snapped down on the bird's neck, then I tried to quickly retract my body so I could return to my hiding spot with my new meal. But the bird was larger than I'd previously thought, and it slammed into the building next to me as I was pulling it, kicking and screaming, into the dark alley.

The rider had fallen off when I grabbed the bird, so dealing with him was most likely unnecessary. I could always find him after killing and eating the Griffin, so I could eat him as well. Speaking of the Griffin, I was actually disappointed in it. Here I was, expecting some grand fight within the confines of the alley... But the damn thing died after slamming into that building. It also wasn't quite as big as I'd thought. Though its wingspan was definitely over twenty feet, the rest of it was fairly small. It was probably about twelve feet long and six feet tall, so it wasn't tiny by any means. Unless you were comparing it to me; then it was little more than a snack.

Solon had stayed back so he wouldn't disturb my meal... or become my next one; I wasn't quite sure which. After waiting for me to finish, he jumped onto my back. Then, he pointed towards a building to my right.

"I think the tower is that way," he said with a slight quiver in his voice. I could tell he was trying to hide it, but I was scaring him. He'd always seen me arguing with his father, or talking with his mother, but he'd never seen this side of me... The monster was always just beneath the surface. The glutton. My hunger had been satiated during my time in the ocean, so he had never seen me truly hungry. But now that these people had given me an excuse... why shouldn't I eat my fill?

I nodded my head to show my understanding. Then, I moved along the side of the building until I reached the end of the alley. As soon as I headed into an open street, I was spotted by a passing patrol of guards. Only one of them managed to avoid looking me in the eye long enough to open his mouth and scream. I bit into him and threw him against a building with such force I could hear his bones being crushed from the impact. He was stuck to the wall for several seconds before falling to the ground. He died only a few seconds later, as my venom saturated his body and melted him from the inside.

"Damn it, I wasn't fast enough!" I quickly smashed the petrified guards. Then, I moved into another alley on the other side of the street. I hid inside for a few minutes before peeking my head out, so I could try finding the tower again. This time, I managed to see it. However, even from a distance, I could tell it was heavily guarded. I could see three guards on the roof of the tower, and I spotted a head peeking over the building and moving from side to side.

"What's that?" I motioned with my head, causing Solon to look in the same direction.

"I... I'm not sure. It looks like a member of the giant race mom used to tell us about... but the color is different. Mom always said they appeared as humans, just a lot bigger. But that one is blue, so it can't be the same race as the one Mom told us about."

I nodded my head, then proceeded to move through the alley on my way to the tower. Staying hidden wasn't as difficult as it could have been, since the guards only seemed to be searching for Solon and were looking in places a young boy might hide. This left me to mostly do as I liked, which I took advantage of at every opportunity. Anytime a group of guards passed in front of me, I would petrify, then eat them. I had eventually eaten several tens of guards and cleared out a good sized chunk of the city. I continued to do this even after eating my fill because I wanted to cut down on the number of possible enemies on our way out. If I succeeded, anyway.

By the time I arrived at the tower several hours had passed, and it was well into the night. The tower was standing in a paved square. The surrounding buildings were positioned about forty feet away from it, in every direction. Most likely, this arrangement was to provide the guards up top ample opportunity to defend the place, should the need arise. The light of a full moon was casting an ominous shadow on the tower and its giant guard. The man was wearing a full suite of leather armor, and he stood about twenty-five feet tall. He was wielding a long pole with an axe and blade at one end. The entire thing was approximately twenty feet long and must have weighed at least two hundred pounds, but he had it resting on his shoulder as if it weighed nothing. His face was covered up by a leather helmet with a metal face shield. His size and stature reminded me of the giant that held up the island. Well, if he was a thousand times larger, he would.

"We'll try going around him... I'd rather not get involved with this giant unless absolutely necessary." I turned and went back through the alley. Then I used the alleyways to circle around to the back of the tower, so I could attempt to find another way in. However, after spotting the iron portcullis being used as an entrance, I quickly realized that I was far too large to fit inside. So, I sat Solon on the ground and thought for a few minutes.

"Alright, brat. Listen up." I looked him in the eyes.

"Yes?" he replied. The quivering in his voice had ceased, for the moment.

"You're going to have to do this yourself." I told him.

His eyes widened, and his face turned pale. "B... but, how?"

"I'll lift you up to the roof, you can start searching from there."

"Wh... what'll you be doing?"

A phantom smile grew on my face. "Eating."

He climbed on my head, and I lifted him up to the roof. He jumped off and ran to hide behind one of the spires. I knocked my head against the roof, causing the three guards to turn and look right into my eyes. Their bodies quickly turned to stone and I smashed them into powder.

The shaking of the tower caused some of the guards inside to come out in order to investigate. It also brought the giant around to the back of the tower. I took the opportunity to move away from the tower and circled to the giant's back, where I waited for the right moment to strike. After a few minutes of walking around the tower without seeing anything, the giant appeared to lower its guard slightly... So, I struck.

Using my size and weight advantage, I bit into its shoulder, my fangs piercing deep into the creature's chest and back. However, unlike my previous victims, the giant didn't seem to be bothered by my venom. Instead, it grabbed hold of my mouth and ripped my fangs out of its flesh. Then it threw me away as if I weighed nothing. I flew through the air for about five seconds before I crashed into a building, destroying it with my massive weight. The building collapsed, burying me under about three tons of stone and wood.

I quickly threw it off of me and turned to face the giant. It had taken the opportunity to rip its chest and helmet pieces off. Presumably, because it realized they would be of no use as my fangs would tear through them. I stared at the creature and realized that it only had one glowing red eye and long soot black hair that draped down to its shoulders. It then picked up its weapon and charged me. A multitude of guards also charged out of the tower and others ran through the surrounding streets in order to surround me.

"Fenris... You better get your ass out here as soon as possible." I bared my teeth and opened my "eyes." Ten guards made the mistake of looking into them, and more would have followed had a man in shiny metal armor not ordered them to look at the ground.

"It's an Earth Basilisk! Don't look it in the eyes, men!" the metal man shouted... But the giant didn't heed his warning and looked me in the eyes... and to my surprise, nothing happened.

"It must be a Tier 5 or higher creature..." The giant spun the weapon over its right hand, then caught it and stood in an attack position. Its weapon took on a glowing red hue as the creature glared at me. I glanced around at the surrounding humanoids, but none of them seemed interested in attacking me. In fact, some of them looked excited at the opportunity to see me fight the giant.

"Well... This should be interesting." It charged at me, then stabbed its weapon at my face. I ducked my head to one side and the blade passed by, then I heard a sizzling noise coming from behind me. I took a quick glance and saw the blade had pierced a standing piece of rubble and caused it to slightly melt.

"Great, the beast can use magic." I slammed my head into its leg, knocking it off balance. Then, I bit into the other leg and lifted the creature off the ground before I threw it into the air, and into a building on the opposite side of the tower. The creature slammed into the side of the building, then continued through it until it landed on the other side. It left a massive hole in the building, but that was soon fixed, as the rest of the building came down, as well.

I quickly followed after the giant and arrived just after it climbed to its feet. I shot my head out, in an attempt to bite the creature, but it used its massive strength to grab my upper and lower jaws. My strike was instantly halted and the creature smiled at me, revealing its sharp, jagged teeth.

"Me no like, Snake." The smile vanished from its face. "So, me crush you!" It twisted its arms and threw me to the side. My head bounced off of the paved road, destroying some of it in the process. Then, I bounced into another building, bringing it down on top of me. I was buried under a massive stone and wood building for the second time during this fight, and it was beginning to annoy me.

It appeared to also annoy the giant since it threw the rubble off of me, then stood above me with its weapon pointed at my body. Though the heat from the weapon was causing me severe discomfort, it was actually the giant stepping on my body that seriously pissed me off.

"Ha ha. Stupid Snake gonna make a good soup."

"I'm sorry... We seem to have gotten off on the wrong foot." The giant looked surprised. His one eye widened, and some of his weight was shifted from my body to the ground beside me.

"Snake can talk?"

I nodded my head, then rotated around to look at him. "Oh, indeed I can. And, may I suggest something?"

"Hmm?" The creature nodded its head.

"Thank you. Now, my suggestion is for you to... Get. The. Fuck. OFF OF ME!" I wrapped my tail around his midsection, then launched him away. He flew over forty feet and slammed into the tower. While flying through the air, he lost his hold on the weapon. After which, I picked it up in my mouth and threw it as hard as I could towards the center of town. Then, I turned to face the giant again.

"Stupid Snake! That was mine!" it yelled, before running at me. Then it wrapped its arms around my body and began squeezing. I took that as a challenge.

"Alright... you want to play this game, do you?" I coiled the free parts of my body around it, then began to squeeze back, while being extra careful not to put more pressure on the part it was holding. And if I'm being honest, the giant was incredibly strong. Under normal circumstances, it could probably beat just about anything in a contest of strength... But you don't challenge a snake to a contest of strength, because we don't play fair in such contests. While squeezing it, I was also biting and injecting copious amounts of venom into any exposed area I could reach.

"Hey... Stop that!" it yelled as it stopped squeezing, so it could focus on escaping. But, of course, I wasn't going to let that happen. Every time the giant tried to escape, I squeezed harder until I heard its bones breaking. Even then, I didn't stop... until. *Pop!* The creature's guts exploded out of its mouth and covered both myself and the ground around me. Afterward, I simply released it, so it could collapse to the ground.

The giant's impact with the ground caused it to shake for a few seconds, then nothing. Everything had gone completely silent in the face of the creature's defeat, and the guards were staring at my gore covered form.

"Hmm? What, do I have something on my face?" I asked as my tongue reached out and pulled a piece of the giant's intestine into my mouth. The action was enough for them to retreat as far from me as they could without leaving the tower grounds... or so I thought until I noticed an orange light coming from my left. I turned to see what it was and saw the giant's eye was glowing.

"I'm just going to assume, that's not good." I scooped up as much of the giant's intestines as I could fit in my mouth, then I retreated from the corpse. I made it about twenty feet when an explosion went off behind me, searing my tail and destroying some of my scales. I looked back to see just how large it actually was and saw a pillar of fire reaching into the sky. Then, it collapsed in on itself and rocketed towards the ground, where it spread out in every direction, cooking several unlucky guards that were in the blast radius and destroying part of the tower.

A few moments after the explosion, a small shadow jumped from a hole in the wrecked tower, then rapidly grew until it was over twenty feet tall and thirty feet long. After it landed on the ground, I realized what it was...

"About time, you damn mutt!" Fenris was glaring at the remaining guards. Meanwhile, three people were sitting on his back and holding onto his fur. It was Lena and the kids. But something was wrong... Lena's clothes had been ripped apart, as had Hali's. Lena's face was set in stone, with a look of fury on her face. Hali was crying, while she clutched onto her brother's shirt. I moved over and "stood" beside Fenris.

"What happened?" I asked while looking from Lena and Hali to Fenris.

He turned his head to look at me, then returned to glaring at the guards. "What usually happens when a man with too much power desires something he can't have..."

It took me a few seconds to understand what he meant, but when I did... "Is the bastard dead?" Fenris nodded and looked up at the top of the tower. I followed his line of sight and saw a humanoid shape impaled on a large stone spike that was sticking out of the roof. I nodded my head and looked back to the guards.

"It's your call. I've eaten my fill already, so whenever you're ready, we can leave." Fenris nodded his head and started walking back towards the harbor. However, he glared one final time at the guards and said, "If I see anyone following us... they're dead. Understand?" The metal man nodded his head and returned Fenris' glare.

I followed behind Fenris and the family as we made our way back to the harbor, where I sunk myself into the water, and the family prepared their ship. It only took them fifteen minutes to get it ready, then we left the island city behind. We sailed for about three or four hours, before dropping anchor and going to sleep.

However, I got this pop-up just as I was going to sleep.

∞∞∞∞∞∞∞∞∞∞

You have eaten the following race for the first time.

Griffin: Tier 4

You have eaten the following race for the first time.

Flame Cyclops: Tier 6

You have unlocked the following evolutionary path: Wind Basilisk

Would you like to evolve?

You have unlocked the following evolutionary path:
Fire Basilisk

Would you like to evolve?

You have unlocked the following evolutionary path:
Elemental Basilisk

Would you like to evolve?

∞∞∞∞∞∞∞∞

"No... No..." I paused and yelled to get Fenris' and Lena's attention.

"What is it, snake?" The two of them looked over the edge.

"I'm about to evolve... Would you mind waiting for me?"

Lena shook her head. "Of course, we don't mind.... Though it would be nice to know how long we need to wait." I nodded my head and decided to ask.

"How long will it take for me to complete the Elemental Basilisk evolution?" A pop-up answered my question.

∞∞∞∞∞∞∞∞∞

15 days

∞∞∞∞∞∞∞∞∞

I passed that along to Lena... then said, *"Yes, I'm ready to evolve."* The white shield quickly formed around me, and I sunk to the ocean floor. Once I was there, another pop-up appeared, and I was forced into a deep sleep.

∞∞∞∞∞∞∞∞∞

Your evolution is underway, and a shield has formed around you until it is complete. Time remaining until completion is 14d 23h 59m 52s.

∞∞∞∞∞∞∞∞∞

CHAPTER TWENTY-ONE

T HE FIFTEEN DAYS PASSED BY AND I AWOKE TO A few new pop-ups.

∞∞∞∞∞∞∞∞

Energy Store/Release: Absorb and store solar energy inside the red jewel on your forehead, then release the stored energy in an explosion of fire.

*Note: Due to the Gluttonous trait, you can use energy gained from eating as a substitute for solar energy, at reduced efficiency and damage.

Resist Elements: As an Elemental Basilisk, you have a minor resistance to all elements.

*Note: This will not protect you from elemental attacks, but will protect you from environmental changes.

Winged: As a Wind Basilisk, you have grown wings.

*Note: Your current wings do not have the strength to fly. However, they can be used to glide.

Name: Torga

Race: Gluttonous Elemental Basilisk

Classification: Tier 5

Skills: Minor Stealth, Heat Detection, Gluttony, Major Durability Up, Major Strength Up, Growth, Minor

Mental Resistance Up, Petrifying Gaze, Greater Acid Venom, Detect Concealment, Energy Store/Release, Resist Elements, Glide

Traits: Gluttonous +2, Growth +2, Strong Willed, Venomous, Aquatic, Winged

∞∞∞∞∞∞∞

"Eh... Wings?" I began to struggle inside the shield and after a few minutes, I successfully broke through and was set free. Once the shield faded, I took a look at my back and saw two large wings. They were covered in thin scales, with what appeared to be very slender bones lining the inside. An extremely thin membrane was stretched across the bones and was, I assumed, what would allow me to glide. Looking a little further down my back, I saw a smaller set of wings. This set was just above my tail and if I had to guess, would allow me to move around while in the air.

Then, there was the pressure that I'd been feeling on my forehead. I assumed this was the stone that would allow me to store solar energy... That line of thinking led to a question.

"Was this the same stone that caused the cyclops to explode after its death?" I was, of course, referring to its red eye, as that is what started to glow, then exploded. So, did that mean, I was also a walking bomb? I wasn't quite sure. But if I was, at least whatever kills me will have one hell of a surprise waiting for them. Of course, it also said that the stone could store the energy I get from eating. But, since it would take more energy to get a lesser effect, I should only do that in an emergency. Otherwise, it might become a crutch... and that could

lead to me dying early, should something happen that removed my ability to use it.

Then, I asked what my future evolution requirements were... and a pop-up answered.

∞∞∞∞∞∞∞∞

Submerge yourself in a "river of fire" to unlock: Elemental Wyrm

Consume the blood of a dragon to unlock: Elemental Serpentine Dragon

Survive 100 years to unlock this path: Elemental Hydra

Consume a Ruby, a Sapphire, a Tiger's eye, a Diamond, an Emerald, an Amethyst, and a piece of ebony ore, all at once to unlock: Elemental Naga

Crush five ships to unlock: Elemental Leviathan

∞∞∞∞∞∞∞∞

"And... if I pass them up, what do I get?" Another pop-up answered.

∞∞∞∞∞∞∞∞

If you pass up the Elemental Wyrm evolution, you will get: Superior Elemental Resistance or Spike Scales

If you pass up the Elemental Serpentine Dragon evolution, you will get: Wind Control or Spiked Tail

If you pass up the Elemental Hydra evolution, you will get: Supreme Regeneration or Elemental Control

*Note: This evolution is a higher tier than the others, so you may pick one of them and still go to this one, but, not vice versa.

If you pass up the Elemental Naga evolution, you will get: The ability to use magic or telepathy

If you pass up the Elemental Leviathan evolution, you will get: Superior Strength or Acidic blood *Note: You will also gain an increase to the growth trait.

∞∞∞∞∞∞∞∞

"I'm going to need a while to think on this since I can't get a description of the races, aside from what I'd get if I discarded them..." Deciding to think more on this later because I'd kept the family waiting for long enough, I looked up at the surface and saw the ship sitting in place, so I swam up to meet them. And, as soon as my head broke the surface, I was intercepted by an irate Fenris.

"You damn snake! What took you so long!?" He glared down at me from the safety of the ship and began a tirade.

Disregarding the mutt, I looked over at Lena and the kids. They seemed to be doing better, now that some time had passed. I thought about asking what happened, but I didn't want to cause them any discomfort after they had finally settled down. So, I kept my mouth shut. Never let it be said that I couldn't be sensitive when I wanted to be. Well, to people I like, anyway.

Which led me to realize *"I actually like these people... some of them, at least,"* I thought as I glanced back at Fenris, who still hadn't shut up.

Lena, after looking at me, gasped and ran over to the edge of the ship for a closer view. Once there, she covered her mouth with her hands and stared at me. "An Elemental Basilisk," she mumbled after a few seconds, causing me to look at her and further ignore Fenris.

175

"What's wrong, Lena?" I asked with a tilt of my head. While I was looking at her, I noticed that everything seemed a lot smaller, than it previously did. For example, I knew Fenris to be over twenty feet tall, but he appeared to have shrunk since I'd last seen him. Because with just my head resting on the ship, I was looking him in the eye. So, I had to be at least twenty feet tall. And I was wider, as well. Using the ship as a base measurement, which I guessed to be just under thirty feet wide and fifty feet long. I was approximately fifteen or sixteen feet wide, as I was a little over half the width of the ship... I didn't even want to guess how much longer I was now.

She shook her head and said, "Nothing... it's nothing." I knew she wasn't telling me the truth because she was acting strangely.

"It's clearly something since you're acting like you've seen a ghost. So, tell me the truth, Lena."

She raised one brow at my words and folded her arms across her chest. "Are you calling me a liar, Torga?" she asked, and I immediately nodded in confirmation.

"Yes." My response surprised her enough that she took a step back and stared at me in wonder.

"That... wasn't the answer I was expecting," she said after a few seconds. I gave her my version of a shrug, which was a slight tilt of my head to the side—an act that probably looked a little strange, coming from a giant snake.

Then, I said, "I'm not your husband. Whether or not you like my answer is irrelevant to me." She looked away and puffed out her cheeks.

I rolled my eyes at her. "Please, do act your age. I already have to deal with one immature brat and I'd rather not deal with another."

Solon apparently heard my words and felt the need to correct me. "Hey!" he yelled before storming over and pointing his finger at me. "I'm not immature!" I tilted my head to one side again and stared for a few seconds, then I started laughing.

"I... I was actually referring to your father. But, if you feel the shoe fits, then feel free to lace it up and wear it."

He looked at me with a blank expression on his face until I stopped laughing, then he asked, "What shoe are you talking about?" He glanced down at his bare feet, then back to me. "I don't wear shoes," he said with a slight shrug, which started a round of chuckles from me and his mother.

"It's a colloquialism, so don't take it literally," Lena said. His face went through multiple changes, before settling on confusion. He looked to his mother, who was trying to hide her own mirth at her son's baffled face.

"Mom... What's a co… co... colocoism?"

She quickly stamped down her mirth, then answered. "Colloquialism, dear. It means it was a saying not meant to be taken literally." She patted him on the head and smiled. "So, don't worry about it." He seemed suspicious for a second, then nodded and walked off. But not before giving me one last glare. Lena watched him walk over to the other side of the ship, then she looked back at me.

"Why do you do that?" asked, tilting my head, puzzled.

"Do what?" she huffed.

"Why do you use words that you know he can't understand? He has enough trouble understanding the simple words, then you go and use words like 'colloquialism.'" I stared at her for a few seconds, then looked over to Solon. "The boy's more intelligent than you're giving him credit for."

She apparently didn't like my saying so because she gave me a hard look in response. "I know my son isn't stupid!"

I turned my head to her, then said, "I realize that. But you do treat him as if he's not as smart as Hali. I think Fenris is the most guilty of this."

Her left brow rose and she said, "Do you have a reason for saying so?"

I nodded my head, then asked, "If I tell you, will you explain why you reacted so strangely upon seeing me?" She thought over my words for a moment, her head shifting from side to side. Then, she tentatively nodded.

I looked back to Solon, who was currently in a conversation with his sister. "The two of you are clearly proud of Hali because of her druid magic. But I sometimes see Solon off by himself practicing with that dagger of his."

Lena folded her arms and interrupted me by saying, "I know he practices, but I fail to see how that means we are treating him as if he was dumber than Hali."

"If you'd shut up and let me finish. I'll explain further." I unintentionally bared my teeth and hissed. She took a few steps back, but her face and demeanor remained the same, so I continued. "I've seen Solon practicing moves that I haven't seen either of you show him. And the moves you do show him only take him a few tries before he has them down pat... And yet, I've seen neither you nor Fenris praise him for it." She opened her mouth to interrupt again, but I beat her to it. "Lena, I'm not saying you're neglecting him, so shut up." Her mouth snapped shut. "All I'm saying is that you pay more attention to Hali's magic than you do Solon's combat training. And Fenris outright ignores his combat training in favor of sleeping all day, while you are left trying to teach them both."

She seemed to consider my words for a few moments, then she looked over at Fenris, who was sleeping, as usual. She stormed over to him and kicked him in the nose. Though she didn't put any real strength behind the kick, Fenris yelped and stood up. "What was that for!?" he yelled, which only served to annoy Lena even further.

"You need to help Solon with his training, instead of expecting me to do everything!" Her sudden shouting confused not only Fenris but the kids as well.

"Mom?" Hali questioned, while Solon just looked confused.

"What's gotten into you all of a sudden? I'm sure Solon's training is going fine." A piece of wood came loose from the deck of the ship and smacked Fenris on the butt, causing him to yelp again.

"Of course, it's going fine. He's my son, after all, but I'm tired of seeing you lounge around all day. So, you have two choices. Either you get off your ass and begin Solon's training or..." She leaned in and whispered something in his ear.

Whatever she said to him, I doubt I'll ever know. But he transformed into his demi-elvan form so fast it just about made my head spin. "Alright, Solon. Training time!" Fenris marched over and grabbed Solon's arm, then dragged him to the back of the ship.

Lena made her way back over to me and bowed her head. "I hate to admit it... but, you're right. We haven't been spending nearly enough time on Solon's training. Hopefully, we can still get him up to speed before something... else... happens." Her eyes went foggy and she lost focus for a few seconds, then she suddenly snapped back to attention. "I just realized, we never thanked you for saving us."

I shook my head. "There's no need to thank me, as I'm not the one that saved you."

She slightly nodded her head, then said, "I'm well aware that it was Solon who did the actual 'rescuing,' but he couldn't have done it without your help. In fact, I feel a spike of dread whenever I think about what could have happened had you not been there." Her eyes grew slightly misty and she just barely managed to choke out her next words. "Seriously, Torga. My family and I are forever in your debt." She bowed at the waist until her head was parallel to the deck and I could see the tears dripping down her face.

"Then, would you mind doing me a favor before you answer my question?"

She quickly nodded her head, then said. "Anything within my power."

I nodded back, glanced over to Fenris and Solon, then looked back to Lena. "Can you please... find that damn mutt a pair of pants?"

Her face went blank, then she slowly turned her head and looked at Fenris, who was currently jumping up and down, completely naked, in front of their son and daughter. "Yes... I can definitely do that."

After forcing Fenris into a pair of loose breeches, she returned and told me that her tribe actually used to worship an Elemental Basilisk as a "protector" of sorts. And this particular basilisk was, according to Lena, Gigantic. It was said to have been over a mile long when it finally passed away from old age, but by that point, it had been their guardian for over a century. So its death didn't really come as a surprise to them, and though they wished for it to continue protecting them, they knew better than anyone that the cycle of life must not be broken by anyone... which made me internally chuckle as I was someone who had deliberately broken the cycle, so I could see and protect Sarah again.

After my talk with Lena, things went back to normal. I swam just ahead of the ship in order to keep an eye out for any predators that may be lurking just beneath the surface. And in this way, another month passed and we finally found what we'd been looking for, The Giant.

~ ~ ~

"There it is!" Solon yelled from his place atop my head—a place he had seemingly taken a liking to since we left the city. Anytime he was free, he would climb on my head and just talk with me. Hali would also join him up there some nights... said it made her feel safe to know that I would, in her words, "Eat anything that tried to harm us." And since their children were usually sleeping on my head, Lena and Fenris had taken the time to get "reacquainted" with one another, despite my frequent requests for them to at least wait until I had gone to sleep before they started humping. I was just as frequently ignored. So, lo and behold, Fenris and Lena came up to the children one day and said, "We're going to have a baby!" It took forever to get my "ears" to stop ringing after Hali began to celebrate by screaming while atop my head.

"There it is," I said in wonder at the sheer size of the thing. Its appearance hadn't changed at all since I'd last seen it. The dark blue skin, tribal tattoos, curved horns, long hair, but most importantly, the island that rested on its shoulders, held there only by the massive chains that wrapped around the entirety of the island's base. I looked back at the family and said, "We're here at last."

The kids started jumping around, while Fenris and Lena just stared at the creature. "H... how are we going to get up there!?" Lena stuttered.

"Climbing it is certainly out," Fenris said, then he looked at me. "Any ideas?"

I looked back at the creature, then at the island above, then at the point where the water began to cover his calves. I nodded and said, "We dig our way to the top."

Fenris, Lena, and the kids just stared at me in confusion, then Fenris asked, "And... how do we do that, when we don't have any tools?"

I tilted my head to one side, then smiled to show off my teeth. "Of course, we do. I have teeth, you have claws and teeth. What more could we need?" Fenris looked back at the giant, then sighed and looked at Lena. "The things I do for you and the kids..."

She smiled at him, then patted him on the shoulder. "And we really appreciate it, don't we, kids?"

They nodded and yelled, "Love you, dad!"

Fenris looked between Lena and the kids, then back at the giant, before finally saying, "Oh well, might as well get us started, snake."

I nodded, then swam ahead of the ship and over to the giant's leg where I started to dig out a path.

"Well, I'm certainly not going to go hungry anytime soon."

CHAPTER TWENTY-TWO

TWO YEARS. TWO YEARS OF NOTHING BUT EATING my way up and around this monstrosity. And that's not counting the several weeks I had to wait for my worn-out teeth to grow back. The giant's skin was harder than stone, so every few days I would lose a tooth or fang, which would severely slow down my digging speed. Of course, I couldn't exactly fault the giant for this, especially after I saw the pop-up.

∞∞∞∞∞∞∞∞

You have eaten the following race for the first time

Colossal Titan: Tier 9

The Titans were a race of prehistoric giants that used to rule Yggdrasil. However, they were overthrown when the first god grew tired of their brutality and killed the Titan king. This giant is all that remains of the first Titan prince.

∞∞∞∞∞∞∞∞

A Tier 9 creature... a creature on the edges of divinity... and it was delicious. I'd been eating or "tunneling" my way in a spiral around the creature. However, as I could not make the inclines too steep, the path wound up, looping around the giant over thirty times before I managed to make it up to the neck. Which

183

is where I was currently waiting for Fenris to make his way up and take over, so I could get some sleep.

The mutt had been getting progressively lazier, ever since his daughter was born last year. Talia was her name, and she was a Warg like her father. Even now, she was probably running around the ship and playing "attack anything that moves," one of the little brat's favorite games. She had dark hair and red eyes like her father and brother and was usually a happy, healthy baby. Well, toddler now, I guess.

I looked off to my right and saw Fenris walking over to me in his complete Warg form. Which leads me to another change that has occurred over the last two years. I've gotten a little bit bigger... okay, a lot bigger. The constant eating actually has had two effects on me. The first has been an increase to my Gluttonous trait, which now sat at a plus three. And that, in turn, further increased my Growth trait to a plus three as well.

This resulted in me having a tremendous growth spurt over the last two years. I'm now over ten times larger than I was before I began to eat the giant. I could no longer even compare myself to the ship, or to Fenris because they were so small. Fenris was so small now, he could easily sit on my head with the rest of the family.

Speaking of, Lena and the kids have been doing quite well, all things considered. Though it did take them awhile to get over what happened back in Edge Haven. I was told that while the man did do some invasive "inspections" on Hali and Lena, neither of them was raped. It was a close call for Lena, however, as the man had been attempting to do just that when I knocked into the building. The impact distracted him enough that Lena was able to force a stone spike to form between her legs, which then pierced through his crotch and slammed him into the ceiling. He was pinned up there until the explosion tore off part of the building, causing him and his spike to be exposed to the sky above. A fitting end for such a man, I suppose.

"What took you so long, Fenris?"

He sleepily glared up at me, then just continued to walk by me. He arrived at the wall of flesh a few seconds later and began to dig into it. I raised a non-existent brow at his silent response, then asked, "Fenris, what's wrong?" He stopped digging and turned to look at me.

"Hali was asking about forming a familiar bond with you last night, so I didn't get any sleep." He yawned again for emphasis, then went back to digging.

I tilted my head to one side and thought back to what Ayla had said about familiar bonds. "Why would she want to potentially tie her life to mine?" Fenris stopped digging and turned back to me.

"I don't know... All she ever talks about is if you'll accept the bond with her. I guess, I shouldn't be too surprised about her decision. After all, you're the only guy she knows that isn't family."

His words confused me, so I asked. "Why does it matter, that I'm male? Shouldn't the partner bond be with whoever she's most compatible with?"

Fenris nodded. "Yes, but if she wants a husband as well, then it needs to be a male."

My eyes went wide, and I blurted out. *"Husband!?"*

Fenris stared at me for a few seconds, then his eyes took on a dangerous glint. "Yes... husband. Does that surprise you? What, were you just going to use my daughter, then discard her... HUH!?" he yelled and took a few steps towards me.

I shook my head. "Actually, I had no idea she wanted me to be her partner until you said something just now. And, just what do you mean by 'use her'?" I stared him down with a questioning look in my eyes.

He stopped his advance after hearing my question, then sat down and said, "Well... I mean... don't you think she's beautiful?"

I tentatively nodded. "I suppose so... Why does that matter?"

His eyes grew slightly wider. "Usually, when a man and a woman find each other attractive they, uh."

"Have sex?"

He nodded.

"I have no desire to have sex with Hali, though. So, again. Why does whether or not I find her attractive mean we would be good partners for each other?"

His eyes widened even further, and I could hear him beginning to growl. "Are... are you saying that Hali isn't good enough for you!?"

I tilted my head to the right, then said. "How did you possibly come to that conclusion?"

"You just told me; you didn't want to have sex with her!"

"So? I don't think of Hali in that way. Besides, shouldn't you be happy that I'm not trying to have sex with her?"

He paused for a few seconds, then opened his mouth to continue yelling at me, when a metal object came flying from the darkness and slammed into his nose. He covered it with his front paws and glared into the darkness... until Hali and Lena stepped out and stared him down.

I looked between them and Fenris, then I just sighed and began to make my way down to the water below. I had to follow the edge of our tunnel, as I was too large to move past the girls otherwise. "Hey, Torga?" Hali called out.

"Yes?" I looked back at her.

"Can we talk... later?"

"Sure." I nodded, then continued on my way.

Later that night, I was resting near the ship when someone landed on my head. I looked up and saw Hali standing there watching me.

"You're ready for that talk, I'm guessing?"

She nodded her head, then sat down and folded her legs underneath her. "Dad already told you what I want to talk about, right?"

I slightly nodded. "You want me to be your partner."

She sighed, then nodded again. "So... will you?"

"Please, allow me to ask you something first."

"Sure."

"Are you doing this because you want a partner, and you're ready to become a full druid or is it simply because you think it's expected of you to find a husband?"

My question obviously confused her, and she opened her mouth to respond... but nothing came out. She went glassy eyed for a few seconds, then after snapping back to reality, she answered. "Well, um, Mom and Dad became partners at my age, and since they eventually married, I guess... both, maybe?"

I shook my head. "Hali, you don't need to follow in their footsteps if you don't want to. You're fourteen years old, and no one important is expecting you to find a husband at your age."

She bit her bottom lip, before responding. "Is... is that a no?"

I nodded. "To the husband bit, yes."

"Why?" she asked.

I sighed, then lifted my head out of the water to look at the stars. "I'm already married, Hali. And, if I'm being honest, I see you as a niece or a granddaughter. To think otherwise would just be... weird."

She was silent for a long time after that. She just sat there and watched the stars with me for about ten minutes before, "You're married!?" she blurted out.

I laughed at her outburst, then nodded my head. "I am."

"Why am I just now hearing about this!? What's her name? What race is she? Is she a snake like you? How long have you been together!?" She continued to rapid fire questions at me for several minutes, so I told her everything. Well, almost everything.

"One question at a time please." I said, and she responded by snapping her mouth shut. "Now, what was the first question, again?"

"Why haven't you said anything about this before?" she asked and moved so that she was looking me in the eye.

I gave her my version of a shrug. "It didn't seem relevant... Also, you never asked."

She puffed her cheeks at me, then asked her second question. "What's her name?"

"Re... Sarah, her name is Sarah."

"Ooh, is she a human?" she asked with sparkling eyes.

I nodded. "She was."

I couldn't tell if she caught on to my slip-up, but since she asked another question immediately after, I decided not to dwell on it. "How long have you been married?" she asked.

"... Thirty-four years." What I didn't say, and she had yet to ask, was how long we were together, not married. We had actually known each other since we were children as we went to the same school and were even in the same class... but our paths went in separate directions after high school.

Before I could get further lost in my memories, Hali asked, "So, where is she?"

I blinked away the memories and answered. "We...we were separated years ago, and I've been searching for her ever since."

"Oh." She was quiet for a while, then mumbled, "I'm sorry... Do... do you have any clues?"

I "shrugged" in response.

She let out a soft sigh, then stood up. "Alright, I'm going to sleep now. Night Torga!" she chirped, then jumped off my head.

I watched her walk over to the sleeping area, then lie down next to her brother. *"False cheer doesn't suit you, Hali."* I sunk down to the ocean's floor and went to sleep.

~ ~ ~

"There you are, you BASTARD!" My eyes snapped open, and I saw my "cousin" heading for us at high speed. I quickly raised my head out of the water and told Lena and the kids what was happening. They abandoned the ship and jumped over to the path we had dug out of the giant, then started running to higher ground.

I turned back to the Leviathan and let out a deep sigh. "Why did this bitch have to find us now? We were so close to escaping, too..." Once it had gotten close enough, the Leviathan shot her head out of the water and attempted to bite me, but I dodged to the side causing it to slam into the giant's leg. Its massive teeth latched onto the Titan's flesh, then tore off a huge chunk and swallowed it. Then, it turned back to face me and rose to its full height, baring its teeth as it did.

"Well... Shit." The Leviathan was still longer than me, though not by much. Its true advantage came from the weight this thing carried around. It was almost three times wider than I was and nearly twice as tall. Which meant it probably weighed several thousand pounds more than I did. Even after the two years of constantly eating Titan meat, I knew that I couldn't match up to this thing in a straight up fight.

"You little shit! Do you have any idea how long I've been waiting for this moment!?" the colossal serpent roared.

I tilted my head to the left, then said. "Hmm... Since I gave you that scar, most likely." I was referring to the circular scar I'd left after eating my way out of its intestines.

"You're damn right! Now, I'm going to finish what I started, but I think I'll chew you up before I eat you this time," it said with a dangerous hiss, then charged at me. Its massive size easily capsized the ship as it charged past. I dodged out of the way again, then quickly bit into the Leviathan's hide. The beast's acidic blood slightly melted my fangs, but the act fulfilled its purpose of pissing it off even more. I tore out a small bit of its meat, then swallowed it before I dove under the water and swam away. It roared in pain, then charged after me. She was probably expecting things to go as they had the last time, but things were different now. I was different now, and I'd be damned if I let some overgrown bitch beat me a second time.

I swam around the Titan's leg, then dove deeper into the water. A few seconds later, I glanced back and saw her right on my tail, literally. I quickly reached my top speed, then did a complete one-eighty and swam directly beneath its jaws. I circled around it, while it was still trying to turn around, then I bit into her hide once again.

Almost immediately after, I had to dodge as she bit down right where my head had been and causing her to bite into her own hide. This only pissed her off further, and instead of aiming for my head, she aimed for my body, which was still wrapped around her... which is what I was waiting for.

She opened her mouth wide, so I shoved my head inside and aimed the jewel at the roof of her mouth, "Fuck off!" The energy that I'd been storing in the jewel over the last two years was released in an instant, and a massive explosion went off inside the Leviathan's mouth. The energy easily tore through the soft flesh inside her mouth, then obliterated her brain, where it then continued to travel through the water for about fifty feet, before finally dissipating just as it reached the surface. However, despite my success in killing the Leviathan, I couldn't celebrate. I was in severe pain from the explosion, as it had destroyed most of the scales on my head, and possibly given me a concussion. I blacked out from the pain shortly after realizing that I'd won.

~ ~ ~

I floated under the water for an unknown amount of time before Fenris and Lena managed to fish me out. Then Lena began to use her druidic magic to heal my scales, though she said that her magic was unable to heal a concussion, so I would just have to suffer.

"It's what you deserve after fighting that thing on your own!" she berated me.

I groaned from the pain. "Listen... I know you're mad, but can you please not yell right now? I have a severe headache."

My words only served to make her even angrier. "A headache!? Oh, you have a headache, do you? Well, sorry, but that's the least of your problems, right now! You could have died, Torga! Do you not understand that!?"

I blankly stared at her for several seconds, then asked. "Hey, Fenris?"

"What is it?"

"I'm hungry. You didn't happen to snag any of that Leviathan meat, did you?"

Lena screamed in anger, then stormed off inside the tunnel. I looked around at Fenris and the kids and asked, "What's her problem?"

Hali let out a deep sigh, then followed after her mother. Solon gave me a bright smile and yelled, "That was awesome, Torga!" Then he too followed his mother, leaving Fenris as the only person to watch over me.

"Why can't you ever make it easy to hate you?" I heard him ask, so I gave him my version of a shrug.

"Don't know. Sarah said it was a quirk of mine..."

As I drifted off to sleep I thought I heard Fenris ask, "Who's Sarah?" A minute later, I heard him sigh and mutter, "Oh, well. I'm sure you'll tell me eventually. Sleep well, you've earned it."

CHAPTER TWENTY-THREE

THE FIRST THING I SAW UPON WAKING UP THE NEXT day was little Talia using her hands to rub something on the side of my head, just below the eye. I lifted my head up, which caused her to get angry and yell at me.

"No! Bad Torga!" She hollered and slammed her little hands on the ground. But since we were currently inside a flesh-and-blood creature, instead of making a thumping sound when she hit the inside of the tunnel, it made a squish.

I moved my head out of the tunnel and over the water below, so I could see what she'd been rubbing on my scales. When I lowered my head down to the water and turned my head to the side... I saw a crude drawing, in blood, of her family and me. I sighed, then pulled my head back inside the tunnel to glare at her.

"Please refrain from turning me into your personal art project." I attempted to stare the brat down, but she just laughed, clapped her hands, and cheered.

"I make Torga pretty!"

I rolled my eyes at her, then lay back down. "Do whatever you want, brat. I'm going back to sleep."

I heard her cheer again, as she started to rub on my side again. I honestly hated how the little brat thought I was her pet snake. But I couldn't really blame her for that, since Fenris was the one to put the idea inside her head. Oh, the mutt thought it was hilarious watching Talia attempt to order me around because I was her pet. Though I returned the favor by convincing Hali and Solon to call Fenris Mutt instead of Dad for a week.

I let out a small chuckle at the memory, then closed my eyes and went back to sleep.

The next day, I had nearly reached the top of our tunnel. Because we were so close to reaching the base of the island, I volunteered to dig the rest of the way, since I dug faster than Fenris.

I'd torn off chunks of Titan meat and had long since eaten my fill. This Titan, whatever or whoever it had been in life, must have been a truly amazing sight to see in motion. Being well over five miles tall, at the very least, and easily a mile or two wide, this thing completely eclipsed anything that could possibly be imagined. However, a being of such massive size must have had an equal strength to match. So, how powerful must the gods be, to not only defeat this creature but to enslave it as well? Is there really such a gap between the ninth and tenth tiers?

"How close are we to the other side?"

I looked behind me and saw Fenris, Lena, and the kids watching me. Hali was carrying Talia around on her hip as she'd been frequently doing, ever since the girl was born. Solon looked bored, as he was standing there with a blank look on his face and was staring towards the sea. While Fenris, who was currently in his demi-human form, was standing beside Lena with his left arm wrapped around her waist.

"Well, we'd be a lot closer if you'd get off your lazy ass and help me."

Fenris rolled his eyes and replied, "You volunteered for this."

I nodded. "Believe me, I'm well aware of that. However, if you're currently not too busy licking your balls or humping the air, maybe you could assist me?"

Lena snorted from her place beside Fenris, then took a step away from him. "Yes, why don't you help Torga dig, while the kids and I go get dinner ready."

Fenris looked away from me and stared at Lena with such hurt in his eyes, you'd think she was divorcing him. "But... but I thought we could go relax together on the ship. You know... like we used to?" He ran his fingers down her arm and was heading as far south as he could.

Lena pulled her arm away from him and glared. "And wind up pregnant again? No thanks. Three kids are enough for me at the moment."

Fenris groaned but didn't say anything as Lena and the kids walked off. Though Hali lingered and seemed slightly disappointed about going, she followed a few seconds later.

I watched her go, then turned to look at Fenris, who was still whining about helping me. "Quit whining, mutt. Just remember, the sooner we get off this planet, the sooner you and Lena can go back to your old lives."

My words seemed to strike a chord with Fenris, as he shifted into his normal appearance and began to help me dig.

~ ∻ ~

A few days passed and with the two of us digging side by side, we "quickly" reached the base of the island. After which, the digging went much smoother for Fenris than it had for me. Fenris' claws could easily dig through the stone and dirt base, in a way I just couldn't duplicate.

"One of the benefits of having legs with claws, snake," he smugly said, and though I tried not to let it show, his words had an effect on me. Having hands would be incredibly useful in a variety of ways, but I still hadn't made up my mind on which evolution I should go for. Though I did rule out the Elemental Wyrm and Leviathan paths, because of the information I have since learned about the two races.

The Leviathan I didn't really need any information on. That had more to do with my personal feelings on the matter, rather than whether it could be a potentially useful path to take. I mean, other than its massive size and the acidic blood I knew it possessed, there simply wasn't anything appealing to me about the creature, so I ruled it out.

And then I asked Lena for any possible information on my evolution paths. Though she was surprised at first, she soon offered what help she could. She didn't have any viable information on either the Naga or the Serpentine dragon paths, but she knew quite a bit about the Wyrm.

Apparently, the Elemental Wyrm is a creature most often found in areas of the purest magic. Now, originally, when she told me this, I assumed it meant places where "pure" creatures could be found, and in a way, I was right. However, she later clarified that by "pure," she meant places entirely composed of magic, where the normal laws of the world didn't apply.

For example, she told me of a place of pure wind magic, where mountains floated on wind currents. Where creatures miles long and made completely of stone floated through the air as if they weighed nothing. But most importantly, a place where if you exposed your bare skin to the air... your flesh would be sliced off as if with a sharp blade. And this, along with the monsters that often inhabited the place, is what made them so dangerous.

The Elemental Wyrm is one such inhabitant. Lena confessed to only ever seeing a fire Wyrm, and not its fully elemental variant. But, she said, the Wyrm was an incredibly dangerous creature while in its element. However, outside of it, they were severely weakened. How this would affect an elemental Wyrm, I didn't know, but I also didn't want to take the chance of being weakened simply because I wasn't in my "element." So, I passed it up as well.

Which left only two choices... Well, three if you count the hydra, but as I didn't want to wait that long, I didn't count it among my possible evolutions... for now, anyway. That would likely change if it became a necessary path for me to take, but for the moment, I was happy with my current choices. Now, if I could only make up my mind.

~ ~ ~

After reaching the base of the island and spending the next two days digging as fast as we could, we made it to the city on the island. More specifically, we emerged into one of the gardens that dotted the cityscape, then we turned and headed back to the tunnel to prepare for the final part of our journey.

Fenris and I gathered the others together and came up with a plan. We needed a way to get from the garden to the branch without the mind-altering effects of the island taking hold of us, and the only thing Fenris and Lena could agree on was that the children shouldn't walk on their own. After all, we didn't want something to happen to them while we were distracted by the island.

So, after about half an hour of listening to them arguing, I suggested they all climb on my back and I'd carry them there. And because they didn't have any better ideas, that is what we went with. The five of them would climb on my back after exiting the tunnel, and I would carry them to the branch. Hopefully, we'd make it there before whatever it is this island does could take effect.

We were just getting ready to put our plan into action when Lena suddenly yelled, "Wait!"

We stopped just before entering the tunnel, then turned to look at her.

"We should take as much of the food from the gardens as we can. There's no telling how long it'll be before we can get home, so we'll need as much food as we can carry." She said this with a slight shrug of her shoulders. Fenris and I looked at each other, then back to Lena.

"Can we empty out an entire garden in a few minutes?" Fenris asked while looking up at me.

"It's certainly possible. If the two of you can snatch up a few plants while we move, I think that would be a better solution than just grabbing the food."

Fenris turned back to Lena. "Do you think you could uproot some of them, while we move?"

Lena gave us a confident nod and allowed a grin to appear. "Of course. Who do you think you're talking to?"

I nodded my head. "Alright, then we need something to put the plants in." I paused for a few seconds, then said, "Think you could make some containers out of the ship?"

She tilted her head to the right and folded her arms across her chest. "Sure, I could... But what are we going to do with the rest of the ship? Are we going to just leave it there?"

I shook my head. "No, I was going to smash it, once it was no longer needed."

Lena's eyes went wide. "What, why!?"

I shrugged. "One of my evolutions requires me to smash five ships. I figured it wouldn't hurt to start with yours since if all goes well, you won't need it anymore."

Lena looked from me to Fenris and quietly said, "But... but we've had so many good memories on that ship..."

Fenris shifted into his Demi-Elvan form, then walked over and wrapped his arms around her. The two of them stood there whispering back and forth for several minutes before Lena nodded and Fenris took a step away, then shifted back. He looked to me, then said, "Give us a few minutes, okay?"

I nodded my head, then left the family to their own devices as I made my way up the tunnel. I stopped just before the island's base, then I decided to lay my head down and wait for the family to catch up. A few minutes passed before I heard someone walking in my direction, so I turned my head slightly to see who it was and saw Hali standing there. She waved at me with a smile on her face, then walked over and leaned against my side.

Neither of us said a word while we were waiting. Though at some point she grew bored and decided to quietly hum a song. I watched her for a few seconds, then turned my back to the stone path ahead.

I let out a small sigh. "Fenris should have kept his mouth shut. I can't even look at the girl without remembering his words now."

She looked up at me and smiled, then went back to humming her song. Awhile later, the rest of the family showed up carrying wooden crates and several large pieces of cloth. They walked over to us, and though Fenris looked at me suspiciously, he didn't say anything.

"Is everyone ready?" Lena asked.

I lifted my head off the ground and nodded, then I began moving through the stone tunnel to the island's surface. A few more minutes passed before I left the tunnel and circled around to the back of the hole. The family exited not long after I did, then they climbed on my back and I began to move around the city.

I traveled from garden to garden on my way to the branch, but I decided to try out something before I got too far from the ship. I made my way over to the edge, then leaned my head over and aimed the jewel at the ship below.

"Are you done with the ship now?" I asked.

I didn't hear anything for several seconds. Then Lena said, "Yes... We're done with it."

I nodded my head and took aim at the ship. "Let's see if this works..." I'd tried to do this before, and though it did work, it had barely left a scratch on the Titan. So, I was eager to see what it could actually do.

"Hey, uh... what're you doi—" Fenris began to ask before I cut him off.

I transferred a small amount of energy from the Titan meat I'd eaten into the jewel on my forehead... Then, *Please... don't give me another concussion,* I expelled the energy from the jewel, causing a beam of condensed power to fly from it. The energy traveled down to the ship below and crushed the back half of the ship into splinters.

While this impressed the family, as they'd never seen the energy used in such a way, I was growing frustrated because not only did it give me a massive headache and crack a few scales, but I'd also missed my target. I'd been aiming for the very front of the ship, but the shot went far left and hit the back.

"Since when could you do that!?" Fenris yelled, and his voice seemed to echo in my now aching head.

I lifted myself back onto the island, then began moving again. "How do you think I killed the Leviathan?"

"I didn't think you did that!" he barked at me, then turned to face Lena. "Stupid snake... First, the bastard grew larger than me, and now he can fire fucking beams out of his head," I heard him mumble to her, causing her to giggle into her hand.

~ ~ ~

A half hour later, we arrived at the base of the branch. The family hopped off, and Fenris shifted into his Demi-Elvan form before making contact with the ground. Then, they turned to face me.

"Well... this is it, I suppose," Lena said after a few seconds.

I nodded my head, then said, "It is. Remember your promise to me, Fenris. I get you here, and you help me evolve."

"I remember, snake. Do you still want me to help you with that evolution?" he asked.

"Yes, collecting the stones will be next to impossible for me, due to my size, and well everything else. So, if you wouldn't mind collecting them for me. I'd appreciate it," I said with a slight nod.

"After everything you've done for us consider it done."

Lena stepped forward and gave me a kiss on the "cheek," then Hali quickly copied her. And Solon, who was standing at the back, just nodded to me and smiled. Talia, who was in Lena's arms, waved at me and giggled.

Then they walked over to the branch. Fenris lifted Hali and Solon into his arms, while Lena used her magic to stick the gathered plants onto his back.

"Remember, snake. The druid home world is Planet Uathea, so if you want your stone, you'll have to come visit us there." Then he reached out and touched the branch, and he and his family were sucked inside, leaving me alone on the island.

I touched my head to the branch shortly after they disappeared and was sucked inside, as well.

∼ ∼ ∼

After being sucked inside the branch, I found myself inside the Bifrost once again and several pop-ups were floating in front of me.

∞∞∞∞∞∞∞∞

Welcome to the Bifrost

Please select your next destination from the available branches.

Geoter: A desert planet.

Neonia: Home of several human kingdoms. Equal parts water and earth.

Thaater: A fire elemental world. Home to several hundred active volcanos and flame guardians.

∞∞∞∞∞∞∞∞

"Hmm... The desert is out immediately." The desert planet was removed from the list.

"And, I'm not ready for the human kingdoms just yet. So, I guess Thaater it is." The pop-up disappeared and I was propelled forward at high speeds.

Chapter Twenty-Four

When I was finally pushed out in the new world, the very first thing I realized was just how different the worlds could be from one another. If the first world was an evergreen forest of darkness, and the second was essentially an ocean, this planet was the embodiment of earth and fire. I stared out at the surrounding area for several minutes, just trying to take it all in before I dared to move.

It was currently nighttime here, so the moon was out in all its glory. The large, blood red moon cast an ominous shadow on everything that touched its light. The stars appeared to be hidden behind a ceiling of fog, as they couldn't yet be seen.

I slowly moved my eyes down and took in the mountains in the distance. They all seemed to glow in a bright red light as if they each had a miniature sun contained within. I could see veins of magma flowing down each of them in a constant stream of red, and pitch-black smoke rose from their open mouths. The mountains were huge, even from where I was "standing," and I was most likely several hundred miles away.

I slowly rotated my head to get a good look of the area around the branch, but a few seconds later, something incredibly hot dripped onto my back. I hissed in pain and moved my massive body away from the branch, then I rolled onto my back and thrashed around until the pain stopped.

I looked up into the sky behind the branch and saw what had dripped on me. A river of lava flowed in a spiral around the top of the branch, but they never touched. The lava spun lazily through the air, on its way to wherever it went. The bright red and orange colors created a pain in the back of my skull, just by looking at it. I "turned off" my heat sensing and a few seconds later, the pain faded away.

"I should probably stick to my normal vision and keep my heat sensing off for the duration of my stay here." After ensuring that I was out from under the lava, I returned to studying my surroundings.

I appeared to be on some form of large hill or small mountain. Now that I was actively focusing on the ground beneath me, I could feel the heat seeping up through the dirt and stone. I looked around for a few more minutes, but as I didn't see anything new, I decided to finally begin moving.

I slowly made my way down the hill and onto flat ground. Then I took another quick look around before picking a direction.

"The Wyrm evolution requires me to completely submerge myself in a 'river of fire.' Assuming that means a magma river, I should probably head for one of the mountains in the distance. But, then what? I can't submerge myself inside a magma river without being roasted alive, so I first need to come up with a way around that."

Now that I was alone again, I didn't need to constantly worry about keeping my stomach full, lest I suddenly decide the family looked appetizing. However, that also meant I no longer had access to Lena's magic. Which, now that I thought about it, probably could have helped me here.

But, as wishing for something to happen never worked, I resolved myself to experiencing some pain while I was here. After all, it wasn't like the answer to my problems would just fall out of the sky. Yeah, no way that was going to happen. So, it looked like I was going to need to do this the old-fashioned way—through stubborn determination and a conceivably good plan.

I decided to head in the direction of the closest mountain and come up with a strategy along the way. I couldn't do anything until I had some lava to experiment with, after all.

After what felt like hours of moving along the ground, I came to the edge of a plateau that was miles above the land beneath it, and when I looked down, I got my first good look at a Flame Guardian, or what I suspected to be one.

It was a colossal tortoise that appeared to be swimming through the earth. Its head was just above the surface layer of dirt, but on its back were three mountains that constantly spewed smog into the air. The beast had to be at least five miles long and three miles tall. It used its massive limbs to tear apart the earth beneath it and move through it as if it were water. I watched it for several minutes, as it moved through the earth in giant, slow strides. Then, something inside me came up with a horrible thought.

"I wonder how it tastes?" I tilted my head to one side. A phantom smile spread across my face as my wings unfurled. This would be the first time in a while that I actually stretched them, as I normally kept them wrapped around me, like a second layer of scales. A neat trick,

which honestly took me longer to come up with than it should have.

During my time tunneling through the Titan, I'd often climb to the highest point and glide down to the water below. This was always entertaining to the kids, as they'd frequently ask me to fly them around for a while. Though it always annoyed me that no matter how hard I tried, I couldn't gain any height with my wings. Not by flapping them, anyway.

I lifted my head as high as I could, then allowed myself to fall over the edge. I quickly fell towards the rocky ground below and my body tensed up in excitement. Then, just before I hit the ground, I spread out my wings and caught air on the thin membrane and began gliding. My upper wingspan was around a thousand feet, while the lower wingspan was about five hundred feet.

I sailed through the air until I felt myself about to lose speed, then I closed my wings and allowed myself to fall again. Once again, I waited until I was about to hit the ground before opening my wings and gliding with renewed momentum.

I repeated this action until I was over the tortoise's back, then I finally allowed myself to touch down on one of the mountains it carried.

After landing on the tortoise's mountain shell, I began looking around for some exposed flesh that I could try digging into. I looked around for several minutes, but the only thing I could find was stone and more stone. So, I did what any sensible snake with a portable laser on his head would do.

"Let's try starting out at a lower output, then slowly increasing it until it's capable of penetrating the stone." I

aimed the jewel at a stone outcropping about twenty feet away, and I transferred the smallest amount of energy I could into it. The jewel slowly began to emit a bright red light and when I released the energy inside, instead of allowing it to explode out all at once, I held most of it back and only let the barest trickle of energy leave. The energy came out as a faint red line, that slowly increased in size the more energy I pushed into it.

After a few seconds of continuously adding more energy into the mix, I considered my experiment a success. The output of energy was now equal to the amount I'd used to destroy the ship, but I wasn't feeling the same effects as before. I was still feeling the pressure on my skull and my head was hurting, but it was a bearable pain. I could most likely keep this up until I either ran out of energy or grew too hungry to continue. The latter was the most likely occurrence, as even now I was suddenly feeling the gnawing hunger that I'd been able to ignore for so long.

"Damn! If I don't get some food soon, I'm going to have to eat rocks again..." I pouted, then increased the beam's output until It finally began to cut through the stone.

I kept the beam going for what felt like hours to my stomach, though it was probably only about ten minutes. It was worth it in the end, as the beam had carved its way deep into the stone, exposing the flesh beneath. A phantom smile spread across my face.

"Jackpot!" I reactivated the beam and began using it to cut out a hole large enough for me to fit inside, though that took me another hour of using my precious energy. Once I'd done it, I was so happy being able to get to the meat, that I no longer cared. Because the stone was

essentially turned to slag, I could ignore it and head straight for the meat, which is what I did.

I slid down the one-hundred and sixty-foot-wide, and two-hundred-foot-deep hole that I'd made, then I quickly dug into my prize. I bit into the flesh of the creature and tore out a chuck larger than Fenris.... It was the most delicious thing I'd tasted since I'd first started eating the Titan. I very quickly tore out another piece, then another, and another. This cycle continued for over an hour and once I'd eaten to the point of bursting, I took a look around and noticed that I'd eaten a fifty-foot hole into the creature's back.

"... I haven't heard the creature react to it being eaten... Does it not feel pain?" I silently wondered.

If it didn't even notice that I'd dug a hole into its back... How tough was this creature, exactly? Never mind the fact that I'd spent an hour carving away bits of its shell, eating a hole into its flesh should've gotten its attention. But I wasn't going to turn away a mostly free meal. I decided not to complain and enjoy it while I could.

A few hours later, and after taking a quick nap, I received this pop-up.

∞∞∞∞∞∞∞

You have eaten the following race for the first time.

Magma Elemental Tortoise: Tier 8

∞∞∞∞∞∞∞

"A Magma Elemental Tortoise... huh?"
I left the hole I'd dug and proceeded to explore my new temporary '"home." I first headed to the top of the mountains on the creature's back. Using my newly

acquired energy, I carved a path down into the mouth of the mountain, then began to explore. Inside, I found molten pits of magma, and caves lined with metal.

"I guess this explains *the 'Magma Elemental' part, but is... is this creature even alive? How can it possibly survive with this stuff inside it?"* I wasn't questioning the magma, as I figured once I'd read the name, that I would find magma inside it. But this metal, I wasn't expecting it. Deciding to disregard it for the moment, I continued to explore the caves I'd found.

I moved past the magma pits and the metal caves in my search for anything that could explain why this creature could live in the way it did, and I found it after about an hour of searching. I'd grown frustrated with the monotony of these metal caves, so I'd tried to use the laser to tunnel my way through the walls. However, something amazing happened instead. The metal walls of the cave actually absorbed my energy, then reflected it back at me. I was just barely able to dodge out of the way in time for the beam to fly past my head and impact the wall behind me, where it was again, absorbed and reflected.

I dodged this one as well and decided to retreat while I was still able. So, I moved back through the caves and retraced my steps to the top of the mountain, then headed back to the hole I'd dug earlier. Once there, I came up with a plan while I was eating to restore my lost energy.

"Since I'm currently unable to mine through that metal, I need to find a safe way to mine it that doesn't involve having my own energy shot back at me. So, I can either try to overpower the metal's capability to absorb energy, which is an incredibly stupid and dangerous idea... or, I can search the planet for anyone already capable of mining it and ask for their help.

Though another option would be to find out if they already have any of the metal, and either steal it or purchase it, somehow?"

My current plan for unlocking the next evolution was twofold. The first step was to acquire enough of this metal to cover my entire body, then I would try submerging myself inside either the floating lava rivers or inside the magma found inside the creature. However, this plan had a few "slight" issues. Namely, that I didn't know if the metal would absorb the heat from the magma. If it doesn't absorb heat, like it does the energy from my jewel, then the entire plan becomes moot.

I also didn't know how large this planet was, so I could wind up searching it for years without ever coming into contact with anyone. And let's say I do find someone within an acceptable amount of time. What are the odds of them being a druid or a beastman? What if I'm unable to communicate with them, and they think I'm just a mindless monster? This plan of mine, there were too many unknowns to completely rely on it, so I was left with only one option.

"Follow through with the plan as best I can and adapt when necessary." That was all I really could do at this point. I didn't want to chance leaving via the branch, only to lose sight of this planet during my travels. After all, I might not come across such a good opportunity again. This metal could not only help me with my future evolutions, but if I could find some way to carry a bit of it with me, maybe someday I could use it to help protect Sarah. So, I couldn't risk losing this metal, simply because it wouldn't be easy to procure.

I left the tortoise after eating my fill and sleeping a while. After dropping over the edge and unfurling my wings, I flew as far as the wind currents would take me, then I would stop to rest. On the first day of traveling, I easily covered seventy miles. However, from then onwards my traveling speed was greatly reduced as I slowly ran out of high places to glide from, so I wound up traveling by land for most of the day.

Eventually, my hunger made its return, so I was forced to travel even slower than I had been because of my need to eat. Since I couldn't find any animals wandering around, I resorted to eating stones and loose soil. But, because of my new Gluttony trait, I needed to eat more now than I ever had before. I easily consumed several tons of stone and soil during the course of a day, and when I would stop to rest for the night, it was to the uncomfortable feeling of stones sitting in my gut.

"I need real food, not this poor substitute..." I sighed after lying down to sleep one night. My stomach had been clenching uncomfortably for hours and I was slowly losing my patience with this place. And at that moment, I felt something I'd not felt since I came here.

My tongue had been "tasting" the air like it always did, when it picked up on the sweat of a living creature. What this creature was, I couldn't know, as I'd never tasted such an odd thing before. It tasted like a perfect blend of flesh and stone... Whatever this creature was, I didn't care as long as I could use it to satiate my hunger. Well, so long as it didn't try to use me for the same purpose.

I followed the creature's "scent" for approximately a mile, and eventually arrived at the mouth of a big cave embedded in the side of a large hill. Upon looking inside, I realized that the floor led into a gradual slope that eventually ended in complete darkness.

I cautiously stuck my head inside and activated my heat sensing, and to my surprise, I was able to detect several small creatures moving around inside. But, that's not all I found inside the cave. A network of tunnels that seemed to stretch on for miles greeted me as I was following the little creatures deeper inside.

I looked around, and after a few minutes in the surprisingly lit-up tunnels, I snapped up one of the creatures that happened to pass by me. I then proceeded to head down one of the tunnels.

"Food, food, here I come!"

CHAPTER TWENTY-FIVE

I MOVED THROUGH THE TWISTING TUNNELS FOR hours before I came to an area with enough light to actually see what I was eating. Of course, the pop-up also helped.

∞∞∞∞∞∞∞

You have eaten the following race for the first time.

Stone Kobold: Tier 2

∞∞∞∞∞∞∞

These creatures were tiny reptilian humanoids. They were perhaps the smallest race I'd ever seen, with the majority of them standing only a little over three feet tall. Though there were exceptions to this, as I'd both seen and eaten several that were much larger. These must have been variations in the race, however, as they also looked slightly different.

The few "variants" I'd seen must have been twice the size of their smaller cousins and stood over six feet tall. The normal kobolds had an odd assortment of scales, in a wide variety of colors. And on top of their scales was a stone substance that covered them like a second set of scales. The variants were monochrome, as they all had burnt orange scales with the same stone-like covering. Also, none of them liked me intruding in the "nest," or so I heard one of them scream before I ate him.

"Mm... Eggs." Obviously, a nest meant eggs, especially for a reptilian race, so I was on my way to help myself to them when my path was blocked by a small army of kobolds. The leader of this army was a large green kobold standing about twelve feet tall. He, like all other kobolds before him, wore simple rags for clothes. Apparently, a brown tunic and pants were the standard outfit in this nest. Though this kobold also wore a bone helmet, which looked strangely like a kobold skull. However, unlike the other kobolds, who were unarmed, this one carried a long staff with a stone spearhead on the end.

He stepped forward and slammed the butt of his spear on the floor of the cave, then shouted at me. "Halt, serpent! You shall not intrude in our nest any longer!"

I quirked a phantom eyebrow at the creature. "Oh?"

The kobold leader and his army took a step back in surprise at my response. Then, they hardened their visage and simultaneously took two steps forward.

"Did you practice that, or does it come naturally?" I questioned with a tilt of my head.

The leader's eyes hardened even further at the remark, then he snarled, "No!" He paused to shake his head, causing the skull to rattle a little, then he continued. "If you're smart enough to understand me, then know this serpent. Our god will not let you bully us like this!"

I nodded my head. "That's nice of them."

My apparent agreement threw him off, and his jaw hung loose for a few seconds. He shook his head, then asked, "So you'll leave us alone?"

I phantom smile appeared on my face. "Oh, of course... Though I do have some questions. Would you mind answering them?"

The moment he answered in the affirmative, I could tell his ego had inflated. He pulled his shoulders back, puffed out his chest, and showed me a cocky smirk.

"Ask your questions, then be gone, serpent."

I nodded my head again. "Of course. First question: Can any of you mine the metal inside a Magma Tortoise?"

His smirk slightly faded, and he growled out, "No, those damn goblins have laid claim to the tortoise mines and refuse to allow us entry. They've even tried to take our mountain before, but as they fear our god, they gave up and now leave us alone."

"Oh, that's not nice... Any idea where I can find them?"

He narrowed his eyes into slits. "Why do you want to know?"

I "shrugged" and replied, "Figured I would teach them to be 'nice.' As a symbol of my apology to you and your people."

His smirk returned, and he let out a laugh. "Ha! Maybe you aren't so bad, after all!" He continued to laugh for a few seconds, then said after calming down a little, "Ahh... They can be found a few mountains to the east of here. Just look out for the giant totem poles and the awful smell. You'll find the bastards there."

I nodded my head in thanks, then asked the second question. "Thank you for the information. My second question is... Who exactly, is your god?"

The kobold turned to his army and yelled, "Who do we serve!?"

The army stomped their feet and unanimously yelled, "Nargas, The Devourer!" The cave echoed from their shout and he turned back to me with an even bigger smile.

"Does that answer your question?"

"It does," I said, with what I hoped to be a pleasant smile on my face. Then I asked my last question. "My final question is... Where is this 'god' of yours?"

The kobold leader's smile slightly fell at my final question, but nevertheless, he answered. "He's... He's outside the mountain."

I stared at him after his answer. Then I showed off my massive teeth. "Well then, thanks for the information. I'm gonna go pay them a visit now if you don't mind… Or do mind, it doesn't really matter to me."

The kobolds had been so fixated on staring me down, that not a single one had bothered to turn away and instead had shown unity with their leader, by staring me in the eye. So, when I opened my "eyes" and used my petrification ability, line by line, and row by row, the kobold army turned to stone; a permanent expression of false bravado etched into their faces.

"Well... time to eat!" I scooped up tens of the creatures with every bite, and I didn't stop until the entire army had been added to the contents of my stomach.

Several kobold variants had been present in the army, including the leader, and the pop-up confirmed it.

∞∞∞∞∞∞∞∞

You have eaten the following race for the first time.

Magma Kobold (Stone Kobold variant): Tier 3

You have eaten the following race for the first time.

Kobold King: Tier 4

∞∞∞∞∞∞∞∞

Normally I would have been worried I'd just wiped out an indigenous population, but I didn't believe for a second I'd seen the last of them. The few hundred creatures I'd eaten before couldn't have mined out this cave if they had a thousand years. I mean, I could fit inside these tunnels with room to spare. The ceiling was easily two hundred feet tall, and the walls were four hundred feet apart. If you add in the fact that these tunnels go on for who knows how many miles... and you're going to need one hell of an army to mine something this large.

An army I wasn't interested in dealing with at the moment.

After growing bored of exploring the tunnels and getting lost, I turned back and retraced my steps to find my way out. I could do this because after the seventh or eighth time finding the same statue carved into the wall, I began digging a small oval at the end of every path, so I could find my way around. I followed my markers all the way back to the remnants of the army and from there I remembered the path out.

However, once I'd exited the cave, I realized that the army I'd been trying to avoid had decided to get the drop on me. I looked around at the mass of kobolds that had surrounded the mouth of the cave. Just from looking at them I couldn't even begin to guess the exact number. But there were easily thousands, possibly tens of thousands of them. It appeared that due to the variations in rock-like scales and colors, no two kobolds looked exactly the same. However, even with the slight variation in appearance, one kobold stood out from the rest.

This particular kobold was the same size as the "magma" variant, but instead of burnt orange, this one had rainbow colored scales and didn't have the stone-like scales. Instead, his scales were smooth and appeared to be incredibly soft... It was also male. The rainbow kobold stepped forward with an intense glare on his face and yelled, "You moronic reptile! Do you have any idea what you've done!?"

I shrugged. "Had a nice meal, then explored your caves for a while. No harm, no foul." My answer only served to piss him off more, as he screamed and stomped his foot.

"You fucking asshole!! It took me years to train up that army... years of being stuck in this body, unable to evolve because my evolution requires me to take over a kingdom! And you... You kill my elite soldiers!!" Steam began to rise from his body, as his anger increased.

"Oh... I didn't realize you needed them that badly. Please, accept my apologies." I gave him a slight nod to emphasize my point.

"Your apologies? That army was my chance to become a human again, you fucking idiot!"

My mind went blank as I processed his words. Then, a true smile bloomed on my face. The edges of my mouth drew back revealing the fangs and teeth within as I let out a quiet chuckle. "Oh man..." The smile continued to pull at the edges of my mouth, and I asked, "Are... are you a 'hero'?"

The kobold puffed out his chest and slammed his fist into it three times. "I am Nargas: Dubbed the Devourer by my enemies, hero to the kobold people, and chosen one of the God of Death!" The army behind him loudly cheered. Their voices seemed to cause the ground beneath me to shake.

I watched the surrounding army while they cheered, and a question popped into my head. *"Niabus said only one 'hero' could exist at a time, so.... what will happen if I kill every hero that shows up? Will my wife be born earlier, or will it not have any effect at all?"* I stared down at the "hero," and for every second I did, that question took over more of my focus. Because I really wanted to know the answer.

Apparently, Nargas didn't appreciate my ignoring him. Because when I finally did focus on him again, his scales had turned a bright red and he was waving his hands through the air.

"Stop. Ignoring. Me!!" He stomped on the ground, causing the earth to shake and a loud roar to echo throughout the air. The ground continued to shake for tens of seconds, but I didn't react to it. My size and strength enabled me to easily ignore a minor earthquake. But it's what was causing the ground to shake that threw me for a loop, literally.

A massive hand came out of the ground and wrapped around my tail, then it actually managed to lift me into the air and throw me over two hundred feet. I landed on the unforgiving earth, then slid for another hundred feet until I came to a stop and lifted myself back up.

I turned back and glared at Nargas, who was now riding on the shoulder of a colossal creature of stone. It stood an easy three thousand feet tall and was the size of a mountain. "Wait..." I focused on the area behind the giant and realized that it wasn't just the size of a mountain, it was a mountain!

"Meet my 'Stone Gorilla puppet,' you dull creature!" The "hero" yelled. The giant let out a deafening roar as it slammed its fists into the ground. The creature stood hunched over with its long arms and short legs both being used to support its weight. Long "fangs" lined its mouth, and glowing red eyes stared at me.

I stared back at the creature, then at the "hero" who had raised a chair onto the creature's back and was sitting in it, a cruel smirk plastered on his face. "Do you have anything to say before my puppet tears you to pieces?" he asked, while folding his arms across his chest.

I gave him a short nod. "I do, actually."

"Let's hear it. I'm an honorable man; I'll give you this at least." His smirk grew even wider.

I gave him my most "innocent" expression and asked, "With the size of that puppet, I have to know... Are you overcompensating for something? A feeling of inadequacy perhaps? Or maybe the female lizards won't sleep with you because of how gaudy your scales are. Oh, I'm sorry. I'm assuming you prefer male lizards, instead? Though, I'll be honest... You should give up on that dream right now. No male lizard who's interested in other males, will ever sleep with you because you look so much like a woman. I mean, I had to double check when I first saw you because I thought you were a woman, and an ugly one at that. Seriously, I've seen a three-eyed shark that was prettier than you, and believe me when I say, that was the ugliest thing I'd ever seen. Well, until you, that is. And what's with that name of yours?" I puffed myself up, in an attempt to imitate him. ***"I'm Nargas the Devourer, Hero of the kobold people, and chosen one of the God of Death!"*** I went back to normal, all the while maintaining eye contact with him. "Seriously, Narg... May I call you Narg? It's like a thirteen-year-old human came up with your name. What, was Nargas 'The Destroyer of Worlds' with double exclamation points taken?" I said all of this without allowing him to say a word, and the entire time I was speaking, he continued to get angrier with every passing insult. The result?

"I'm going to fucking take you apart Piece. By. PIECE!!" The smirk was long gone off his face, and his scales had been dyed the color of blood. His eyes seemed to glow with rage, and he threw out his arm, causing the puppet to start for me.

"Well, here comes the fun part." I charged up the jewel and held my ground.

The puppet rushed at me like an angry bull: head down, in a full sprint. And as soon as it was close enough I ducked my head down and fired directly into its face. The force of the shot drove my head into the ground. But, unfortunately, Nargas had ordered the puppet to jump to the side at the last second, so all I managed to damage was its left arm. However, that wasn't all I was aiming for. The shot flew past him and impacted the ground in the middle of the kobold army. Thousands died from the impact and subsequent explosion, which served to infuriate Nargas even more.

"You bastard!" he snarled at me.

I tilted my head to one side, as I dodged a swipe from the puppet. "Why do you keep cursing at me?" I asked, while ducking under another swipe and winding through the puppet's legs. "If you put half as much effort into finding a boyfriend, as you do cursing at me... you might have gotten laid by now." I said from directly behind the puppet.

Nargas screamed in rage and the puppet attempted to backhand me, but I charged up another blast and took off its other arm at the elbow. The puppet howled in apparent pain, and Nargas screamed, "I'm going to kill you!!"

I let out a laugh and said, "You know... It's funny because I thought you were already going to do that!"

The puppet lifted up its left foot and attempted to stomp on me, but I moved around it and wrapped myself around its waist, then used my weight to throw the creature off balance. The puppet fell onto its back, and Nargas was sent flying off.

Without its master there to control it, the puppet became inert. I charged up a final blast and sent it directly into the puppet's face, causing its head to explode and its body to begin dissolving... I looked over to where Nargas had landed, only to notice that he wasn't there.

"Do... do you know why they call me the Devourer?" I heard from just beneath my head.

I glanced down and saw Nargas, who was beaten and bloody. He reached out to touch me, and as soon as he did a pressure instantly attacked my mind.

"They call me the Devourer... because I devour the 'heart' and souls of my enemies!" The pressure increased a hundred-fold and I almost fainted, until Nargas said, "Oh ho... What's this then?" He paused as he went through something that had appeared in his mind. Then, he began laughing. "I can't believe it. You want to marry an elf? Please, a monster like you will never be able to make her happy." The cruel smirk reappeared on his face. "But a hero like me? I think I can make her an incredibly happy woman indeed!"

I glared at him, and I lowered my head until we were nose to nose with each other, then I said, "Oh... I'm sure a piece of you might make her incredibly happy indeed. Maybe I'll rip off that ugly mug of yours and make her a glass out of it? Or better yet, you can just become my food and I'll pass her your regards." I opened my "eyes," and though he wasn't affected by the petrification ability like I thought he would be, he still staggered away from me while holding his face. I used the opportunity to snatch him up in my mouth, then crunched down on him. His bones snapped, his blood gushed inside my mouth, and I bit down on him until he was little more than mush inside my mouth.

I ignored the screaming protests of the innumerable kobolds and left shortly after my fight with Nargas. A few kobolds attempted to stop me, and those that did ended up inside my stomach, while I left the rest alone.

After falling asleep that night, I was visited by someone in my dreams. He was a tall, thin man in a red tuxedo. His slicked-back hair and thin mustache would make the average person think him a man of nobility. Except both his hair and eyes were pitch black without the slightest bit of color, and he was a skeleton.

"Greetings ol' chap. Amaar's the name, and death is my game." he said, with an over-the-top flourish. A few seconds later, a top hat and a cane appeared in his hands. He placed the hat on his head and slammed the cane's end into the "floor."

I stared at him for a few seconds, then looked down at my body, only to realize that I was back in the "shadow" body. I let out a sigh, then asked, "Why are you here?"

He snapped his finger and Nargas appeared between us... Though he appeared to be bound by a thick rope and had a gag in his mouth.

"It has come to my attention, that you killed my champion."

I looked between the two, then said after a few moments' pause, "You're the God of Death?"

He gave me a nod. **"Indeed I am."** He paused for a few seconds to look me over, then smiled, somehow. **"But fear not, mortal. I have no desire for revenge. In fact, you actually did me a favor by killing ol' Nargas here... isn't that right, Francis?"**

Nargas' eyes grew wide, and rage built within them. He began to thrash around in an attempt to free himself, but it was to no avail.

"You see, Francis here made a deal with me ten years ago. In exchange for allowing him to reincarnate as a powerful monster, he would champion my cause."

I nodded so he would continue.

"However, I don't really have a 'cause' per se. So, I told him that as long as he entertained me, I would grant him his wish. But, ol' Francis here isn't the humblest man around. So, I turned him into what he is now."

"Why?" I asked, while tilting my head in confusion.

He shrugged his bony shoulders and replied, **"Because I just love pissing people off... which is why I'm going to help you this once."**

"I'm guessing that by helping me, you're going to be annoying someone?"

He gave me a slight chuckle. **"Oh, you have no idea how many people this will piss off. There are gods and goddesses, heroes and villains, kings and queens, and a hell of a lot of monsters that will despise me for this... which is why I'm going to do it."**

I scrutinized him for a few seconds, then finally asked, "Why risk yourself to help me?"

His eyes glowed an ominous red and he said, **"Because, my boy, I'm Death, and I don't give a**

flying fuck what they like." He snapped his fingers and both of them disappeared.

A few seconds after they vanished, I received several pop-ups.

∞∞∞∞∞∞∞∞

You have gained the following skills and a trait, due to consuming Nargas, the Kobold Hero.

You have unlocked the following trait: Immunity to Mind Control.

No one but you may control your mind.

You have unlocked the following skill: Puppet Maker

The ability to consume the mind and turn the body into a puppet under your control.

*Note: You must touch the target with your jewel to use this skill.

*Note: Because of the Gluttonous trait, you gain a small amount of energy from consuming the mind of your target.

You have unlocked the following skill: Body Possession

 The ability to consume the soul and possess the body.

*Note: Your body will be drawn inside of your target for the duration of this skill.

*Note: You must touch the target with your jewel to use this skill.

*Note: Because of the Gluttonous trait, you gain a large amount of energy from consuming the soul of your target.

∞∞∞∞∞∞∞∞

"Oh... Well, that certainly solves some problems." Just before I tried to wake up, I received yet another pop-up.

∞∞∞∞∞∞∞∞

Note from Amaar:

Oh, I'm also not supposed to tell you this, but your theory is correct. If you eliminate the "Heroes" that are in line before your wife, then she can be born sooner. However, despite the entertainment I would no doubt receive from watching you interfere with my "siblings" plans, this course of action will draw unwanted attention onto you. So, be absolutely certain that this is what you want to do before you act against them.

They aren't as nice as I am...

∞∞∞∞∞∞∞∞

A few moments after reading the note, I finally drifted off into a deep sleep.

Chapter Twenty-Six

WHEN I WOKE UP THE NEXT DAY, THE FIRST thing I decided to do was test out my new skills. However, unfortunately, I'd eaten the last kobold in the area before I fell asleep. As such, I needed to find another "volunteer" to test my powers on. But I had a pop-up to read before I could do anything...

∞∞∞∞∞∞∞∞

Because of gaining an ability pertaining to souls, you have unlocked a new evolutionary path.

Consume 100 souls to unlock: Dark Serpent

*Warning: Continuing down this path may lead to corruption.

∞∞∞∞∞∞∞∞

I was rendered speechless after reading the warning... What was it about this path that could corrupt me? Another pop-up gave me my answer...

∞∞∞∞∞∞∞∞

The Dark Serpent

The dark serpent, otherwise known as the "demon serpent" is a creature of ancient power. This race is believed to be responsible for the corruption, and eventual fall, of the angels, and is known as the first demon.

There have only been three dark serpents in history, and all of them were attacked and killed before they could control their power.

This race is the natural enemy of the gods because only this race possesses the ability to consume the vital essence that all gods need to maintain their power.

This evolution does not cause your physical body to evolve. Instead, it evolves your soul. Should you continue down this evolutionary path, then your soul will never be the same again. When you die, your soul will be consumed by your power and you will never know peace. You will also forever be forbidden from becoming a god. But with great risk, comes great reward.

The antithesis of a god. The ancient power of a devil is what awaits you instead.

∞∞∞∞∞∞∞∞

I read through the pop-up several times, just to make sure I understood exactly what was being said. Then I asked if I could pass up the evolution and gain something from it.

∞∞∞∞∞∞∞∞

No, if you unlock this path, then you will evolve.

∞∞∞∞∞∞∞∞

The Dark Serpent was apparently some form of demon, like the kind I'd eaten back on Iorus. Only, this one seemed to be different somehow. From the description the pop-up had given me, this wasn't just some evolution I could unlock to gain power, then forget about. If I gained this power, then it was for good.

Which meant, using my new powers will have consequences. If I use the Body Possession skill too often, I could accidentally unlock this path and then I'll have no choice but to evolve. The only good thing is if I do decide I want this "devil power," then even if I evolve, it won't affect my current evolutions.

According to the description, this path will evolve my soul and not my body. So regardless of my choice, my evolutionary paths will remain the same. Whether or not that's a good thing, I honestly don't know.

If I go down this path, then it's fair to assume that I will eventually gain the power to kill anything, even the gods. But is my desire to protect Sarah really worth my soul? I stayed where I was for approximately five hours before I decided that I needed to take a break from this train of thought. So, I got up and followed the kobold's directions to the goblin nest.

I searched the area until I found a large stone totem pole, then I searched more until I found a peculiar scent. Though I had prepared myself for an "awful" smell, what I actually found surprised me. The smell of burning flesh, mixed with that of a pig is what I was currently smelling. In other words, I smelled burnt bacon.

I lifted my head into the air and had to tilt my head back to keep my venom from leaking onto the ground. The smell was so appetizing, that I actually forgot what I was worried about. However, that same smell kept me from realizing that I'd been seen until an army of goblins had appeared in front of me.

I stared down at the army and took the opportunity to look the goblins over. The creatures varied in size, build.

Hell, most of them weren't even of flesh and blood. But those that were "normal," had green skin, a long-hooked nose, pointed ears, and black eyes. Most of them were naked, though some did wear loincloths, or a tunic made of "leather." And the largest goblins even wore skulls on their heads, as if they were helmets. Much in the same way the kobold king did.

The other goblins were even more bizarre looking. Some of them were made of a dark stone and had white glowing eyes. Then there were "flame goblins." These creatures were composed entirely of a bright orange flame that turned blue at the top of their head. And lastly, there were "metal goblins," goblins composed entirely of a reflective metal, that would reflect the sun with every movement.

Individually, I doubted that any of these creatures was much of a threat. But when they teamed up to attack a singular foe? Then they could be dangerous. Which is why I was further surprised when instead of attacking me, they just held their position, and a single female goblin, wearing a large skull for a helmet, stepped forward. This goblin advanced on me until she was about ten feet away from my mouth, then she took a quick bow and began to speak.

"Please serpent, be at ease for we mean you no harm," the goblin said in a squeaky voice.

I focused my attention on her. "Is that so?" I asked, after a few seconds' pause.

She gave me a quick nod and continued. "It is. Our spies saw what you did to the kobold and their 'god.'" She said the last part while rolling her eyes. "And we have no desire to see our own nest be attacked in such a way, so I have been sent to make a deal with you."

"What kind of deal?"

A small smirk flitted across her face before it disappeared and was replaced with a blank expression. "One where we give you whatever you want, in exchange for your word that you won't destroy us."

I scrutinized her for a few more seconds, then asked. "You'll really give me whatever I want?"

She shrugged. "It's what the king declared."

I turned away from her and looked at the goblin army that was blocking their cave from my sight, then looked back to her. "Very well, you have my word."

A small goblin came running out of the depths of the army and only came to a stop when it was standing beside the female. It gave me a quick bow, which is when I realized that it was a little boy goblin.

"Greetings lord serpent, I'm Nato, and I'm here to deliver your demands to the king." The tiny goblin was carrying what appeared to be a quill and a sheet of very thin leather.

I nodded to the little goblin. "I only want a few things, then I'll leave you alone. Are you ready?" I asked while looking down at the sheet he was carrying.

He nodded then brought the quill up to the sheet.

"Number one, I want ten goblins of various elements to be offered up to me. Male or female, it doesn't matter. However, I would prefer them being without child or partner and past the age where they are able to help the tribe." I figured since I needed to test out my skills anyway, and I'd prefer not to attack the tribe after they'd already agreed to do what I'd asked, getting the ones closest to death seemed the most "Humane" alternative to simply attacking the tribe and killing hundreds, possibly thousands, in the process.

Nato wrote on his sheet, then looked up at me.

"Number two, I want you to give me several tons of the tortoise metal for my personal use. Though I may decide to leave the metal with you to safeguard until I can come to retrieve it."

More was written down on the sheet.

"Number three, I would like for one goblin to become my assistant and travel with me. There are plenty of things that I am unable to do because of my size, and I need someone who can move around and do what I can't."

He wrote this down as well.

"And lastly, I want to know if you have a hero hidden among you?"

Nato looked up at me in confusion, then said, "Not as far as I'm aware."

I stared into his eyes, as I thought over his answer. Then I shrugged and brushed it off. "Oh well, fulfill my other requests, and I shall leave."

Nato nodded, then he and the female turned and walked back to the army. The army parted like water to let the two pass, then closed up to continue guarding the entrance.

"Now, the waiting game begins."

An hour after I released my demands to the goblins, the first demand was met. Ten goblins were now standing before me. Three of which were normal goblins, two were flame, two were metal, and three were stone. Each of them was male and appeared to be very advanced in age. I appraised each of them in turn, then told them why I needed them.

"You are going to help me test out my skills, understood?"

I got a simultaneous nod from each of them.

"Good, then we'll start with the base goblins and work up from there, shall we?"

The first of the goblins stepped forward, and though he appeared to be terrified, he didn't complain as he followed my instructions. I tilted my head down so it could touch the jewel on my forehead, then I activated the Puppet Maker skill. A dark energy traveled down the length of his arm and then pierced his head through the nose. The goblin fell to the ground and began convulsing. He thrashed around for almost two minutes before he finally stopped and laid still. He remained like that for another minute or two, then he slowly climbed to his feet and I felt something. It was almost like I'd gained a limb that I hadn't quite learned to control. I tried to make him walk around, but he stayed immobile with a blank expression on his face.

I frowned as I attempted to work out how to control him, when an idea came to me. I focused on that "feeling" and tried to send energy to it. And it worked. The blank expression vanished, and a look of focus entered his eyes. I mentally ordered him to pat himself on the head, and he complied. Then I ordered him to jump up and down, and again, he complied. A few seconds later, I received a pop-up.

∞∞∞∞∞∞∞∞

You have consumed the following race for the first time.

Goblin: Tier 2

∞∞∞∞∞∞∞∞

And then another.

∞∞∞∞∞∞∞∞

Goblin Puppet

Classification: Tier 2

Skills: Night Vision, Consume and Adapt

∞∞∞∞∞∞

After reading through both pop-ups, I ordered a stone goblin to touch the jewel and the same thing happened to him. Though the first goblin turned to ash after the second had been created. "I can only have one puppet at a time, it seems..." I turned one of each element into a puppet and read their pop-ups in turn.

∞∞∞∞∞∞

You have eaten the following race for the first time.

Stone Goblin: Tier 3

Stone Goblin Puppet

Classification: Tier 3

Skills: Night Vision, Major Strength Up, Major Durability Up

∞∞∞∞∞∞

"Hmm... Good for manual labor."

∞∞∞∞∞∞

You have eaten the following race for the first time.

Flame Goblin: Tier 3

Flame Goblin Puppet

Classification: Tier 3

Skills: Night Vision, Fire Control, Explosion

∞∞∞∞∞∞

"Alright, they could be useful as well..."

∞∞∞∞∞∞∞∞

You have eaten the following race for the first time.

Metal Goblin: Tier 3

Metal Goblin Puppet

Classification: Tier 3

Skills: Night Vision, Absorb and Reflect Energy, Major Strength Up, Superior Durability Up

∞∞∞∞∞∞∞∞

After reading that pop-up, a smile grew on my face and I ordered the remaining metal goblin to step forward. He reached out and touched my jewel, as the others had done before. But this time I activated the Body Possession skill, instead of Puppet Maker. Almost instantly, my body became a beam of ebony energy and penetrated his skull. Over the course of the next hour, the energy that had pierced his skull was drawn inside and mutated his body to fit my mentality... First, his metallic body formed shiny silver scales that further increased his defense. His head became more snake-like in appearance, losing the nose and ears altogether, and his eyes turned bright yellow with slit pupils.

Following this, I received another pop-up.

∞∞∞∞∞∞∞∞

Name: Torga

Race: Metal Goblin (Gluttonous Elemental Basilisk Possession)

Classification: Tier 5

Skills: Minor Stealth, Heat Detection, Superior Durability Up, Superior Strength Up, Petrifying Gaze, Detect Concealment, Energy Absorb/Store/Release, Resist Elements, Night Vision, Puppet Maker, Release Body Possession

Traits: Gluttonous +3, Venomous, Strong Willed, Sturdy, Immunity to Mind Control

∞∞∞∞∞∞∞∞

Once the transition had ended, I gained as much or perhaps, even more, energy than I did from eating the magma tortoise. However, with this energy came a feeling of extreme pain as my mind fought against itself while trying to adapt to the new form... My instincts were telling my mind that I was still a snake, but my new body wasn't sending the signals my brain was expecting. Hence the pain. I collapsed to my knees and grabbed my head in a futile attempt to suppress the pain, then I started screaming.

The goblins had frozen in place after I'd collapsed, my puppet turned to ash because I lost the necessary focus to keep it active. And I blacked out not long after...

When I came to the next day, I realized that I was alone outside the cave and the goblins offered to me had fled, which was just as well. I didn't actually need them anymore anyway.

Shaking my head from left to right, I slowly fought to stand up. First, I climbed to my knees, then into a kneeling position. And from there, I stood up, though I fell many times while trying to stand. Once I was actually on my feet, it became much easier, until I tried walking for the first time, and repeatedly fell after taking the first step.

It took me another five hours of repeatedly falling on my face or butt before I managed to successfully walk around without issue. And another two hours for me to learn how to run and jump. However, I did discover something a little disconcerting. My weight didn't appear to have changed from before. Though it was incredibly easy for me to move around, with every step I took the ground would cave in.

"Hmm... It seems like I'll need the stone Fenris uses to change his size after all. Even if it's just to get rid of my weight." Following this decision, I slowly made my way over to the goblins and requested that a stone goblin be given as a sacrifice to replace the ones that ran away.

"We aren't giving you anything!" one large goblin yelled after hearing my request.

"Why not? Are you saying that you are going back on your word?" I asked with a tilt of my head.

"We only agreed to your ridiculous demands because of what you are." He stepped up until he was towering over me. "Now that you're just a metal goblin we have nothing to fear," he finished while glaring into my eyes.

I stared at him in complete shock. Then I started laughing.

"What's so funny!?" he yelled, then he continued in a quieter voice. "You think I'm joking, but I'm completely serious. You will leave now, or we will kill you."

I laughed for a while longer, then I looked at him with a smile on my face. My metal fangs glinting in the light of the sun, and the serious look in my eyes must have given him some warning because his face turned pale. I grabbed him by the nose and pulled him down to my eye level.

"I'm ever so glad you decided to refuse my demands because the list just got longer. And I'm starving." I tore his nose off, causing him to scream and attempt to backpedal away from me, but then I grabbed him by the neck and slammed him into my knee, bursting his head open and splashing blood and gray matter everywhere. Then my jaw unhinged itself from my skull and I shoved his corpse into my mouth. I chewed his body into unrecognizable mush, then I simply swallowed it down.

I gave the other goblins a smile, making sure to show off my gore covered teeth, then I asked, "Now, who wants to take down my new demands?"

The same tiny goblin as before came running not long after with his sheet of leather and quill. "I'm dreadfully sorry about the inconvenience, sir!" He yelled as he bowed his head repeatedly.

"Yeah, yeah. Here is my new demand. I want a stone goblin, a metal goblin, and a flame goblin to also come with me, bringing the total up to four, and they must be two female and two male goblins... Understood?"

Nato nodded his head and quickly ran away, while I turned on my heel and began walking away. "I'm going out for a while; I expect my demands to be met by the time I return," I said, while looking over my shoulder at the now terrified goblins, then I began my hunt to find a "river of fire" that I could test this new body on.

Chapter Twenty-Seven

FTER LEAVING THE GOBLIN NEST, I DISCOVERED another "problem" with being this small... It took forever to get anywhere! Though I could walk for hours at a time before I needed to stop to eat, my travel speed was slow enough for that not to matter. In the five hours since I started walking, I doubted I'd gone further than twenty miles. And that's a high estimate.

"Note to self: Don't travel while using Body Possession. It only leads to aggravation and slowed down travel speed," I said with a small sigh.

Another thing I discovered was that the longer I spent in this body, the more uncomfortable it got. At first I believed the feeling of my skin being too tight was a temporary thing and it would go away after I'd gotten used to it, but it didn't. In fact, it got so much worse that it had become almost unbearable. It felt as if my skin were going to strangle me, or would burst trying.

Luckily for me, I'd remembered a lava river not far from the goblin nest and I should be there soon. Then, after performing my experiment, I could ditch this body. And about an hour later, after walking up a steep incline and falling down several times in the process, I finally made it to a magma river.

I stood on the precipice and looked at the flowing magma that was roughly a hundred feet below the crust.

I breathed in through my nose and looked up at the sky above. I held my breath for a few seconds, then slowly exhaled through my mouth. Then I jumped.

I rotated my body in the air until I was facing the cliff wall, then I reached out my arms and shoved them into the stone. They easily penetrated the wall and as my weight dragged me down to the awaiting magma, my arms ripped great swaths of stone from the wall. After falling for approximately fifteen feet, I spread out my legs until they were just past the width of my arms and I shoved my feet into the wall as well.

My massive weight dragged me down at a rapid pace and treated the wall as if it were paper. But it did slow me down enough that when I finally reached the bottom, I was able to completely stop myself by leaning forward and pressing my arms further into the wall. The result of this action was me dangling just inches above the magma with my toes brushing against it every few seconds. Which proved part one of my experiment. Though I could feel the heat, and it did seriously hurt, no actual damage was done. My toes passed through the magma like it was water and the only thing I had to show for it was a slight discoloration at the tips of my toes.

I let out a sigh, then slowly pried one arm loose from the wall. It took a few tries, as my arms were lodged in much deeper than I'd originally thought, but I eventually got it loose. Then after resting for a few minutes, I pulled my other arm loose and allowed myself to fall in. The magma splashed on the walls and melted through them almost instantly, and I quickly sunk to the bottom. I kept my mouth and eyes shut once I was under, and I covered any other places the magma could breach with the palms of my hands, lest they be damaged.

I floated along the bottom for several seconds, until I heard something ding... I forced open one eye while keeping the other lid tightly closed and read the pop-up.

∞∞∞∞∞∞∞∞

You have unlocked the following evolutionary path: Elemental Wyrm

Would you like to evolve?

∞∞∞∞∞∞∞∞

While I was reading the pop-up, I felt my eyeball burst from the heat of the magma. Just when I was about to scream in pain, I clamped my mouth down even tighter and inside my mind, I screamed out. *"No!"*

A few seconds later, I heard another ding. Against my better judgment, I forced open my other eye and read the pop-up.

∞∞∞∞∞∞∞∞

Very well, you have passed up the Elemental Wyrm path. As a result, this path has forever been locked to you.

Please select your reward for unlocking it:

Superior Elemental Resistance

Spike Scales

∞∞∞∞∞∞∞∞

"Superior Elemental Resistance!" I quickly replied as my other eyeball burst, and I felt the goblin body begin to die.

∞∞∞∞∞∞∞∞

You have been granted the Superior Elemental Resistance skill, due to unlocking and rejecting the Elemental Wyrm path.

∞∞∞∞∞∞∞∞

I activated the Release Body Possession skill, just as the new skill was granted to me. The goblin body I'd been possessing exploded into ashes that were quickly melted away, and I reformed inside the magma.

However, I was no longer in pain. In fact, I didn't even feel the heat coming off the magma anymore. I knew that I was still completely submerged, but the magma flowed around me as if it were water. I rose my head out of the river and looked up at the sky above.

I let out a deep sigh, as my mind fought to recover from the shock of my eyeballs bursting. After taking a few deep breaths and doing my best to forget the pain I'd just endured, I lifted myself out of the river and onto land once again.

"Okay, I am never. Doing. That. Again..." I laid down a few hundred feet from the river and passed out.

~ ~ ~

When I woke up the next day, I made my way back to the goblin nest to collect what I was promised. However, when I arrived, I received some disappointing news.

"So... You're saying that you can't get the metal for another three years?" I asked Nato.

He gave me a tentative nod. "Yes. The metal can only be mined for one week every ten years. And we still have three years to wait before the next 'harvest.'"

I gave him a slight nod. "I see... Can you explain why that is?"

He swallowed, then answered. "Every ten years the Magma tortoise stops swimming through the earth and goes to sleep for one week. During this time, the metal behaves like any other ore. It can be mined, melted, even broken. But once the tortoise wakes up, the metal goes back to being nearly impossible to mine."

"I see... And how does this affect the metal outside of the tortoise? Once it's outside, can it be smelted into armor?"

He nodded. "It can, though for whatever reason the same rules apply. The metal seems to be linked to the physical activity of the tortoise, and even the metal that has already been mined follows the same principles. For one week every ten years, the metal loses its unique properties and will become little more than iron armor. So maybe it's best if you keep that in mind?" he finished with a nervous laugh.

I smiled down at him. "I will, thank you for the information, Nato."

"No problem... sir." He quickly shook his head, then continued. "In the meantime, the goblins you have requested have been prepared and are ready to go at any time."

"Good. Good... Please bring them here to meet with me, then I will be out of your hair for three years."

"Right away!" Nato nodded his head, then ran off.

I watched him run inside the cave, then I turned my eyes up to the floating magma streams. I let out a deep sigh. *"Sarah, I'm getting closer to the power needed to keep you safe, but..."* I shook my head. *"No matter what happens from this moment on, I swear that the world you will be born into will be a safe one. Even if I don't make it to the end, I promise that you'll get to live your life, as you wish..."* I silently prayed that Niabus would pass my message on to her, but I doubted he actually would.

About half an hour later, the goblins showed up. There were five of them, six if you counted Nato, who was leading them. I took a close look and realized that I recognized one of them. The base goblin walking beside Nato was the female goblin I'd spoken to the first time.

I nodded to her and she responded with a slight smile. "Hello again," I said after they'd come to a stop in front of me.

"Greetings," she replied in her squeaky voice.

The other goblins remained silent as they stared up at me. At least they didn't seem to be afraid of me for the moment. In fact, one of the stone goblins appeared to be quite hostile towards me. Just from his facial expression alone, I could tell that he would betray me at the first opportunity. So I rectified that problem immediately.

"You're going to be my new puppet," I said, while looking directly at him, so it was clear which one I meant.

His face instantly switched from angry to worried. Then he slowly turned his head as someone stepped up and put a hand on his back. The other stone goblin stood there with a smile on his face.

"Sorry about this," he said in a gravelly voice, before throwing a right haymaker into the chosen goblin's jaw, causing stone and blood to fly out of his mouth and onto the ground. Then he grabbed the chosen goblin by the throat and dragged him over to me.

The goblin looked up at me with a slight smile and said, "One puppet for the master." The other goblin kicked and screamed in a desperate attempt to escape his fate, but the metal goblin grabbed him by the arms and lifted his hands into the air, while the stone goblin held him still. I tilted my head down, and the metal goblin forced his hands to touch the jewel and I activated the Puppet Maker skill. The two goblins held him in position until I told them to release him, and no matter how loud he screamed or how hard he struggled, the two refused to let go.

Eventually, the skill took effect and I received the pop-up.

∞∞∞∞∞∞∞∞

Stone Goblin Puppet

Classification: Tier 3

Skills: Night Vision, Major Strength Up, Major Durability Up

∞∞∞∞∞∞∞∞

"You can let him go now."

They instantly released him and allowed him to fall to the ground. I then directed my energy into making it stand up and rejoin the line of goblins.

"Now, I believe some introductions are in order. My name is Torga," I said.

The two male goblins and the other female goblin didn't seem to understand what I wanted, but the larger female did understand. She stepped forward and said. "My name is Siofs: Hobgoblin, and a warrior by trade." Then she stepped back in line and pushed the large metal goblin forward.

"Uh... My name is Holstig: Metal Hobgoblin, and a defender." He said while scratching the back of his head, then he stepped back in line.

The small flame goblin took a large step forward and gave a dainty salute. "Hi!" she chirped in an oddly smooth voice, then she introduced herself. "I'm Findral: Flame goblin, and a spy. Pleased to meet you!" Then she stepped back and the last one stepped forward.

"I'm Hogunn: Stone goblin, and Berserker," he said, then stepped back.

I nodded my head. "Good, I'm glad that you are a varied group. Thank you Nato, you may leave now."

The small goblin seemed surprised that I was actually letting him go, but rather than question it, he turned and ran back inside.

I watched him go, then looked down at my new "followers." "I would like some details on your classes."

As each one stepped up to tell me about their class, I took the opportunity to memorize everything I could about them. The first to step forward was Siofs. She was tall, with a thin build and short black hair that almost covered one eye. She wore a tightly bound leather tunic that covered her body down to her knees, and a large skull helmet that looked almost like a kobold skull. She carried a long-rusted sword and a dagger in a belt that she had tied around her waist. She held out her hand and pressed it to my nose.

"We goblins are used to serving those stronger than us, so we can bond with you and allow you to see our status plates... Is that okay?" she asked, with a tilt of her head.

I thought it over for a minute or two, then asked. "What does that entail?"

"We bind ourselves to your service until you release us. And in return, you help us to evolve and gain power."

"How?"

She gave me a questioning look, then said, "The same way you gain power and evolve... We need to eat certain things to evolve our bodies and we need to fight to evolve our classes."

I nodded, then asked, "How do you bond with me?"

A smile appeared on her face. "Oh, that's easy. You just have to allow us to ingest some of your blood and we'll do the rest."

I stared down at her for a few seconds. "If you do anything other than bond with me, and your status plate doesn't appear within twenty seconds, then I'll not only kill you, I'll turn you into my new puppet... Understand?"

She gulped and slowly nodded. Then she pulled a black dagger off her belt and nicked my scales with it. But it didn't do anything. She stared at my scales, then at the dagger and gave me a weak chuckle. "Um... would you mind?"

I rolled my eyes at her, then bit down on my tongue with my non-venomous teeth. Some blood pooled in my mouth and I slowly let it leak out onto the dagger she held.

She brought the dagger up to her mouth, then licked the blood off. A few seconds later, a pop-up appeared.

∞∞∞∞∞∞∞∞

Siofs

Race: Hobgoblin

Classification: Tier 4

Class: Warrior: Rank 3

∞∞∞∞∞∞∞∞

The other goblins all repeated her actions, and each of their pop-ups appeared in turn. The first was Holstig. He was tall, with a wide build and cropped black hair.

He wore a loincloth to cover his groin and wielded a club and shield combo that he kept strapped to his back via a strip of leather.

∞∞∞∞∞∞∞∞

Holstig

Race: Metal Hobgoblin

Classification: Tier 4

Class: Defender: Rank 2

∞∞∞∞∞∞∞∞

Then Findral bounded forward. She was tiny and stood at about half the size of Siofs and Holstig, at three feet tall. She wore a small tunic that went down to her stomach and a loincloth that reached down below her knees and she was unarmed. I asked her how she wore leather without it bursting into flames. "Oh! The inside is lined with metal that absorbs the heat. And I don't carry weapons because I make my own!" She finished with a smile as she rotated her hand and multiple flame daggers appeared and began rotating around her.

∞∞∞∞∞∞∞∞

Findral

Race: Flame Goblin

Classification: Tier 3

Class: Spy: Rank 4

∞∞∞∞∞∞∞∞

She stepped back and the final one stepped forward. Hogunn was widely built and was the same height as

Findral. He wore a loincloth and nothing else, and he carried around a stone hammer that was larger than he was. He kept it strapped to his back via a leather cable that wrapped around his chest.

∞∞∞∞∞∞∞

Hogunn

Race: Stone Goblin

Classification: Tier 3

Class: Berserker: Rank 6

∞∞∞∞∞∞∞

I nodded to them. "Good, then it's settled. In exchange for your service, I will help you evolve and you'll have my protection for as long as you serve me faithfully."

Siofs, who I assumed was the de facto leader of the group, then stepped forward and asked, "So, what's first boss?"

"I have a meeting to get to, so we'll be leaving this planet after I go back to the tortoise for a while...Climb on my back and we'll get moving."

Though they appeared confused that I would let them ride on my back, they didn't question my orders and quickly complied. The puppet also climbed on after I gave it the order, and then we set off to find the tortoise.

CHAPTER TWENTY-EIGHT

I TRAVELED FOR DAYS TO THE LAST SPOT I'D SEEN THE tortoise, but unfortunately, it was already long gone. The tracks it left behind had been filled in by something, and since there was no way for me to track it without those tracks I gave up. Turned my back on it and headed for the branch.

However, the trip wasn't a complete waste, as I'd used the travel time to practice controlling the puppet, and what better way to learn fine control than to have it fight against its peers? One at a time the goblins fought against the puppet and each battle helped me learn the various ways it was different from them.

For instance, because the puppet doesn't feel pain, it can endure a tremendous amount of punishment. And I can heal any damage it does receive by simply transferring more energy into it. Though there is a limit to this, as I can only completely heal it two or three times before I completely exhaust my supply of energy. So, keeping the puppet out of long, drawn-out fights, would probably be in my best interest. But, having it serve as an intermediary for everyday use would most likely be the best role for it. Especially after I discovered that I could make it share its vision with me, and I could make it speak as if it were still alive.

A neat trick that I may have, and I was definitely abusing it. I actually refused to speak for three whole days and would only respond if someone addressed the puppet directly. Though this did annoy the goblins, they kept their mouths shut and allowed me to have my fun.

And eventually, I returned to the branch, but before I entered, I stopped and addressed my new "companions."

The puppet had everyone sit down and began to speak in my place. "Alright everyone, the meeting I need to get to is on the druid home world of Uathea, so we have some ground rules to go over first."

Through the puppet's eyes, I watched as Holstig, Findral, and Hogunn adopted a bored look and began to ignore my words. However, Siofs, who was the only one paying attention, slapped the three of them around until they focused. Then she apologized for their behavior and sat down herself.

The puppet rolled its eyes, then continued speaking. "Rule number one: Don't attack the inhabitants of the worlds we travel to unless I give the order, or they attack you first.

"Rule number two: Under no circumstances are you to give away my existence to the populace of any planet we travel to. The only exception to this is if I give you direct orders to do so.

"Rule number three: Should you find yourself in a fight with the inhabitants, do not, under any circumstances, allow survivors. I don't care if you die in the process, but you must ensure that all enemy combatants are eliminated... with extreme prejudice."

The puppet looked around at them to ensure they were still paying attention. Once I was satisfied that they were, it continued.

"Any questions?"

Siofs raised her hand, so the puppet motioned for her to speak.

"What if we get separated from you?"

The puppet assumed a thinking pose, then said, "If we are separated without a place to rendezvous, then make your way to the branch and wait there for me to arrive. Any more questions?" Because none of the others raised their hands or spoke up, I assumed they had nothing else to ask, so I entered the branch with the goblins and the puppet still riding on my back.

∞∞∞∞∞∞∞

Welcome to the Bifrost

Please select your next destination from the available branches.

∞∞∞∞∞∞∞

Before it could show the destinations, I said, "I would like to travel to Uathea. Is there any way for me to go there directly?"

A few seconds went by with nothing happening. Then a pop-up appeared.

∞∞∞∞∞∞∞

It is impossible to travel to Uathea from this location. However, you can travel to the connected branch from here.

∞∞∞∞∞∞∞

"Alright, take me there." I was shot off towards my destination at high speed.

I was deposited on a relatively normal looking planet. Blue skies, green trees, and no abnormal animals to be seen. Honestly, this planet made me more nervous than Thaater ever did, simply because of how "normal" it seemed. And if I've learned anything since this journey started, it's that nothing is ever "normal" in this place.

But despite my reservations about whether this planet was safe, I still needed to get to Uathea. So, I would just have to deal with it.

I turned around to access the branch when a pop-up appeared.

∞∞∞∞∞∞∞∞

Welcome to the intersected world of Neonia. Your destination is only accessible from the branch on the other side of the planet.

∞∞∞∞∞∞∞∞

I let out a soft sigh and said, "Damn it..." Then I started moving in a random direction. I didn't decide on a direction beforehand because, at the moment, it didn't matter. I couldn't wait by the branch, as Neonia was a populated world, so It was impossible to know when someone would come by and discover me. That meant I needed to leave as soon as possible and regroup after I was sufficiently far away.

During my time on Rualea, I spent the majority of my time in the dark because of the trees blocking out the sun. However, with my current size, I no longer needed to worry about that. Even while lying down on my stomach, I was taller than the trees by several feet... which made me more nervous than anything, as I could no longer use the darkness to hide from pursuers or anything else I happened to be hiding from at the time. But... That's what the goblins were here for.

The whole reason I brought them along was because of my inability to hide. I needed something to scout the area so I could avoid any unnecessary conflicts. They were also going to help me enter places that I normally could not, like towns.

We arrived at the outskirts of a small town and I burrowed my way into the ground, so I would not be discovered. I dug out a cave just large enough for me to hide in, then I sent the goblins to scout the town, while the puppet went out hunting for me.

Controlling the puppet while looking through its eyes wasn't as difficult as I'd originally thought it would be, though it was a weird experience. The puppet moved very smoothly, and as I had access to both its eyes and ears, exploring wasn't too difficult. However, I couldn't "smell" the forest. I'd grown so used to using my tongue to "smell" the areas I was exploring, that when I suddenly lacked that ability, it was disorienting.

However, the sense I lost was replaced by another. Stone goblins have a unique trait that allows them to sense vibrations through the ground. Because of this, even though I could no longer "smell" the area around me, I could find any moving creature that traveled along the ground. So, when I managed to find a lone boar walking through the forest, I was ecstatic. Granted, one boar wouldn't do much to fill me up, but it was a start.

I crouched down behind a tree and watched the boar for a few minutes. During this time, I noticed it walked with a slight limp that favored its left front leg—a weakness that I could very easily exploit if I did this right.

I pulled the metal dagger out of my belt, then I waited until the boar began to limp away before I struck. I dashed out from behind the tree and jumped as high as I could over the boar's back, then, just before I landed, I rotated in the air and slammed the pommel into the top of the boar's head.

The strike threw the boar off balance enough that it had to press down on its hurt leg, causing it to fall over in pain. I used the opportunity to jump on its side and stab my blade into its neck.

Unfortunately, the boar still had some fight left in it, as it swung its head up and pierced my puppet with its tusks. Though the strike didn't do much damage, it did knock me back far enough for the boar to climb up to its feet and attempt to run.

I jumped on its back and pulled the dagger out, then plunged it into the neck three more times in quick succession. Each strike caused it to wobble on its feet until it finally collapsed on its side. I plunged the dagger deep into its chest, piercing the heart and putting the creature out of its misery.

After climbing off and wiping my dagger off on the grass, I sheathed the blade and hoisted the boar onto my shoulders, then retraced my steps back to my real body. Upon arriving at the cave, I threw the boar inside, then turned around to go hunt down some more creatures, while my real body made short work of the boar.

I used the puppet to hunt down an additional five boars, three deer, and two rabbits with long horns on their forehead, and I read each pop-up in turn.

∞∞∞∞∞∞∞∞

You have eaten the following race for the first time.

Boar: Tier 1

You have eaten the following race for the first time.

White-tail deer: Tier 1

You have eaten the following race for the first time.

Rabbicorn: Tier 2

ᴔᴔᴔᴔᴔᴔ

Then I went to sleep to await the return of the goblins.

The goblins returned just before sunset, and while the others were preparing their dinner, Siofs went over the events of the day with me.

"The town is mostly populated by humans, though we also saw beast-kin and elves walking around. Starting from the edge closest to us there are twenty-seven buildings positioned in three rows, with nine buildings per row," Siofs said while reading from a piece of paper she'd "borrowed."

As I was still using the puppet as an intermediary, it nodded its head, then asked. "Are there any specialty shops?"

"Yes: one blacksmith, one tailor, one bakery, and one butcher. However, this town also has a guild building, so there is a fairly high chance of adventurers being present." she said with a slight grimace.

"What's a Guild?"

She reached behind her and pulled out another sheet of paper. This one had a large red emblem in the shape of a sleeping dragon on the top-right corner. The puppet reached out and took the paper from her, then allowed me to read it.

ᴔᴔᴔᴔᴔᴔ

Neonia Adventurers Guild

Are you looking for a grand adventure?

How about wealth beyond your wildest dreams?

Do you desire to be known throughout Yggdrasil as a Legendary Hero?

Then come inside and sign up for your guild card and jump on the fast track to achieving all of your dreams...

*Note: you must be 18 years old or older to sign up.

*Note: The Neonia Adventurers Guild is not responsible for any of the following: sickness, corruption, injury, loss of personal property, loss of life and or limb, rape, being kidnapped, being vaporized, being eaten, being touched inappropriately, STDs you may contract while in our employ, being cheated, being cheated on, your stupidity, your 5th grade math teacher being a bitch, the fact that you are still reading this sheet when you could have signed up already, or the evil in the world.

∞∞∞∞∞∞∞∞

I stared at the paper with a blank expression on my face, then I looked up at Siofs. "Okay... Who the fuck wrote this?" I asked while balling it up and throwing it over my shoulder into the fire the goblins had just started.

Siofs shrugged her shoulders. "Who knows. Humans are a weird race."

I desperately tried to forget what I'd just read, while Siofs and I went over the rest of the details. Apparently, there weren't very many guards patrolling during the day, and we guessed that after dark that number would drop further.

The first thing we needed to do was "acquire" some better gear. That meant we needed armor, weapons, first aid equipment, and possibly a new puppet for me to use. Not that there was anything wrong with my current puppet, but if I wanted to get a closer look at the civilized areas, then I would need a better guise than a goblin.

I called over Findral and had her stand beside Siofs, then I told them what I needed. "I want the two of you to explore the surrounding area tomorrow. Look for any humans, elves, or beast-kin walking through the forest. If you find anyone, follow them around for a few days and see if they have anyone that would miss them: a spouse, a child... hell, even a pet would be too much. If, after three days, you haven't seen them speak or interact with anyone, then I want you to abduct them and bring them to me... Understand?"

"Yes, Master," Siofs said, while Findral just quickly nodded, then bounded away to eat her fill. The two of them joined up with the male goblins and I ordered the puppet to bring me more food, so it went hunting again.

The next day, after the females had left, I ordered the males to help me with my puppet control, so we fought again. But this time, I assumed direct control instead of just giving it orders.

Hogunn and I threw our weapons to the side, then we rushed at each other. Because I was slightly faster than him, I reached the middle of the campsite first and I jumped into the air. I pulled my knee up and impacted with his nose, slinging his head back as his feet continued moving forward. He fell and landed on his back, while I landed on the other side of him.

I spun around and swung my fist in a downward arc aimed at his face, but he rolled to the left before I could make contact, and my fist slammed into the ground. He jumped to his feet, then swung his left arm backward, hitting me in the temple and knocking me over. I fell onto my side, then rolled onto my back just in time to see his next move. He attempted to follow up his strike by stomping on my chest with his left foot, which I caught. Then I kicked his right leg, which buckled out from under him and dropped him to a knee.

I drew back my leg and tried to kick him again, but he caught it, then pulled me closer to him and commenced beating my face in. I raised my arms up to block most of the punches, but a strong strike to my left forearm rendered it useless and knocked it to the side. Hogunn then threw a left haymaker into my ribs, followed by an uppercut that snapped my head back, immobilizing the puppet and ending the fight in Hogunn's favor.

After the fight had been called, Hogunn fell to the ground holding his knee, prompting Holstig to walk over and check on him. Holstig grabbed Hogunn's leg and straightened it out as best he could, then he started prodding it around the knee that had already begun to swell. A few minutes went by without any sign of Holstig or Hogunn saying anything, so I healed the puppet and ordered it to set up the campfire again.

Ten minutes later, Holstig stood up and walked over to the puppet. "Master, his knee appears to be dislocated. When Siofs returns she should have a look at it, as she may be able to fix it."

The puppet gave him a nod, prompting him to walk back over to Hogunn.

After a few more minutes of getting the campfire ready, I sent the puppet out hunting, while Holstig, Hogunn, and I settled in to wait for the females to return.

Later that night, after a rather disappointing day, Siofs had Findral and Holstig hold down Hogunn, while she snapped his knee back into position, then, after allowing Hogunn to settle down, we all went to sleep in preparation for the next day.

Interlude:
The serpent and the highwayman

Valkas Heiqen had never amounted to much in his life. As the only son of an elf shaman and a human woman, he was born an outcast. His father, a disgraced shaman warrior, was the only member of his tribe to survive the "purge"—the kingdom of Guisea's attempt to cleanse the land of the races they deemed too "impure" to live.

His father, while being severely injured, crawled over seventy miles to the small border town of Silverglen. It was here that he met Sophia, the oldest daughter of the local blacksmith and fiancée of the town's young lord.

Naturally, as with all stories of this nature, the two fell in love... But they didn't get to live out their fairytale ending, as the father was executed for impregnating the lord's fiancée. And Sophia was locked up inside the lord's keep until the day of her wedding. Then, after giving birth to her son, she was forced to hand him over to the local orphanage.

Valkas lived at the orphanage for ten years. But once he'd gotten too old to continue living there, he was kicked out and was forced to turn to a life of petty crime to survive. This life would eventually land him a job as a highwayman for a local bandit boss. A semi-lucrative job to be sure, and one that would lead to his eventual doom.

The road he was ordered to toll was near an area that until recently had been teeming with wildlife... But something had recently driven the animals away and forced the nearby town to start importing their food, as the hunters could no longer find enough meat to keep the town sustained.

While this led to even more tolls for Valkas, his success in the area had caused his ego to swell enough that he lowered his guard for the first time in weeks.

Valkas was slowly stirring his pot of rabbit stew when he heard the sound of a stick being broken. He quickly looked away from the campfire and stared in the direction the sound had come from. His half-elven eyes quickly adjusted to the darkness of the surrounding forest and he saw a large shadow standing just out of the fire's light. He squinted his eyes in order to get a better look, but the shadows were simply too deep for him to see through.

Adopting a fake smile—the kind he always used to get inside women's pants and disarm travelers—he stood from his squatted position and introduced himself with an alias that he'd recently come up with.

"Whoa! You gave me one hell of a fright, my friend. The name's Mathias, would you care to join me for a meal?" Valkas asked in a falsely jovial tone, while moving his hand towards the scabbard on his side.

The shadow stayed completely silent as it stared at him. A few seconds later, another stick was broken, but this time the sound came from directly behind Valkas.

He turned his head to see who was standing behind him, and he drew his sword from its scabbard in a show of force. But a strong strike to his jaw rendered him unconscious before he could fully unsheathe it. The last thing he saw before passing out completely, was a nearly invisible foot about to kick him in the face.

He came to an unknown amount of time later. His arms and legs were bound by strong cords of leather and he'd been stripped of his clothes and weapons. His back was pressed against a solid wall of... something, and he was in complete darkness. He struggled in an attempt to free himself, but that was brought to a halt when a strong strike hit him in the chest. The blow knocked the breath out of him and brought tears to his eyes.

"You should probably stay still. We transported you here safely, but should you try to escape... Well, let's just say, you won't like our response." An oddly two-toned voice spoke from inside the darkness.

"You can't keep me here!" Valkas screamed. "Do you have any idea who I work for!?" He thrashed around, prompting another strong blow against his chest. Spittle flew from his mouth as he yelled in pain and he thrashed again. "Release me!" Another blow came, but this one struck him across the jaw. His head spun to the side, where it impacted a solid surface and he became severely dizzy.

The two-toned voice let out a sigh, then spoke again. "If you'll just answer my questions, then I'll set you free."

Valkas used his head to right himself, as he was still pressed against the wall, then he acquiesced. "Fine... What do you want to know?" A chill went down his spine after he answered. but he wasn't sure why.

"What is your name? Your real name, not that fake one you gave my associates," the voice demanded.

Valkas stared into the darkness in an attempt to see his abductors, but it was still too dark, so he instead asked, "How do you know it's fake?" A heavy open-handed blow struck him across the face, and his head was slammed into the "wall." Valkas let out a groan of pain, then answered. "My name is Valkas Heiqen, I'm a highwayman for the bandit boss Grukag!"

Silence followed his statement. Then the voice spoke again. "I'll be honest and say, I didn't expect you to give up who you worked for so easily. But you've saved me a question, so I thank you for that. Next question: Are you expecting anyone to come find you?"

Valkas didn't want to say anything on this subject, so he remained silent. Until a kick to his stomach loosened his lips. "Yes! Four members of my group are supposed to come join me in the next week and if I'm not there, then they'll assume the town did something to me. And trust me when I say, you don't want boss Grukag mad at such a small town. He's destroyed towns of that size for less than what you've done to me," Valkas said, in an attempt to rattle his captors.

"Oh well, that isn't my problem. Next question, and this is the final one: Has anyone from the town seen your face?"

Valkas shook his head. Then quietly said, "No... I wore a mask every time I 'tolled' someone, so no one has seen my face. You're not letting me go, are you?" It was the 'That isn't my problem' statement that alerted Valkas to the fact that he wasn't dealing with a vigilante from the town like he'd thought.

Ever since he awoke, he'd been thinking that someone from the town had come back to punish him for what he'd done since coming here. A vigilante, if you will. But now, he knew otherwise. Whoever this was, they didn't grab him because of what he'd done. They most likely didn't even care who he worked for.

"What are you going to do with me?" Valkas asked.

Suddenly, two sets of arms hauled him into the air and slammed him against a cold smooth surface. "I thank you for your cooperation. The last eight travelers my associates grabbed weren't as accommodating and had to be... 'dealt with.'" The voice paused for a few seconds, then a hand grabbed him by the hair and pressed his forehead into the cold surface. "As for what I'm going to do with you... As I said, I'm going to set you free... from everything."

A pain, unlike anything Valkas had ever felt, penetrated his head. Along with the pain came an ambient glow that revealed just what he was pressed against.

"A... jewel?" He passed out shortly after and never woke again.

Chapter Twenty-Nine

THE STONE GOBLIN PUPPET TURNED TO ASH, JUST AS I finished turning the highwayman into a new puppet, and a few seconds later I got the pop-ups.

∞∞∞∞∞∞∞∞

You have eaten the following race for the first time.

Wood Elfling: Tier 3

∞∞∞∞∞∞∞∞

"So, he wasn't an elf like I thought..."

Siofs and Findral had watched this guy for days. Though his outward appearance had caused his victims to underestimate him, I made sure to order the females to take him out without giving him the opportunity to fight back, lest they be injured in the attempt.

He appeared young, possibly in his early to middle twenties, and he was a little on the short side. He kept his long blond hair pulled into a ponytail and his face was cleanly shaven, which only served to make him look even younger. His eyes were dark blue, and he had long pointed ears.

He was wearing a pair of loose brown pants, a long-sleeved green shirt with a brown pocket on the right breast, and a pair of brown leather boots. As Siofs was the one to carry him back to me, Findral had stayed behind and looted his camp. She brought back one complete set of leather armor, a long wooden bow with metal spikes on each end and a metal grip in the center, a quiver with twenty-three arrows, a dark lower face mask, and all of his camping gear.

Naturally, as I had no use for the armor, the camping gear, or the mask, I distributed them among the goblins: I gave the armor to Siofs, and I gave the camping gear to them as a whole. And as Findral begged for the mask with huge eyes, I wound up giving it to her.

Before I got too invested in the bow, I'd decided to keep for myself, another pop-up appeared.

∞∞∞∞∞∞∞

Wood Elfling Puppet

Classification: Tier 3

Skills: Major Agility Up, Light Stepper, Thievery, Observe

∞∞∞∞∞∞∞

Because three of the skills were fairly self-explanatory, I only asked about Observe, and thankfully, the pop-ups took pity on my ignorant self and I received another pop-up.

∞∞∞∞∞∞∞

Observe: Gives detailed knowledge on creatures, objects, or places you have prior experience with.

*Note: If you do not have any knowledge of the target of this skill, then it will fail.

∞∞∞∞∞∞∞

"That's useful."

After reading the pop-ups and doing some light exercise to get used to controlling the new puppet, I made it pick up the bow and quiver, then head outside to practice. Because the puppet could be ordered to complete a simple action, then left on its own, I could simply tell it what targets to hit, and it would shoot at them. Though it wasn't accurate in the slightest and out of ten shots, it only hit with three of them.

I made the puppet call over Siofs, then it handed the bow to her. "The puppet can't hit with this thing, so I'll just stick with a melee weapon for the time being. Can any of you use a bow?"

"Well..." Her expression turned thoughtful for a few seconds." I believe Findral can use a bow, but I'm not sure how well she can use it."

I hummed to myself, then called to Findral. Her ears perked up and she came bounding over with the grace of a large Alpha Deer: loud, fast, and dangerous to anyone standing in her way. Thankfully, she slid to a stop just before running into Siofs.

"Hi, Master! What can I do for you?" she asked in her annoyingly cheerful way.

"Can you use a bow?" I asked, even though I dreaded the answer. But her response honestly surprised me.

Her cheerful expression faded a bit and was replaced with a more serious one. "I can. Does Master wish for me to use the bow?"

I nodded, handed over the bow and its quiver, then I ordered the puppet to go hunting. It picked up the blade that had been confiscated earlier and disappeared into the forest.

The next morning, I assumed the role of the puppet's eyes and ears and ordered it to head into town. It made the thirty-minute journey in about ten and came to a stop outside the town proper. I took direct control of it and made it begin looking around the town.

The buildings were simple things: wooden walls and dark tiled roofs, and they were just large enough to fit a small family comfortably. However, I wasn't interested in the homes for the moment. No, I was interested in the blacksmith and the tailor. The first of the two I came to had an anvil on a sign hanging above the door. I pushed the door open, causing a bell to chime, then I walked inside.

The inside had a bare center floor, but each of the four walls had five shelves apiece, which stretched from one side of the building to the other. And a chest-high counter blocked off the shelves from any would-be thieves. Behind the counter was a young human with black hair. He was wearing an apron, denoting that he worked here. But instead of greeting me, he had his nose buried in a large book that he had placed on the countertop, so I took the opportunity to look at the items that lay on the shelves.

I took my time and tried to memorize every detail I could about the shop: where everything was located, what appeared valuable, and what was useful to us. Not once during my time inside did the boy look up from his book, so I left without saying anything to him. From there I wanted to go inside the tailor shop, but according to a sign on the door, they weren't opening today, so I turned on my heel and headed for the camp.

After returning to camp, I had the goblins gather around the puppet and I laid out the plan for the next few days. The females would observe the town and count the number of guards they saw in the area around the blacksmith shop for the next two days, while the guys would do the same for the tailor.

Then, the following night, Siofs and I would break into the blacksmith shop and steal the equipment we needed. Findral and Holstig would break into the tailor shop and steal clothes and any repair supplies they could find, provided I could get inside and look around first.

"Remember... The rules still apply. No one is to be harmed unless I give the order. If you are discovered, then you can knock them out, but No. Killing... Am I clear?" I looked at each goblin in turn, to ensure they understood. As none of them said anything, I accepted their silence as confirmation, and I sent the puppet out hunting again.

CHAPTER THIRTY

THE NIGHT OF THE BREAK-IN CAME AND SIOFS AND the puppet were crouched outside of the blacksmith shop. Because Findral had given two sets of lockpicks to the puppet, it was currently crouched down in front of the door, while Siofs stood watch. *Click* The lock successfully turned, and the door swung open.

"Yes!" I quietly celebrated, then I turned to Siofs and motioned with my head for her to go inside.

She stepped around me and quietly walked inside, while drawing the sword I'd given her. Once she was inside, she searched the building for any residents while I began to search for the items we needed. I jumped over the counter and looked on the shelves for anything we could use, but they were gone.

"Damn, the clerk must move the items after closing." I mumbled to myself, then I headed into the backroom where I found Siofs still looking around. I joined her for a few minutes, then I headed up the stairs and started looking around up there. Searching through the five rooms I found up there netted me several barrels that contained swords, daggers, maces, and a number of other weapons.

I began throwing the weapons each goblin claimed they could use inside a rucksack Findral had found with the elfling's camping supplies. I tossed three sheathed daggers, two iron longswords, and a morning star into the sack, which I then tied closed to prevent any of it from falling out. Then I headed back down and found Siofs standing at the foot of the stairs holding a similarly filled rucksack.

"Got everything?"

She nodded, then threw the sack to the puppet. "Have the puppet carry this, so if we happen to run into any trouble, it can escape while I hold our pursuers off," she said, then turned and headed for the door. Luckily for us, we didn't run into anyone and managed to get back to camp safely. Approximately thirty minutes later, the other goblins arrived.

"Did anything go wrong?" I asked Findral.

"No Master! We got the stuff you asked for and made it back without being seen," she said with a slight smile, then she held out the full rucksack for my inspection.

I took the bag from her and set it on the ground, then I motioned for them to go over to the sacks Siofs and I had brought back. The three of them eagerly ran over and began to plunder through them, while I looked through the tailor supplies.

"Four shirts of various colors, four dark pairs of pants, four pairs of boots, and sewing tools." I closed that sack and opened the other one. *"Four rucksacks, and a tarp... Good, that's everything we need for the time being."* I picked up the sack of clothes and threw it over to the goblins.

They stopped playing with their new weapons and looked at me with a confused expression on their faces.

"Everyone but Findral pick a shirt, a pair of pants, and a pair of boots. I'm tired of seeing you lot walking around almost naked."

They gave me a downcast look and grumbled a bit but complied with my order. After they'd finished getting dressed, I ordered them to pack up so we could get moving before the townspeople woke up and discovered they'd been robbed. After all, it wouldn't be very convenient if we had to fight our way out because somebody got lucky and found me.

An hour later, the goblins had everything packed up and were sitting on my back as we moved off.

We traveled through the forest for three days. Along the way, I cut off the majority of the puppet's long, blond hair, leaving it short, messy and just barely long enough to cover its ears. Then I made the puppet fight with Holstig, so I could get used to fighting at the new size, which led to the discovery that I'd been controlling the puppet wrong this entire time.

Ever since I started controlling puppets, I'd assumed the only way they could move was like their counterparts. But that couldn't be further from the truth. The puppets will move according to my direction, regardless of how I tried to make them move. As such, if I ordered them to run around like a big cat, they would do it without much issue.

This led to an even bigger discovery for me. The puppet wasn't bound by the limitations of its body, at least, not like normal beings were. Sure, it wasn't able to climb vertical surfaces or fit in areas that were too small for it. But in terms of flexibility and strength, there were magnitudes of differences between it and the being it was imitating. It could fold its body into a ball and roll around without difficulty, and its strength was magnified to the absolute peak for something of its size. It never tired, so it could run at its maximum speed for as long as it needed to.

And the only thing keeping me from realizing this sooner was I'd unknowingly put limitations on it. I'd assumed it needed to function like the original, so it responded in kind by behaving like the original and its body took on the original's characteristics.

After I made this realization, the puppet was no longer bound by the strength and flexibility of its muscles or by the hardness of its bones. It could run, dodge, or flip around an enemy for as long as it took to wear them down, then it would strike with brutal efficiency. And in the cases where it couldn't avoid being hit, it could withstand any blow that didn't immediately immobilize it.

Broken bones were ignored and being impaled only slowed it down, unless it was through the head or heart. Then it was only incapacitated until I restored it. Even having its head caved in barely deterred it.

However, the farther from its original capabilities I pushed it, the more energy it took to control. At its maximum potential, I only had enough energy to keep it sustained for ten minutes before I was completely depleted and needed to eat.

Because of this, I decided to only use it for combat purposes as a last resort. After all, running out of energy while I was in the middle of a fight would defeat the purpose of using it in the first place. And in such a case, I would be better off fighting as myself instead of the puppet.

But, for the time being, I was going to enjoy "playing around" as the puppet.

Holstig, Siofs, and Hogunn stood across from the puppet with their weapons drawn. As I had stopped to eat, there was time for a quick bout between the goblins and me. So, I'd assumed control of the puppet while my real body focused on eating its way through a mountain.

The puppet tilted its head to the right until it was parallel to the ground. It smiled at the goblins. "Ready?" it asked.

The three of them gripped their weapons tighter, then they charged. They closed the twelve-foot gap in only a few seconds and they each swung at a different part of the puppet's body. Siofs swung in a horizontal slash aimed for the head, Holstig stabbed at the stomach with his longsword, and Hogunn swung his morning star at its left knee.

The puppet lifted its right leg and kicked the handle of the morning star, deflecting its arc. Next, it tilted its body back until it was staring up at the sky, so the blades passed safely overhead. And with one quick move it launched into a back tumble and came up in a crouched position.

The puppet rushed at the goblins and began its "dance." It would dodge around Siofs and Holstig, while it focused on Hogunn. The two larger goblins swung their swords at its head and legs from behind in an attempt to catch it off guard, but the puppet jumped into the air and double kicked Hogunn in the face. The puppet used the sudden momentum to push itself into a corkscrew spin that allowed it to pass between the blades. Hogunn was launched headfirst onto the ground, where he lay motionless.

The puppet, after passing through the blades, stuck out its right arm and pressed it into the ground, stopping its spinning and allowing it to move again. It kicked out with its left leg, hitting Siofs in the back, and jumped over its arm to land back on its feet.

Siofs stumbled forward, but then turned around and leaped at the puppet, swinging her sword through the air as she did. The puppet stepped out of the way and swung its fist into her jaw. Her downward momentum only added to the force of his fist, and she was instantly knocked out. The puppet reached out with his other arm and caught the front of Siofs shirt before her head could slam into the ground, then let her down gently.

Holstig waited for the puppet to put her down, then charged with his shield raised. The puppet let him get as close as possible before it jumped into the air and placed its right hand on Holstig's head, then pushed off and vaulted over him.

It landed in a crouch, spun around and attempted to sweep his legs out from under him. *Clang!* His metal skin bent the puppet's legs in the wrong direction. He turned around and kicked the puppet in the face while stomping on its foot, causing the puppet's neck to snap backward.

Holstig bent down and grabbed the puppet by the shirt and started bashing its face in with his shield. Three smashes later, the puppet was immobilized.

Holstig stood up straight and said, "You lost again, Master."

I let out a sigh. "Yes Holstig, I'm aware..."

I healed the puppet while Holstig woke up the other goblins and they sat down to wait for Findral to return from exploring the area. Two hours later, she returned and informed us that all was well, and we could continue moving without issue, as the surrounding area was barren of civilized life. So, I took her word for it and continued to dig my way through a mountain.

Three days later, I finally completed carving a tunnel through the several mile-long mountain range—which may have seemed like an incredibly long time to waste. But since it would have taken over a week to go around it and going over it would have been impossible due to the sheer cliff wall that prevented me from climbing up, through the mountain it was. And once I was through, I continued moving towards my goal of finding the other branch.

~ ~ ~

Two more weeks passed while we were traversing the land, and we eventually arrived at the ocean that separated this continent from the rest of the world. I stopped and allowed the goblins to do whatever they pleased for one week, while I rested.

Two of those days went by without much happening but on the third day...

∞∞∞∞∞∞∞

Findral

Race: Lower Flame Princess

Classification: Tier 4

Class: Spy: Rank 4

∞∞∞∞∞∞∞

Findral had finally eaten enough to evolve into her next race. No longer was she the small, bald goblin that I'd come to know. She grew to around six feet tall and short, orange, flame-like hair grew from her head and hung down to her chin. Two small horns grew from her forehead.

She celebrated her new form by shooting balls of fire into the air and jumping around. However, her celebration was cut short after Siofs smacked her head and pointed to the fire she'd started with her antics.

While Siofs berated Findral, Holstig and Hogunn were forced to put out the fire by filling the leather sacks up with water and dumping it on the flames. But even after her mishap, Findral wouldn't be deterred from her celebration, and she spent the next week with a smile on her face.

The good news didn't stop there, as she wasn't the only one to evolve during this period of rest. On the fifth day, another goblin evolved—only she didn't complete her evolution until the seventh day.

∞∞∞∞∞∞∞∞

Siofs

Race: Water Hobgoblin

Classification: Tier 4

Class: Warrior: Rank 3

∞∞∞∞∞∞∞∞

Siofs had apparently caught and eaten enough water creatures to finally unlock her element. Her skin turned a bluish green color and gills grew on her neck, but otherwise, she didn't change physically.

The two of them evolving in such drastically different ways prompted me to ask Siofs about the goblin evolution tree.

"Well, Goblins are... adaptors. Unlike other creatures that require certain stones to evolve or are required to eat creatures that are saturated by the elements, goblins have the inborn ability to draw out small amounts of elemental energy from everything we eat. Because of this, we don't have a strict path to follow like most races do. For example, Holstig over there…" she motioned to Holstig who was fighting with Findral over the last fish. "He used to eat small bits of metal every day until he eventually evolved into a metal goblin."

She pointed to Hogunn. "Hogunn did the same, but with normal stones instead of metal. And Findral used to heat stones until they began to melt, then she would put them in her mouth and literally suck the fire energy out of them."

I looked over at the cheerfully fighting Findral and tried to picture her having the discipline required to torture herself in order to evolve.

Siofs must have recognized the look on my face, as she quickly added, "Don't let her appearance fool you, Master. Findral is a lot tougher than she looks."

"I'll keep that in mind." I shook my head, then refocused on Siofs. "Why does she look so different from the rest of you, though?"

Siofs glanced over at Findral, then back to me. "Because of her fire element magic, she was given the opportunity to evolve beyond the goblin forms and she took it," she finished with a lazy shrug.

"I see..." I turned away from her and called to the other goblins.

"Let's go. We've got a long way to go and I want to get there before I die of old age!"

The goblins quickly packed up their stuff with some help from the puppet, then they all climbed on and I slid into the water.

"It's good to be back in the water... I hope there's plenty of fish in this ocean because I'm starving," I said aloud as I swam further out into the water.

Chapter Thirty-One

I T ONLY TOOK A FEW DAYS OF SWIMMING IN THE ocean for me to realize that while there were plenty of fish, there was sadly a lack of anything higher than a Tier 1 creature. Which meant I stayed perpetually hungry, even while surrounded by literal tons of food.

Eventually, I grew tired of constantly slowing down to catch the small fish, so I just focused on swimming and made the puppet go fishing for me. It dove into the water with the dagger in its mouth and swam along with me, while it caught any fish that happened to come near.

Three hours into our trip, the puppet threw the goblins some fish for Findral to cook so they wouldn't be too hungry to fight in case something was to happen.

And when something did happen, I let out a sigh. *"I'm glad I prepared for these instances, but why is my luck always so bad? It's almost like every time I wish to be left alone, something decides to send trouble my way."*

It was Findral who'd seen them first and she'd been all too eager to yell out her discovery to the rest of us. Thirty ships, all of various makes and sizes, were floating on the horizon, and between them flew three flags: a red flag, with a golden lion's head insignia; a purple flag, with a silver bird insignia; and a black flag, with a white skull insignia.

The red flags were flown on ships that appeared to have been created for combat, massive in size and scope. They were well over three hundred feet long and one hundred feet wide and lined with enough cannons to pulverize a mountain, with an especially large cannon mounted at the bow. They easily had the most firepower, but they also had the least number of ships, with only four ships total.

The purple flags were flown on ships that appeared to be defenseless. They were small in size, being about the size of the ship Fenris and his family used. They had no cannons to speak of, but each ship had multiple sails and oars sticking out of the lower part of their hulls. So, I assumed they were meant for speed. There were eight ships bearing the purple flag.

Lastly, the black flags were the most numerous, and also the most diverse. The black flags were flown on an amalgamation of ships that ranged from the combat ships of the red flags to the travel ships of the purple flags. Their numbers were even further padded out by many other types of ships, with the largest ship being tens of stories high, and resembled a floating city. Ships of every size imaginable were used as supports for the three "castles" that rested atop it to further emphasize their majesty, as if the castles weren't enough. The owners of the floating city had each castle lined with cannons, and on the roof of each sat a wooden, high-backed chair.

I let out a deep sigh. "What's with that overly grandiose display? It's almost like they want someone to aim for the chairs at the top."

Siofs, who'd heard my words, voiced out her agreement. "I agree, Master. Truly a foolish move to put yourself on display as such an easy target—"

A cannon fired at the top of a castle in an attempt to destroy the chair... But a golden shield manifested before the cannonball could get near it and sent the ball flying off into the distance.

"Well... It seems I was mistaken," I said in a quieter voice.

That first cannon shot led to an all-out war between the ships. The red flags versus the black flags, while the purple flags tried to flee.

However, this action led to an idea. I still needed to gain the Leviathan evolution and as the ships with cannons were currently distracted, well, let's just say I had no intention of allowing this opportunity to pass me by.

"Findral, can you survive underwater?" I asked, while staring at the fleeing ships.

"You underestimate me, Master... You're underestimating all of us it would seem," she replied with a giggle.

I turned my head around to look at her and when I did, she proved that I had indeed been underestimating them. The flames on her body turned from bright orange and yellow to blue and purple. The heat that came off her was enough to evaporate the nearby ocean water almost instantly.

"We're adaptors, Master... There's not a climate in existence where we cannot thrive," she said with a mad grin—an action the others quickly copied as they each moved.

Siofs jumped off my back and landed in the water, staying submerged for ten seconds before she rose to the surface and stepped out of the water to stand on top of it.

Hogunn and Holstig both jumped in and swam towards Siofs, who caught them and began to pull them out of the water where they joined her on the surface.

"You see, Master. Though we are not the physically strongest race, we make up for it by being the most adaptable," Findral said, before she jumped into the air. A second before she touched the water, a micro explosion beneath her feet sent her flying into the air.

She would cause one of these explosions every time she began to drop towards the water, and this allowed her to, for all intents and purposes, run across the water as if it were dry land.

"I must say... I've never been happier to be wrong," I said. Then I ordered the puppet to follow Siofs orders for the time being. "Your target is one of the purple flag ships. Clear out the people aboard, then get out of the area."

"What will you be doing, Master?" Holstig asked.

The puppet gave them a toothy grin in my place. "It's lunchtime, Holstig... I'm going to eat my fill," I replied, then I dove under the water and swam as fast as I could towards the ships.

I swam until I was directly underneath one of the purple ships, then I launched myself out of the water and barreled into that ship and two others, turning them into splinters.

Suddenly, everything went quiet, as if the entire world had turned off the sound. I stared down at the humanoids clinging to their ruined ships and they stared up at me in turn.

"I'm truly sorry about this, but I'm starving over here," I said with a polite bow of my head.

"..........." The humanoids were silent for ten more seconds, then. "M... Monster!!" one of them yelled, causing the active cannons to cease fire on the black flags and focus on me.

"Oh well, let's get this over with," I sighed, as I opened my "eyes" and activated my petrification skill.

Almost instantly, forty percent of the humanoids were turned to stone. But the ones who weren't, were either too powerful to be petrified or had looked away at the right time. I left my "eyes" open, while I charged up my next attack, and it finished charging, right after the red and black flags had fired a volley at me.

"Twenty percent power should suffice..." I shot out a consistent beam of energy and quickly twisted my head, causing the beam to turn ten ships to dust and killing who knows how many people.

A pop-up appeared almost immediately after...

∞∞∞∞∞∞∞∞

You have unlocked the following evolutionary path:
Elemental Leviathan

Would you like to evolve?

∞∞∞∞∞∞∞∞

Before I could respond, multiple cannonballs smashed into me, causing severe pain and a few cracked scales, but otherwise it just pissed me off.

"No." I growled out. The pop-up disappeared and a new one took its place.

∞∞∞∞∞∞∞∞

Very well, you have passed up the Elemental Leviathan path. As a result, this path has forever been locked to you.

Please select your reward for unlocking it:

Superior Strength

Acidic Blood

∞∞∞∞∞∞∞∞

"Superior strength!" I quickly said, while ducking under the water again to prevent my attackers from firing another volley at me.

However, despite my quick answer, I'd actually thought about this choice for a long time. And I'd come to the decision that Superior Strength was the more useful of the two for one reason. Superior Strength is transferable to my possessed bodies, while Acidic Blood most likely was not.

Just like I'd lost my wings while I was inside the goblin body, I guessed that I would also lose the acid blood if I possessed a body. Could I be wrong? Sure I could, but I would rather take a certain bet over a gamble, any day.

Another pop-up immediately followed my choice.

∞∞∞∞∞∞∞∞

You have been granted the Supreme Strength skill, due to unlocking and rejecting the Elemental Leviathan path.

*Note: The Leviathan Superior Strength combined with your already increased strength to unlock its current level.

*Note: Your Growth trait has been increased by 7, bringing it to Growth +10

∞∞∞∞∞∞∞∞

"That's going to be a problem in the future," I said with a sigh as I launched myself out of the water and slammed into the barrier around the bottom of the floating castles. My massive size and weight launched one castle off the ship and sent it flying into the air. It flew over one hundred feet away, then it crashed into the water. The other two castles collapsed under their own weight and the ship as a whole fell onto its side.

Then I turned my attention to the red flags. I snapped my head out and bit one of the ships completely in two, with the back half of the ship becoming my meal.

Another volley of cannonballs came flying my way, but I picked up a red flag by its mast and used it to take the brunt of the volley. Then I tilted my head back and used my tongue to pull the ship into my mouth, where I quickly chewed it up.

The black flags decided to use this opportunity to flee, but I cut them off by thrusting my head into the water behind them, causing a massive wave to capsize over half the ships, while I destroyed the rest by another charged shot.

This left only one red flag and four purple flags, after the goblins took over one of the remaining purple ships and left the immediate area. These five ships were the only witnesses. Then suddenly, a loud roar echoed from one of the castles.

I and the remaining twenty humanoids turned to look at the now glowing castle.

"That's going to be a problem..." Before whatever was about to happen actually happened, I quickly scooped up two of the purple flags and ate them, then I blasted the red flag with an energy beam. And finally, I picked the second-to-last purple flag out of the water and slammed it into the remaining ship, leaving only me and

whatever was about to burst out of the now swelling barrier. A large black tentacle came out of the barrier that easily stretched over a mile into the sky. It came crashing down, causing massive waves to knock me about for a few seconds. The tentacle was then followed by a truly massive octopus, which was attempting to pull its body out of the barrier.

"As if I'm going to allow that," I scoffed, as I swam as fast as I could towards the creature. Then I launched myself out of the water and body slammed it back into the barrier. My quick response stopped it before it could get more than two tentacles and part of its head out. Its glowing yellow eye glared at me as it drew back one of the free tentacles, then it came flying at me... and right into my waiting mouth.

It screamed in pain as I bit off its leg, then I pulled the massive tentacle into my mouth as far as I could before I started chewing it.

"You're a big one, that's for sure... But you're not very strong, are you?" I asked while I was chewing its leg into mush.

My accusation seemed to piss it off because its other tentacle wrapped around my body and attempted to throw me away, so it could further free itself. But I bit into its revealed eye and yanked it out just as the creature lifted me out of the water and tossed me away.

I landed back in the water after flying for three hundred feet, but even though I wasn't severely harmed, I was stunned enough that it had time to pull the rest of its head through the barrier.

Luckily, I tackled it in time to prevent it from getting any further; otherwise, my next action wouldn't have worked. I slammed it against the barrier using my newly enhanced strength, then I pressed the jewel against its head, and sent a full-powered blast into the creature's bulbous head.

Its head turned into mush and the barrier behind it made a sound like glass breaking, as it completely shattered, releasing the rest of the creature's body into the water. And this thing was truly massive. Each tentacle easily stretched over a mile in length and was about one hundred feet thick. But as its main body was similar in size to me, it was only about one thousand four hundred feet long.

However, even with its massive size, the creature wasn't as powerful as the Leviathan I'd killed, a theory that was later proven when I got this pop-up.

∞∞∞∞∞∞∞∞

You have eaten the following race for the first time.

Kraken: Tier 6

∞∞∞∞∞∞∞∞

After reading the pop-up, I began to feast on the floating carcass. But I was interrupted by someone calling out to me.

"Master!"

I tore off the leg I'd been chewing on and turned to see who'd called out to me. It was Siofs and the goblins on their newly acquired ship.

"What?"

"We have someone on board that wants to speak with you. Do you have a minute?"

"I'm busy...Tell them I'll talk with them after I finish eating."

Siofs nodded her head, then went back inside the ship's cabin.

I tore off another piece of the kraken while I grumbled about stupid people interrupting my precious mealtime. *"Can't a snake ever eat in peace?"*

I decided to forget about them and everything else and just enjoy my meal while I still could.

I managed to consume over half of the kraken before I was satisfied, then I offered the rest to the goblins. However, all but Siofs declined to dine on the colossal mollusk for one reason or another.

Personally, I think they are just being overly picky, but I wasn't going to force them. After all, more food for me is never a bad thing.

Siofs jumped off the ship and swam over to the carcass and started ripping pieces off and stuffing the raw meat into her mouth. "Thank you for the food, Master!" she said with a cheerful smile on her face. Then she went back to eating and I refocused my attention on the ship.

The first thing I saw was Holstig, Hogunn, and Findral lounging around on the top deck. Holstig and Hogunn were lying down at the front of the ship and Findral was hanging by her feet from the mast. I tilted my head while looking at her. I opened my mouth to question her about her choice of "resting" spot, but I snapped it shut after deciding it wasn't worth the effort or the headache her answer might bring. So, I instead turned my attention to the two newcomers on the ship.

One of them was a large green-skinned, pig-like humanoid. He was around eight feet tall and looked like he could weigh as much as five hundred pounds. His head was covered by a dull gray bucket helmet that left his face open to the world around him. The rest of his body was covered by a similarly colored suit of metal armor that only left his forearms and hands exposed. As for his weapons, he had two large hammers strapped to his back via corded leather.

Overall, he had the appearance of a brute, and his first words confirmed that you could, in fact, sometimes judge a book by its cover...

"Big snake destroy castle... You have goblin fix!" he yelled, the fat around his mouth jiggling with every word.

I stared down at him, and the fact that I was amused by the pig's order didn't go unnoticed. The pig's green face turned a remarkable shade of purple as the creature continued to yell at me. However, I opted to ignore him in favor of observing the companion.

A mass of moving black cloth and a frowning harlequin mask where the head should have been stared up at me. As no skin was exposed beneath the thing's peculiar robe, I couldn't be sure what it was. However, that didn't stop me from trying to figure it out.

I first tried my heat sense, but it appeared as if the robe was encapsulating its body so completely, that not even heat could escape. So, I moved on to what I could see, instead.

Even through the robes, I could tell the creature was tall and had an extremely thin body. If I included the metal horn that stuck out of the mask's forehead, then it was around twelve feet tall.

The robe moved and shifted as if it were alive. "Must you stare like a mentally impaired monkey?" the masked figured suddenly asked in a dull tone.

Its abrupt question had me tilting my head in confusion. Then a smile appeared on the puppet's face. "Oh, now you, I like. What's your name?"

Its masked face stared at me and said, "My name is none of your concern." Then it paused for a few seconds and appeared to look me over before it continued. "However, if you'll tell me what a Tier 5 Elemental Basilisk, with the Elemental Wyrm and Leviathan paths unlocked but discarded is doing on a Tier 3 world... then I'll answer you."

I squinted my eyes and slightly opened my mouth. "How could you possibly know what evolutions I've unlocked and discarded?"

"It's my job to know everything there is to know about monsters."

"That doesn't answer my question."

"And you never answered mine, so I guess that makes us even," it said with a slight scoff.

"Yes, I suppose it would," I replied, while making the puppet show a toothy grin.

The masked figure then turned to the pig, who was still loudly yelling in my general direction. "Master, we really should get going... It's obvious these animals won't comply with your wishes."

"No! Snake repair castle!"

"Master, you're forgetting our lessons again—"

"No! Lessons make brain hurt. I no care about your 'lessons' anymore. I'm king and I get what I want!" the pig yelled while stomping his foot.

The masked figured stared down at the pig for a second or two, then it turned back to me. "It seems I've wasted my time with this one... Do with him as you like; I'm leaving." Suddenly, the mask on its face started to vibrate, and the creature let out a deep sigh.

"Great timing Prudens... You just had to get the last word, didn't—" Its words were cut off when the mask suddenly collapsed in on itself and turned into some form of liquid. Then the robe fell to the ground and rapidly began to shift through every color of the rainbow.

"What is happening?" I asked the pig, who, after seeing his companion "melt," for lack of a better word, had calmed down and started watching the now kaleidoscopic goo.

"Prudens is coming. I like Prudens. He's the nice one," he said, while bouncing in place.

The robe finally settled on a bright pink color, then it sprung into its former position. The previously moving "shadow" robe was gone and in its place was a normal, if outrageously colorful, one. But that wasn't the only thing to change, as the mask had turned into a smiling harlequin that constantly cycled from one color to the next. Even the horn had shifted into what appeared to be a long nose.

"Ahh, that's better..." It lifted its arms to the side and pulled them behind its back as if it were stretching.

"I'm guessing you're Prudens?"

The mask tilted up and it looked up at me. "Wow, you're huge!! What are they feeding you snakes nowadays!?" it yelled, taking several steps back.

I flicked my tongue at it and narrowed my eyes.

"Oh... Whoops." it said in a contrite tone. It swung its arm in a grandiose display and bowed low to the ground. "Please excuse both my, and my alter ego's rudeness... We, uh, don't get out much." It stood up straight. "To answer your question, yes, my name is Prudens... And in case you're wondering, my alter ego is called Gorre."

"Well, that answers two of my questions, but I'm still wondering how Gorre was able to know which evolutions I've passed up." I answered.

It shrugged. "Sorry, I can't tell you that."

"Can't or won't?"

"Can't. Gorre and I may share the same body, but our skills and abilities are completely different." It paused and looked at each goblin for a few seconds, then it settled on Findral. "Madam, could I have your assistance for a moment?"

Findral looked over to me first. After I gave her a tenuous nod, she walked over to Prudens.

"For example, my power enables me to understand the history of any humanoid race I come into contact with. I can see their past, their present, and even parts of their future, should they allow me to. But Gorre, his specialty is 'monsters.' And how he knows what he does, I honestly couldn't tell you."

"Very well... Then what can you tell me about miss Findral here?"

Prudens rubbed its sleeves together, as if they were its hands, then turned to her and held out a sleeve. "If you would allow me, madam?"

Findral studied it for a few seconds, then placed her left hand on its sleeve.

"Very interesting... You are six years old, so barely out of puberty by goblin standards and yet, you have already evolved twice."

"Is that rare?" I interrupted

"Oh, incredibly so. For any race to evolve once in ten years is a rare thing and the individual would be considered a genius in most circumstances... But evolving twice is beyond the level of a genius and is approaching 'hero' levels."

My mind immediately went to the fact that I'd already evolved twice and unlocked two more evolutions. And I was only three years old... Or was I?

I shook my head to clear it of those thoughts, then asked, "When you say 'hero' what exactly do you mean?"

"'Hero' is a title given to those who have been reincarnated through the power of a god. These beings are usually humanoids of some description. Though monster 'heroes' have been known to appear from time to time, as well."

"I understand... Please, continue."

Prudens returned its focus to Findral. "You are the epitome of what it means to be a goblin. Born with a high resistance to fire, due to your elemental parentage. You quickly adapted to the flame element while you were still in your first year of life. However, before you reached the point of evolving, you chose to gain the spy class for the stealth bonuses it would bring. Then, you finally allowed yourself to evolve during your second year."

"What were her parents?"

Before Prudens could answer, Findral yanked her hand away. "My mother was a Flame empress and my father was... a very powerful fire elemental that disappeared before I was born," she said with a downcast look.

"If neither of your parents were goblins, then how come you were born as one?"

"Goblins are unique in a variety of ways and that is one of them."

"What do you mean?"

"Well, the goblin race can evolve into almost any other race imaginable... provided they consume enough of that race. However, no matter what race they evolve into, their offspring will always be born of the goblin race."

"Interesting...Then how come I didn't see any other races during my time at the goblin nest?"

"The goblin king doesn't wish for the goblin race to be diluted with the insertion of the other races' needs. He believes that would weaken our adaptability. So, once a goblin evolves beyond their goblin form, they are forbidden from ever living inside the nest again."

"I understand," I said with a nod.

Prudens lifted its arm and acted like it wanted to say something, but its mask suddenly started to vibrate.

"So sorry, but it appears I'm going to have to cut this meeting short. Otherwise, I'll never hear the end of Gorre's complaining." It waved its arm and a silver portal opened in the air.

"Please, do what you like with him." It waved to the pig. "Ditching him is the only thing Gorre and I have agreed on lately." Its body melted down just as it stepped through the portal. Then it and the portal vanished, leaving us alone with a tantrum-throwing pig.

"Fix castle now! Wait... Where Prudens go?"

I turned to the goblins. "Who can gain something from eating him?"

"I'm already at its tier, so I can't gain anything from it," Holstig replied. Findral and Siofs both said something similar, so it was Hogunn who eagerly raised his hand.

"If I eat the whole pig, I can become a stone variant of its race."

"Good, then if you can kill it, it's yours."

A vicious grin appeared on Hogunn's face as he drew his weapon.

"What you doing?" the pig asked.

"In the words of my master... It's lunchtime, pig!" He dashed at the creature.

The pig squealed as it reached to its back and tried to pull the two hammers out of their straps. However, Hogunn was too fast and he slammed his morning star into the pig's right leg. The force of the impact severely dented its armor and dropped the pig to one knee. Then Hogunn drew back and slammed the morning star into the pig's face.

It squealed again, as it was knocked onto its back, further preventing it from unsheathing its weapons. Hogunn reached down and grabbed the pig by the throat and began to squeeze. A few seconds into this, the pig decided to cut its losses and forget the hammers. It drew back its right fist, then punched Hogunn in the jaw hard enough to knock him to the side.

But the punch only brought his anger to the surface, and he activated his "berserk" mode. His normally white eyes turned blood red, then he started tearing the pig apart.

The pig swung its right arm into Hogunn's ribs, and a crunching sound rang out, but Hogunn ignored the pain and grabbed hold of the pig's arm. Then he placed his foot on the arm's shoulder and began to pull.

Snap! The pig squealed as its arm was forcefully dislocated. The pig rolled onto its stomach in an attempt to throw Hogunn off, but all that managed to do was give Hogunn access to its neck.

He wrapped his arms around the pig's neck and began to squeeze as hard as he could. Then he put his knees into the pig's back and yanked backward.

Snap! The pig's head hung lifelessly from Hogunn's arms until he let go and it hit the deck with a *Thump!*

Hogunn fell onto his back and panted from exhaustion, as his eyes slowly returned to their normal color.

"Very well done, Hogunn. As promised, the pig is yours. Do what you will with its equipment," I said with a proud grin on the puppet's face, then I went back to eating the kraken.

Findral walked over to the exhausted Hogunn and patted him on the shoulder. "Good job Hoggy! Want me to cook him for you?" she asked with her usual enthusiasm.

Hogunn was still on his back, trying to catch his breath. He lifted his head enough to nod, then he passed out from the pain in his ribs.

When he awoke that night, Hogunn feasted on the pig's corpse and told Findral that she could have some if she wanted. Then he went into his evolutionary cocoon where he would stay for two days.

I ordered the goblins to take the next few days to rest while I handled some stuff, namely, stuffing my stomach with as much of the kraken as possible.

When the cocoon finally opened, Hogunn emerged a completely different being than when he went in: He was now as tall as the pig he'd eaten. But whereas the other had been fat and pig-like, Hogunn was muscular. He had short black hair that he pulled into a topknot, his stone-like skin had become darker, and two tusks jutted out from his bottom lip.

I got this pop-up a few minutes after he emerged.

∞∞∞∞∞∞∞∞

Hogunn

Race: Stone Orc

Classification: Tier 4

Class: Berserker: Rank 6

∞∞∞∞∞∞∞∞∞∞

"How do you feel, Hogunn?"

He looked down at his body for a few seconds, then he looked back to me. "I feel great!" he said with a genuine smile.

"Good... Then we've wasted enough time here. Let's move out!"

The goblins got the ship moving and so we continued our journey across the ocean.

Chapter Thirty-Two

Two months later...

I T TOOK US A LONG TIME, BUT EVENTUALLY, WE MADE it to the other continent and our destination was within sight. As the other branch of Yggdrasil loomed over us, we were infused with renewed energy. I increased my travel speed and made a mad dash for the branch.

Completely disregarding the concept of subtlety, I overran everything in my path. Any tree in my way was either knocked over or eaten, and with the puppet running ahead of me. The animals met the same fate. The puppet would chase them down, slit their throats, then throw them in the air for me to catch. So, overall, it was a good system we had going. And when we finally did reach the branch, I barreled straight into it without slowing down.

I, and my followers, were sucked into the portal and propelled into the Bifrost.

∞∞∞∞∞∞∞∞∞

Welcome to the Bifrost

Please select your next destination from the available branches.

Uathea: An earth elemental world. Home of massive forests and the "guardian" of the druids.

Seleth: A wind elemental world. Home of floating mountain ranges and constant hurricanes.

Jitia: A water elemental world. Home of many small human kingdoms situated on hundreds of small islands.

∞∞∞∞∞∞∞∞

"Druid guardian? But Lena said the guardian was dead... didn't she?" I asked myself, while I was reading this message.

"What is it, Master?" Siofs asked, after seeing me pause at the pop-up.

"Conflicting information." I shook my head. "Never mind, I'll just have to figure this out later."

"Uathea!" I yelled, and my body went flying forward at high speed.

When I landed outside of the branch, the first thing I noticed was how odd this world seemed. The sky was bright green and the sun that was just about to reach its peak was a dark blue. Which looked quite strange floating in the green sky.

On the ground, I saw the blue foliage that covered the landscape. The tree leaves were mostly dark blue like the sun, though I saw several orange and purple leaves hidden among the masses. The grass was differing shades of blue, ranging from almost black to nearly white, creating patches that formed stripes along the ground.

However, aside from those extreme examples, the world looked relatively normal. The wood was still varying shades of brown. I didn't sense any weird animals skulking around, nor did I see any bad weather or floating lava streams. So all in all, not a bad place.

After looking around to my satisfaction, I ordered the puppet to stand in front of me and the goblins to jump off, so they wouldn't be hurt from what I was about to do.

"What are you doing, Master?" Holstig asked in a bored tone.

I let out a sigh. "I'd rather not scare the druids too much, so I'm going to possess the puppet."

"Oh..." he finished lamely.

One thing that made itself apparent during the two months I'd spent traveling with the goblins: They were an odd bunch.

I'm assuming it's because they've gotten used to my presence, but each one of them has begun to show more and more of their personalities.

By observing Holstig, I'd come to understand some truths about him. For starters, he's a very dull conversationalist and prefers to keep to himself unless he's around Siofs, which brings us to point two. He's very protective of Siofs, but he refuses to say why. However, from what I've witnessed, his desire to protect her isn't weaker than my own desire to protect Sarah, so he must have a reason.

Moving on to Hogunn. He's become more cooperative, ever since he evolved into an orc. And he's no longer the standoffish one. I'm assuming it's because I allowed him to evolve and catch up to his peers, but you never know. It could be for another reason.

Siofs is still the strait-laced one of the group and is usually the first to fall into the leader role whenever I'm not around. I had, however, learned a few things about her.

For instance, I learned that she is a goblin "princess" and is the youngest daughter of the goblin king. But that led to my questioning why the king would send his own daughter to accompany me.

"I'm a goblin princess, and as such, I'm expected to one day form a nest of my own, as are my siblings. But with you showing up and demanding some goblins accompany you on your journey, I figured this would be a good opportunity for me to travel to an acceptable planet to form my nest, so I volunteered. Oh, but don't worry. I was going to ask for your permission before I started the nest," she replied in a straightforward manner with a slight smile on her face.

I didn't question her further about her nesting plans because I honestly had no issues with her starting up a nest. In fact, a goblin horde could be extremely useful one day, so why would I reject it? No, I definitely wasn't going to deny her request to form a nest, though I might have a suggestion or two for her when the time came.

And then there's Findral, our resident pyromaniac and ball of explosive energy. Ever since the meeting with Prudens and Gorre, Findral has become a bit… sharper?

No, that isn't right. It's more like she just isn't hiding behind the facade of innocent exuberance as much as she had before. I've been seeing more and more of her serious side, and I have to say, I'm impressed. It's obvious that she'll never be a natural leader like Siofs, but Findral is a definite second.

However, with this more serious side came a feeling of familiarity that I just couldn't seem to place. Now, I knew that I'd never met her before that time in the goblin nest. So why was I feeling this way?

"Just another thing to add to the 'figure it out later' list. Now that I'm thinking about it, that list is getting pretty long. I should probably make some time to think over things before I start forgetting them altogether," I whispered to myself, as I touched the puppet with my jewel.

~ ~ ~

SOLON

A bright red light flashed over the treetops as I and a group of elven hunters were returning home from another successful day of hunting.

"Did you guys see that?" Alok Norro, a dark elven kid around my age asked.

"Yes... Ruehar and Rathal, you two head back to the village and tell the Elder that we've gone to investigate." Elwin, our de facto leader and veteran hunter told the twin trackers.

They gave him a salute, then ran off.

"Form up on me and remember, at the first sign of trouble the young hunters need to flee."

"But Elwin—"

"No, Einar! Either follow my orders or you can go back to the village with Ruehar and Rathal," he told his younger brother Einar.

Einar's lip trembled a bit, but he swallowed down his frustration and nodded.

"Good, now... Move out!" Elwin ordered.

We assumed our positions and began running towards the red light's origin.

We'd been running for around fifteen minutes when I smelled something I recognized... Torga.

"Wait!" I yelled, causing my group to slide to a stop.

"What is it, Solon?" Elwin asked, while raising his head to sniff the air. Like me, Elwin and his younger brother were demi-elves, but I was half Warg and they were half fox.

"A friend," I replied with a smile on my face. Then I motioned for them to follow me, while I followed my nose to Torga.

"Who's this friend of yours, Solon?" Alok asked.

I simply smirked at him and refused to answer as I continued to follow my nose until I arrived at a break in the trees. The area had been completely flattened, as if a mountain had been dropped on the area, and standing in the center of the destruction was an extremely tall snake-man.

It towered over its companions at around fifteen-feet tall and was almost as wide as two men standing side by side. It was bald with a thick crest on its forehead that housed a bright red jewel, two yellow eyes with slitted pupils, and a mouth that I just knew was filled with razor-sharp teeth.

Its scales were almost completely dark green, except for a patch of dark gray scales around its stomach… and it was naked.

"Oh my!" Alata, our resident dryad exclaimed with her eyes locked on a certain part of the snake-man's body.

"My eyes are up here, girl." The snake-man said in a dual-toned voice.

Alata quickly covered her eyes and turned around. "Sorry!" she yelled once her back was turned.

The snake-man softly chuckled as it held out its hand to a blue goblin standing to its right. *"Pants, please."* It said to the goblin.

"Sorry Master, but we don't have any in your size," she said with a contrite look.

"I'm aware, Siofs. Still, there must be an extra pair in there from the orc, yes?"

"Well... Yes, but what good will they do you?"

"Just hand them over."

She wordlessly passed over a pair of extremely large black pants and the snake-man slipped them on. Then he tore a long strip out of the left leg and wrapped it around his body to form a makeshift belt.

"Much better!" it said with a smile as it looked down at the pants.

"Torga, is... is that you?" I tentatively asked.

The snake-man raised his head and looked me in the eye. "Hello, Solon. How's the family?"

A smile grew on my face and I ran over to him.... And drop kicked him in the chest. "You're late!"

~ ~ ~

TORGA

I followed along behind Solon and his group as they led us back to the druid city. And while I was walking, I made it a point to look at each of them in turn.

Solon still looked the same, though he was a little taller and his hair had grown more wild, so I passed over him and looked at the others.

The first was a plant woman. She had blue skin covered in green foliage, which led me to believe she wasn't from this planet originally. Her "hair" was made of vines that hung down to her lower back and she had orange eyes, and she walked around naked. Because of course she did.

Then, there were the fox siblings. Both of them had short red hair and long fuzzy tails that ended in white patches. The taller brother was wearing a suit of brown leather armor that covered loose fitting pants and a shirt. The shorter brother was wearing a simple brown robe with leather accents.

And finally, there was the young dark elf. He had long silver hair that hung loosely around his neck, except for one long braid that hung past his temple, and he had bright red eyes. He was wearing a green robe with leather accents and carried a wooden staff.

"So, Solon. How's your family?" I asked.

He turned to look at me with a sad expression on his face that he then tried to quickly hide. "Oh, they're fine! Mom and Dad are the same as usual. Hali's been acting a little weird, but she's a girl so that doesn't count, and Talia's been causing as much havoc as her little body can handle."

"I see... So, there's nothing bad going on? You and your family are safe?"

"Well... We've had some issues, but there's nothing you can do to help in that regard."

"Try me."

"There's—"

"Solon! The Elder's already explained this to you!" The taller fox brother yelled.

"But—" Solon tried to say something, but he was again cut off by the fox.

"No buts."

"How about if you interrupt him again, I'll shove your head so far up your ass, you'll have a reason for that brown nose of yours?"

The fox-boy clamped his mouth shut.

"Now, what's this problem you're having?"

Under the glare of fox-boy and his younger brother, Solon told me everything that had happened since their return.

Three years ago, the druids adopted a new guardian. However, this guardian required something for its protection: live sacrifices. And in an effort to delay his own sacrifice, the city's Elder had been sending out young children to be sacrificed to the guardian.

This, I understood and could accept. But something Solon said later truly pissed me off.

"When this Ayla girl was to be sacrificed, her grandmother took her place and was sacrificed in her stead. But even after her grandmother's sacrifice, Ayla is still set to be sacrificed within the next few days... And then it's supposed to be Hali's turn," Solon said dejectedly.

"I see... And what exactly, is this guardian?" I asked through clenched teeth.

"It's an earth dragon," Solon replied, looking at the ground.

"Solon."

"Yeah?" He turned to look at me.

"Does your dad have what I asked for?"

"Oh! Yes, he does. We stopped to get them in Neonia before we came here."

"Then go get your father and tell him to come meet with me... We have some planning to do."

Solon nodded, then ran off into the forest, leaving me and the goblins with the hunting group.

"You can't stop Lord Arroth's will—"

"Shut up before I eat you."

"Hey! You can't talk to him like that—"

"Silence!" I roared, causing everyone to take several steps away from me.

"I just found out a friend of mine was killed and two more of my friends are on the chopping block... So the next person to open their fucking mouth will get their tongue ripped out! Understand!?" I snarled, then I headed over to a tree and sat down to wait for Fenris to show up, with the goblins immediately copying my actions.

The hunters were frozen in fear for ten minutes following my outburst, then they too, settled in to wait.

CHAPTER THIRTY-THREE

PPROXIMATELY TWENTY MINUTES LATER, Fenris in his Demi-Elvan form, Lena, Hali, and Solon ran up to me. Lena and Fenris slid to a stop to stare at me, Solon made his way over to the goblins and started chatting with Findral, while Hali slammed into my side and hugged me.

"Torga!" She cried out as she attempted to burrow deeper into my scales.

I stayed frozen there for a few moments. Then I raised my right hand and began to softly rub her hair.

"It'll be alright..." I whispered to her.

She lifted her head and looked up at me with tears in her eyes. "I didn't think you would make it in time..."

I heard someone clear their throat off to my left. When Hali and I turned to see who it was, we saw Ayla standing there with a devious smile on her face. "Sooo, Hali, this the man you've been talking about?" she asked in a teasing tone.

"Ayla!" Hali yelled, then she quickly extracted herself from my side, blushing a brilliant shade of red. Ayla giggled in satisfaction at her embarrassment, then she turned to me. "So, what's your name—" She began, before pausing midsentence.

"Haven't we already done this, Ayla?" I asked.

"Wait..." She squinted her eyes. "Old man?"

"In the scales." I said with a chuckle. Then the humor left me. "Ayla... I'm sorry I wasn't here to—"

She did an almost perfect imitation of Hali and dove into my side so she could hug me.

"Those bastards killed her, old man!" All traces of her previous amusement were gone as she cried into my shoulder. Her long hair became a tangled mess as she rubbed her face into my neck.

I repeated my earlier action and reached up and patted her hair. "Ayla... Listen to me, Ayla."

She stopped long enough to look up at me.

"The people that did this... the ones who made the deal with the dragon... Can you take me to them?"

The first emotion to appear on her face was confusion, but that was quickly replaced with all the anger her tiny body could muster. "Will you kill them?" she asked.

"With extreme prejudice."

She watched me for a few seconds amidst the watchful eyes of our audience. Then she nodded her head and stepped back.

Hali quickly walked up to her and grabbed her arm, then she dragged her off to the side. She apparently began to question Ayla, but I couldn't listen in as my focus became occupied by Lena and Fenris.

"Well, now that my daughter has had her moment, I think we need to have a talk," Fenris said with the most serious expression I'd ever seen on his face.

"Of course," I agreed, then I stood up and began to follow them. "Siofs!" I called over my shoulder.

"Yes, Master?"

"Guard the children..."

"Of course," she nodded.

We walked just out of earshot of the children, then we began to plot.

~ ~ ~

"Do you have what I asked for?" I asked, as soon as we were alone.

"Who do you think you're talking to? Of course, I have them." Fenris replied with a scoff as he tossed me a small brown pouch.

"Thanks, Fenris." I said, as I snatched the pouch out of the air and dumped its contents into my palm. Multiple colored gems and stones fell out, then I quickly threw them into my mouth and swallowed them whole.

With my potent stomach acid, the stones were dissolved within moments and I got the pop-up.

∞∞∞∞∞∞∞∞

You have unlocked the following evolutionary path:
Elemental Naga

Would you like to evolve?

∞∞∞∞∞∞∞∞

"No." With my hatred for a certain dragon influencing my actions, I declined the Naga evolution for two reasons: The first was because if I accepted it and began to evolve, then by the time I was released, it would most likely be too late to save the few people in this world I cared about.

And the second reason, If I didn't at least severely injure that damn dragon, then I just might go crazy.

A few seconds later, another pop-up appeared.

∞∞∞∞∞∞∞∞

Kenneth Arant

Very well, you have passed up the Elemental Naga path. As a result, this path has forever been locked to you.

Please select your reward for unlocking it:

Magic Manipulator

Telepathy

∞∞∞∞∞∞∞∞

Because of my ability to communicate through the puppet, I chose Magic Manipulator.

∞∞∞∞∞∞∞∞

You have been granted the Magic Manipulator trait due to unlocking and rejecting the Elemental Naga path.

*Note: You now have the ability to use magic, but without learning the spells, incantations, and movements of the differing magics, you will be unable to use this trait to its fullest potential.

∞∞∞∞∞∞∞∞

"You done yet?" Fenris asked as I finished reading the pop-up.

"Yeah, I'm done." I replied, while waving off the pop-up. "Now, tell me everything you know about this situation and the dragon."

"Why do you want to know about the dragon, Torga? What are you planning?" Lena asked.

"That should be obvious, Lena. I'm going to kill it."

The two of them stared at me in shocked silence for several moments, then, "What!?" "Are you fucking joking, right now?!" they simultaneously yelled.

"No, I'm not joking."

Fenris scoffed. "Then you're just suicidal."

"What the fuck is your problem, Fenris!? What did you think I was going to do? Just let it live?" I yelled at him.

"I was expecting you to help us leave this damnable planet, not run off to commit suicide by dragon!" he snarled back at me.

His words caused me to pause. "Why can't you leave?"

Lena and Fenris glanced at each other, then Fenris motioned for Lena to take over while he went to check on the kids.

"Do you remember what I told you about Master Uriel?"

"He's the enchanter, right?"

"Yes," she agreed. "Well... He was forced to put a barrier around the branch."

"I didn't see one when I came through."

"It only appears when someone tries to leave." She sighed. "It was originally supposed to keep children from wandering through the portal into the outside world, but Elder Ayas forced him to alter it so no one can leave."

"Why would he do such a thing?"

She walked over to a tree and sat down, then she buried her head in her hands. "Elder Ayas is the one who led the dragon here."

"What!? What the hell possessed him to do that!?"

"Have you ever met a druid of the dominator faction?" she lifted her head to ask.

"Unfortunately."

"Then you know why. He wanted power."

I watched her for a few seconds in an attempt to make sense of what she told me. Then it hit me.

"He tried to dominate the dragon, didn't he?"

She pulled her knees up to her chest, then she nodded. "Yeah."

"What kind of arrogant—" I began to ask, but after looking at her face again, I stopped.

"You're not as angry about this as I expected you to be."

She snorted. "Oh, I'm furious..."

"Then why haven't you done something about it?"

"I don't know. If it were anyone else, we wouldn't be having this conversation... and the gods know, Mom would have killed him for this—"

"Wait. Mom?"

"Caught that did you?" she asked with a derisive laugh. "Yeah... Elder Ayas is my stepfather. He married my mom after dad died a few centuries ago and they had a daughter together."

"So, you have a stepsister? And what does she think of this?"

"Probably not much, since she's been dead for a few years."

"Ah... Sorry."

"No, don't apologize. Aurea wasn't the easiest person to get along with. It was only a matter of time before her actions caught up with her," Lena said with a discontented sigh.

The name Aurea struck a chord with me, but I played it off as concern. "What happened to her?" I asked.

"No one knows. I asked the druids who were on the expedition with her, but all they would tell me is that she disappeared in the Myrkr forest one day. She probably wound up on the wrong end of an Alpha Deer's horn."

"Or inside the stomach of a large snake." But of course, I didn't say that out loud. Instead, I directed the conversation back onto her stepfather.

"I'm assuming Ayas didn't take the news of his daughter's disappearance well?"

"Understatement of the year," she scoffed. "I'm told that after her disappearance he became erratic, and for some reason, he believed himself to be losing control of the tribe. That coupled with my banishment to Iorus led him to... drastic measures."

"Like trying to dominate a dragon?"

She nodded silently.

"But why sacrifice the children? Wouldn't animals or even the adults be better?"

"That's the part I don't understand as well. Elder Ayas loves his grandchildren dearly. Hell, he calls all of the children in the tribe his grandchildren, so this sudden change of heart doesn't make any sense. The Ayas I knew would have gladly killed or died to protect the children, but he would never have done this... Shows what I know, huh?" she said with a self-deprecating tone.

I stared down at her. "Maybe you know him better than you realize," I quietly said.

"What?" She raised her head and looked me in the eyes.

"The dominator I knew tried to enslave me to her will, but I was able to fight her off—"

"That doesn't surprise me," she laughed.

My mouth quirked to the side for an instant, then I continued. "Anyway, what I was trying to say was... Maybe the dragon did so as well?"

The humor drained from her face almost instantly and she stared at the ground.

"What is it?" I kneeled in front of her to ask.

She glanced up at me, then back to the ground. "I was thinking of an old horror story my mother used to tell Aurea and me when we were kids."

"About?"

She locked eyes with me. "She used to tell us that the true danger of the domination path came not from its inherent wrongness, but from the animal's wrath. Of course, Aurea never believed in the old stories, which is why she turned out the way she did."

"Lena!" I called out to get her to focus. "What did she say would happen?" I asked.

"She said, 'If you open your mind to the creature and accept it as a partner, it shall accept you in return. But if you try to dominate the mind of a predator, be very careful, lest you be dominated in return.'" She paused for a few seconds, then she continued. "The thought of my mind being taken over by such a predator is what ultimately made me decide to follow in my mother's footsteps."

"So... You're saying that it's possible your father is being dominated by the dragon?"

She nodded. "If the old stories are true... then yes, it's possible."

"Well, we'll have to fix that, won't we?"

She slowly shook her head. "If it's true, and he is being dominated, our best course of action is to kill him and get it over with."

"Why? Couldn't we save him?"

"No. To be truly dominated is to have your mind completely devoured by the dominator. It's why so many of us look down on the dominators as evil people. They don't just enslave the animal they dominate, they completely erase its sense of self. Can you imagine such a thing? To erase someone's sense of self is possibly even worse than killing them, because they can no longer function without the dominator. Tis truly an awful thing to do to someone."

My mouth formed a firm line, then I nodded my head in agreement. "Very well, then we kill him. Then I'll deal with his dominator."

Her lower lip started to tremble and she had to run the back of her sleeve over her eyes a few times to wipe away the tears. "Thank you, Torga... You're a true friend."

"Right... friend."

After our little heart-to-heart, Lena and I made our way back to the group, then we all started walking towards the city. The group of hunters was out in front, while the family, Ayla, and I followed closely behind them.

"What can you tell me about dragons?" I asked Lena, who was walking to my left.

"Are you still going on about that?" Fenris butted in. "You should give up and focus on something else before you—"

I reached over and grabbed him around the neck, then I pulled him into a headlock and covered his mouth with my hand. "Do you see that little girl over there?" I asked, nodding to Ayla.

"Yeah?" he mumbled through the gaps in my fingers. His feet became tangled up and he almost tripped, so I lifted him off the ground by his head and carried him while we talked.

"I met her and her grandmother long before I met any of you... And if I'm being honest, I'm rather fond of the little brat. Now, imagine my feelings when I'm suddenly told by Solon that the only family she had left was offered as a sacrifice to a piece of shit dragon."

"Anger?" he mumbled out.

"Yes, genius. I'm very angry. Now, as I've already promised that I would avenge her grandmother, I'm left with two choices: keep my promise and avenge her or break my promise to one of the few people I care about." I looked down at him. "Which do you think I'm going to do?" I asked.

"Keep your promise?"

"Exactly. And you can either help me avenge her or not. The end result will be the same... So don't tell me to Let. It. Go. Again." After I whispered the last word, I turned him loose and he fell onto his ass.

"Sorry. Please, continue." I motioned to Lena.

She cleared her throat, then she began speaking. "Dragons are called the 'Apex monsters' for a reason. They are often very large, very tough, and insanely strong. However, it isn't their bodies that make them so dangerous."

"Powerful skills?"

"Insanely so. Depending on their element, dragons are almost undefeatable while inside of a corresponding terrain. For example, 'Lord' Arroth is an earth dragon. As such, he has almost complete control over the ground beneath our feet and the plants around us."

"So, we're fighting an uphill battle?"

"That's putting it lightly."

"Can a group of druids hold him down long enough for me to—"

"No." She interrupted with a shake of her head.

"I'm sorry?"

"Magic doesn't work on dragons."

"They can't be completely resistant to it."

"It's not their resistance to it that's the problem. It's because dragons *eat* magic."

"So... Any magic you send at it will get eaten?"

She shook her head. "Any magic, period. If one of us so much as gets too close to it, then it could suck the magic out of our bodies, killing us in the process."

"Is that why it wants the sacrifices? It's hungry?" If it was, then I completely understood the feeling. I was still going to kill it, though.

But again, Lena shook her head. "No, definitely not. Dragons eat ambient magic, so the paltry amount of magic they would gain from eating one of us wouldn't be worth the effort... unless it just likes the taste." she conceded.

"I see."

"Hey, Mom! Come over here!" Hali called from her spot off to the side of the groups. She and Ayla and been talking privately ever since Ayla hugged me.

"Coming!" she yelled back. "Sorry, but we'll talk more after I find out what Hali wants."

"Don't worry about it. You've answered all of my questions."

"You sure?" she asked with a tilt of her head.

"Just go," I said with a chuckle.

Lena nodded her head, then she walked over to the younger girls.

"Hey, Fenris?" I called out to the Warg.

"What, snake?"

"Regardless of whether or not you help me... You'd better protect them all, with your life. Am I clear?" I whispered just loud enough for him to hear me.

"As if you even needed to tell me that," he scoffed.

"Ayla too, Fenris."

"Not like I was going to leave her to fend for herself. You're not giving me enough credit, snake," he replied with a smirk.

I responded with one of my own as I looked him in the eyes. "Whatever you say, mutt."

Upon arriving at the city, we were stopped by a group of armed guards. Ten of them stepped in front of us and pointed their spears at the goblins and me.

"Halt!" the apparent oldest of them said as he stepped forward. It was a fox-man with yellow hair.

"Virion, what the hell are you doing? Put those down!" Lena yelled as she ran to the front of the group.

"I can't do that, lady Lena. Your father received word of a flash of light in the forest and has ordered any suspicious people to be detained until he can meet with them."

"Well, I suppose this is as good a time as any." I reached out and grabbed the spear closest to me, pulling the dryad holding it into a backhand. Then, I swung the blunt end of the spear at the guards.

"Watch out!" the leader yelled, as he ducked under my swing. But his warning came too late, as the spear collided with five of them and sent them flying.

"I would prefer it if you would let us pass without resistance," I said to the remaining guards. However, they ignored my request, and the remaining guards charged at us.

I let out a sigh as I swung the blunt end of the spear into a charging wolf-man. He was much larger than the rest of his compatriots, so when the spear smashed into him it broke against his chest.

"You'll have to do better than that!" he laughed.

"Okay," I shrugged, then slammed my right foot into his stomach sending him flying away from me.

"Reinforcements!" Fenris yelled.

I turned in his direction and saw another fifteen guards running towards us. I sighed. "Fenris, you take Lena and the kids and go find Uriel. Force him to remove that barrier if you have to!" I barked out as I backhanded a charging elf.

"What about you!?" Fenris front-flipped over a spear and dropkicked his attacker in the face, then he rotated in the air so he would land on all fours. After a flash of light, Fenris had returned to his normal form.

"Didn't you hear? Ayas wants to see us, so it's only polite for me to comply."

"If you were going to surrender anyway, then why attack them!?" Lena yelled as she caused large vines to sprout from the ground and wrap up the hunting group to prevent them from assisting the guards.

"Who said anything about surrendering? I'm just going to go find him." I picked up a yellow-skinned elf in a dark green robe and slammed my head into his.

"Enough chitchat, we need to go!" Fenris jumped into the air to avoid a group of spears, then he dashed around to each of his family members and threw them onto his back.

"Don't forget this one!" I pulled Ayla out of the way of a spear thrust, then I threw her into the air, which made her scream. "Holstig, You and Siofs follow after the mutt and guard Ayla with your lives!"

Holstig nodded as he grabbed her out of the air and sat her on his shoulders. "Hold on, little one!" He blocked a sword-strike with his shield, then he sliced the attacker in two. He and Siofs then fought their way out of the mob and dashed after Fenris.

I watched them go until I felt a dull pain in my side. When I looked down, I saw a broken spear poking me, so I grabbed its wielder and lifted them into the air. "You're the one that tried to stab the girl, right?" I didn't wait for an answer, and I instead crushed his head between my hands.

"Enough!" A booming voice echoed throughout the camp.

The guards stopped attacking us, but maintained their positions, as an old dark elf came into view. He wore an open black robe that dragged the ground. Beneath it was a set of leather armor, and the pommel of a sword poked out from behind him. His long silver hair was braided and hung over one shoulder, and he had piercing red eyes.

"You must be Ayas," I said, while discreetly motioning to Findral. Out of the corner of my eye, I saw her nod, then she walked behind Hogunn and disappeared.

"And you're the one causing a ruckus in my city!" he accused.

"Yes, I suppose I am."

"Why have you come here?" he asked, as he came to a stop fifteen feet away.

"Well, I promised a friend of mine that I would help you."

"And, just how does attacking my city 'help' me?"

"Because it allows me to do this in a public place." I snapped my fingers and a few seconds later Ayas' head fell to the ground.

The surrounding guards and civilians watched as their leader's head slid off of his neck, his body dropping a few seconds later. Panic quickly ensued as people began to scream, but I silenced them by roaring out, "Be silent!" A hush fell over the crowd as they stared at me.

"Now, you have two options: Stay here and be eaten by me or flee with Fenris and his family... You have ten seconds to choose," I declared, but before I could begin counting, a majority of them had already begun to flee.

"That's what I thought." Not long after seeing the civilians flee, the guards decided to cut their losses and fled as well. Findral took this time to fade back into view.

"Good job, Findral. You too, Hogunn. Now, split up and search the city. I don't want anyone here for the dragon to feed off of."

"Of course, Master!" The two saluted, then they left the area to search for any remaining humanoids.

"Now I just need to set up my backup plan."

"Master, I believe that is everyone inside the city," Findral said, as she and Hogunn returned.

"Excellent work you two, but now, I need you to do something else for me."

"Yes?" Hogunn asked.

"Get these bodies out of here, then I want the two of you to stay with Ayla."

"Understood, Master—" Hogunn began to say, but Findral interrupted him.

"I'm not leaving you, Master."

"That wasn't a request, Findral."

"I understand that, Master... But I'm not leaving you here to die."

I stared her down for several seconds, then I sighed and turned to Hogunn. "Then you stay with Ayla." I turned back to Findral. "However, you both will get these bodies out of here, Am. I. Clear?"

"Crystal, sir." Findral replied with a smile.

"Then get moving."

They nodded and began to follow my orders, while I continued to prepare for the upcoming battle.

~ ~ ~

Three days later…

A colossal reptile approached the city. It had brownish yellow scales, spikes along its spine, and on the back of its head rested four horns with a fifth on his nose. The reptile was easily twelve hundred feet long, over four hundred feet wide, and six hundred feet tall. Its tail made up almost a third of that length and its apparent weapon of choice was displayed prominently: A three-pronged spike stuck out of his tail for all to see.

"Ayas, where is my sacrifice!?" the beast roared. But his words were only met by silence.

"Don't try to hide from me, mortal. You won't like what happens." The beast reached out for the connection it shared with Ayas for the first time in over a month, but nothing was there.

"What the—"

~ ~ ~

Meanwhile, high above the dragon's head, Findral, with a familiar blade sheathed on her back, was using micro explosions to keep herself afloat in the air.

"Here I go, Master.... Protect me, father!" She flipped upside down and triggered a massive explosion to propel herself downwards.

~ ~ ~

At the same time, just below the dragon's feet. I was lying in wait for the signal from Findral. I listened as the dragon came to a stop just above me and began to speak.

"There you are." I tilted my head up to look at the ceiling of the cave I'd dug. It wasn't big, which is why I was waiting down here in my "human" body. I heard the dragon roar for Ayas, then it went quiet until... *Boom!*. The dragon roared in pain and I exploded out of my body.

～ ～ ～

FINDRAL

I used the momentum from the explosion and the fall to slam a mallet of fire into the dragon's head. The impact caused it to drop its head and scream in pain.

Almost immediately after, Master came bursting through the ground on a collision course with the dragon's neck. He opened his mouth and clamped down on it, then he lifted the dragon up and carried it far away from the city and out of sight. I ran across the sky after them.

When Master's wings could carry them no further, he angled his head down and slammed the dragon into the ground.

"Get off!" The dragon kicked with its back legs and threw Master over its head.

"Now Findral!" I heard Master shout as he impacted the ground.

I launched myself forward and slammed the mallet into the side of the dragon's head, which distracted him enough that Master was able to get off a beam to the dragon's front left leg.

"Yes, finally! Something that fights back!" the dragon laughed as it lifted its other leg and slammed it back down, causing spikes of stone to rise from the ground and fly towards master.

I created an explosion behind me and propelled myself towards the centermost spike, then I created a large flame sword and slashed the spike in two causing it to barely pass on either side of Master's head.

The dragon attempted to summon more spikes, but Master stopped him by springing off his tail and slamming into it. He bit down on the dragon's neck and lifted it up... then he slammed it back into the ground. The impact created a tsunami of air and dirt that further destroyed the area.

"Not... bad," the dragon choked out as it used its claws to rip apart Master's flesh in an attempt to throw him off. Master held on.

Then the dragon raised its tail until it was positioned directly behind Master's head. "Watch out!" I yelled, and Master let go and dodged out of the way. However, he was just too slow to completely avoid the attack, so the leftmost prong sliced into Master's neck and he spurt blood onto the dragon's face.

The dragon opened his mouth and began to drink the blood that fell into his mouth. "Mmm, it's been a while since I've had basilisk blood. I'd almost forgotten how bitter it was."

"Don't worry.... I'll make sure that was your last taste!" Master gurgled out, then he bit into the dragon's neck again and lifted it once more into the air. Master coiled himself around the dragon's body to hold it in place, then he turned to me.

"Cut him Findral—" And again, the dragon slammed his pronged tail into Master's neck.

"I can't wait to see how you taste. Maybe I'll even forgive the elves for their lack of sacrifice this month," it said with a laugh.

I roared and unsheathed the sword Master had taken from the elven leader, slicing into the dragon's neck. A single thin line appeared on the dragon's hide and the beast actually laughed at me.

"Oh, come now, girl. You can do better than that!" it roared as it yanked out its tail and slammed it into another part of Master's body.

"No!" I began to frantically stab the blade into the dragon's neck until finally, I was rewarded with blood.

"Move!" Master yelled.

I back-flipped off of the dragon's neck just in-time for Master to bite down on the barely bleeding wound.

"Congratulations, girl," the dragon said. "You managed to make me bleed. But now what? Are you going to just let me—"

The dragon stopped when it saw Master begin to glow.

"No! what are you doing!?" It became frantic as it repeatedly smacked Master with its tail.

"Findral... Run." Master grunted, as a white shield slowly began to cover him.

"No, I won't—"

"If this doesn't work, you'll die... But I'll be safe until I evolve. So... Go!" He quickly opened his wings and completely encapsulated the dragon within his body, even managing to catch its tail while it was still pierced into him.

"I'll... see you soon... Findral."

That was the last thing I heard Master say before the shield covered him completely, and all that remained of my Master and the dragon was a giant egg-shaped shell in the middle of a destroyed forest.

"See you soon... Master," I whispered. I briefly ran my hand along the outside layer of the shield. Then I turned around and ran in the direction the others were fleeing. I bounded for three steps before leaping into the air, detonating a micro explosion beneath my foot that sent me flying through the air.

I followed the road we'd previously agreed upon for hours before I caught up to my charges and landed deftly beside Holstig. They'd set up camp inside a forest a few miles from what appeared to be a harbor town. "I hope they aren't doing what I think they're doing," I sighed.

"Master?" Holstig asked.

I shook my head. "He took the dragon with him into the evolutionary shield. I don't know what happened after that."

"Wait, you can do that?" Fenris asked from where he was lying beside the fire.

I shrugged. "Master did it."

"That tells me absolutely nothing. Snake-face is always doing shit that doesn't make any sense."

We were tense, most of us concerned for our futures and for the fate of Master. But we actually began to laugh. What started as a chuckle erupted into full-blown laughter after a minute or so of silence.

I looked back towards the "egg" that held my master's body and wept tears of laughter… and sadness at the loss I felt in my chest.

∾ ∿ ∾

TORGA

∞∞∞∞∞∞∞∞

Warning!!

Because both of your bodies were inside the evolution barrier when it sealed, they are locked in a state of suspended animation until one mind is destroyed.

When only one of you remains, the loser's body will be absorbed into the winner's, and they will gain all of the loser's skills and traits.

Good luck!

∞∞∞∞∞∞

After reading the pop-up, I shifted my gaze to the dragon and stared at it. It stared back.

We smiled at each other and launched across the space that separated us. However, upon slamming into each other, something was made abundantly clear. Because of the lack of magic or earth in the area, I had a clear advantage.

"Oh... I'm going to enjoy this far more than I should," I told the dragon as I pinned it beneath my body. It growled at me, so I laughed and hissed back. I sunk my teeth into its neck and lifted it off the ground, only to slam it back down a moment later. The dragon's body buckled beneath my weight, and I felt bones snapping inside its body.

"What's the matter? You were so talkative outside."

"Quiet you—" The dragon used its powerful legs to push my head away from its throat, or so it thought. I purposely released its neck, bit the leg reaching for me to hold it in place, then coiled my tail around it. I tightened my hold on its leg until it roared in pain.

"Shut up," I hissed. I twisted my body enough to pull the dragon into a sitting position. My body coiled around the dragon's until I had its entire body engulfed in mine.

I stared into its eyes as my face drew closer. Our foreheads touched.

"You… killed a friend of mine."

"So, what—Urk!" Its words were cut off as my tail worked its way around the dragon's body to wrap around its neck.

"You took her away from one of the sweetest children I've ever had the pleasure to meet. I wanted you to know that your death is because you gave me enough time to make this gamble, when you could've easily killed me at any time. That was your second mistake." I tightened my hold on it even further, causing its bones to snap in rapid succession and its eyes to roll back into its head. "Your first mistake was making Ayla cry… because that shit just pissed me off."

"Thanks for the meal," I hissed. I opened my mouth as wide as I could and swallowed the dragon whole.

∞∞∞∞∞∞∞∞∞

Congratulations!

You have won the battle of souls and you will remain the dominant one.

Your evolution is underway. Time remaining until completion is 10 y, 9m, 20d, 23h, 59m, and 52s.

∞∞∞∞∞∞∞∞∞

I read through the pop-up several times, then I smiled. "Well, time to test if this will work..." I closed my eyes and focused.

EPILOGUE

Somewhere with the goblins and the family...

THE LARGE GROUP WAS BEING ROCKED BACK AND forth by the waves lapping at the ship they'd "borrowed."

"Why are we on a ship, again?" Solon asked the dark elf man sitting beside him.

The man was wearing an ornate blue robe, with a silver lining around the collar. He had medium length raven hair that hung to his shoulders, and his eyes were milky white. However, in spite of this odd coloring, the man in question acted as if he could see perfectly well. "Because your father decided it was best to get as far from Uathea as possible," the man said with a chuckle.

"Yeah, yeah. Laugh it up, Uriel."

Most of the people aboard the ship snickered... until they heard something they didn't expect.

"Alright, whose idea was it to get back on a ship. Damn, you'd think after being on one for as long you were, you'd be sick of them by now."

Almost as one, the group looked to the final person aboard the ship... a yellow-skinned elf wearing a dark green robe. He was running his hands through his long brown hair and picking at his clothes.

"T... Torga?" Hali squeaked out.

"In the... flesh? Wow, I can't believe it actually worked." He was immediately tackled to the ground by three crying women: Findral, Hali, and Ayla. He patted them on the head, then looked up at the others. "What?" he asked.

"How... How are you here?" Lena asked.

"That's a long story."

She folded her arms across her chest. "We've got time."

He chuckled. "I suppose we do. Well, settle in. Because this is going to take a while." Everyone aboard the ship crowded around as he began to tell his story... his full story.

"It all began, when I met a god..."

Books, Mailing List, and Reviews

If you enjoyed reading about Albert and the rest of the gang in *A Snake's Life* and want to stay in the loop about the latest book releases, awesome promotional deals, and upcoming book giveaways be sure to subscribe to our email list at:

www.ShadowAlleyPress.com

Word-of-mouth and book reviews are crazy helpful for the success of any writer. If you *really* enjoyed reading *A Snake's Life*, please consider leaving a short, honest review—just a couple of lines about your overall reading experience. Thank you in advance!

About the Author

Hello, everyone. My name is Kenneth Arant and I like to pretend I'm a writer in my spare time. A bit about myself: I'm a retired martial artist with fourteen years' experience, six of which I used to teach others how to not knock themselves out with a pair of nunchucks.

Currently, I'm a full-time night owl with a minor caffeine addiction and a penchant for letting my imagination run wild. My dream is to write awesome books that people will enjoy for years to come.

Books from
Shadow Alley Press

If you enjoyed *A Snake's Life*, you might also enjoy other awesome stories from Shadow Alley Press, such as Viridian Gate Online, Rogue Dungeon, the Yancy Lazarus Series, Path of the Thunderbird, Zero.Hero, School of Swords and Serpents, American Dragons, Dungeon Bringer, or the Jubal Van Zandt Series. You can find all of our books listed at www.ShadowAlleyPress.com.

James A. Hunter

Viridian Gate Online: Cataclysm (Book 1)
Viridian Gate Online: Crimson Alliance (Book 2)
Viridian Gate Online: The Jade Lord (Book 3)
Viridian Gate Online: The Imperial Legion (Book 4)
Viridian Gate Online: The Lich Priest (Book 5)
Viridian Gate Online: Doom Forge (Book 6)
Viridian Gate Online: Darkling Siege (Book 7)

<<<>>>

VGO: The Artificer (Imperial Initiative)

<<<>>>

VGO: Nomad Soul (Illusionist 1)
VGO: Dead Man's Tide (Illusionist 2)
VGO: Inquisitor's Foil (The Illusionist 3)

<<<>>>

VGO: Firebrand (Firebrand Series 1)
VGO: Embers of Rebellion (Firebrand Series 2)
VGO: Path of the Blood Phoenix (Firebrand Series 3)

<<<>>>

VGO: Vindication (The Alchemic Weaponeer 1)
VGO: Absolution (The Alchemic Weaponeer 2)
VGO: Insurrection (The Alchemic Weaponeer 3)

<<<>>>

Strange Magic: Yancy Lazarus Episode One
Cold Heatred: Yancy Lazarus Episode Two
Flashback: Siren Song (Episode 2.5)
Wendigo Rising: Yancy Lazarus Episode Three
Flashback: The Morrigan (Episode 3.5)
Savage Prophet: Yancy Lazarus Episode Four
Brimstone Blues: Yancy Lazarus Episode Five

<<<>>>

MudMan: A Lazarus World Novel

<<<>>>

Two Faced: Legend of the Treesinger Book 1
Soul Game: Legend of the Treesinger Book 2

<<<>>>

Kenneth Arant

Rogue Dungeon: Rogue Dungeon Series Book 1
Civil War: Rogue Dungeon Series Book 2
Troll Nation: Rogue Dungeon Series Book 3
Rogue Evolution: Rogue Dungeon Series Book 4

eden Hudson

Revenge of the Bloodslinger: A Jubal Van Zandt Novel
Beautiful Corpse: A Jubal Van Zandt Novel
Soul Jar: A Jubal Van Zandt Novel
Garden of Time: A Jubal Van Zandt Novel
Wasteside: A Jubal Van Zandt Novel

<<<>>>

Darkening Skies: Path of the Thunderbird 1
Stone Soul: Path of the Thunderbird 2
Demon Beast: Path of the Thunderbird 3

Aaron Ritchey

Armageddon Girls: The Juniper Wars 1
Machine-Gun Girls: The Juniper Wars 2
Inferno Girls: The Juniper Wars 3
Storm Girls: The Juniper Wars 4

<<<>>>

Sages of the Underpass: Battle Artists Book 1

Gage Lee

Hollow Core: School of Swords and Serpents 1
Eclipse Core: School of Swords and Serpents 2
Chaos Core: School of Swords and Serpents 3

A Snake's Life

<<<>>>

Shadowbound: Ghostlight Academy Book 1

J.D. Astra

Neon Dark: Zero.Hero Book 1

Morgan Cole

Inheritance: The Last Enclave Book 1

Kenneth Arant

A Snake's Life Book 1

Shadowbound: Ghostlight Academy Book 1

BOOKS FROM
BLACK FORGE BOOKS

Aaron Crash

War God's Mantle: Ascension (Book 1)
War God's Mantle: Descent (Book 2)
War God's Mantle: Underworld (Book 3)

Denver Fury: American Dragons Book 1
Cheyenne Magic: American Dragons Book 2
Montana Firestorm: American Dragons Book 3
Texas Showdown: American Dragons Book 4
California Imperium: American Dragons Book 5
Dodge City Knights: American Dragons Book 6
Leadville Crucible: American Dragons Book 7
Alamosa Arena: American Dragons Book 8
Alaska Kingdom: American Dragons Book 9
Wyoming Dynasty: American Dragons Book 10

Barbarian Outcast: Princesses of the Ironbound 1
Barbarian Assassin: Princesses of the Ironbound 2
Barbarian Alchemist: Princesses of the Ironbound 3

<<<<>>>>

A Snake's Life

Raider Annihilation: Son of Fire Book 1

Nick Harrow

Dungeon Bringer 1
Dungeon Bringer 2
Dungeon Bringer 3

Witch King 1
Witch King 2
Witch King 3